CW00670115

THE LOST HEIR

Jane Cable

SAPERE
BOOKS

THE LOST HEIR

Published by Sapere Books.

24 Trafalgar Road, Ilkley, LS29 8HH,
United Kingdom

saperebooks.com

Copyright © Jane Cable, 2023

Jane Cable has asserted her right to be identified as the author of this work.

All rights reserved.

No part of this publication may be reproduced, stored in any retrieval system, or transmitted, in any form, or by any means, electronic, mechanical, photocopying, recording, or otherwise, without the prior written permission of the publishers.

This book is a work of fiction. Names, characters, businesses, organisations, places and events, other than those clearly in the public domain, are either the product of the author's imagination, or are used fictitiously.

Any resemblances to actual persons, living or dead, events or locales are purely coincidental.

ISBN: 978-0-85495-073-7

For Sally — beta reader, fellow literary adventurer, and most of all, friend

PROLOGUE

Illogan, Cornwall, 1838

From her family pew the woman watches as her daughter stands at the altar. The Bassets built this pew with its high wooden walls, setting the woman apart, trapping her in her place above them all. The proud Bassets, the powerful Bassets, of whom only she remains; once tall but even now refusing to stoop, glowering at the world through her small grey eyes. If she cuts a lonely figure it is because she is lonely; the great house of Tehidy is silent around her, save for the click of the dogs' claws on the marble floor of the hall.

Her dear, devoted Harriet had been the first to leave, then Mama, God rest their souls. Finally Papa and his new bride, married almost straight out of mourning quietly, nay, one could even say secretly, in London. Such behaviour she would never comprehend from the man who would brook no scandal; who had ruined her life because of it.

And now, her daughter, being wed to this mine captain Tolcarne, was to be taken on the morrow far across the seas to Mexico, most likely never to return. Not in her lifetime, certainly. And what is worse is that she will leave without knowing who her true mother is.

The vicar intones, "If any man can show just cause why they may not lawfully be joined together, speak now…"

Any man? But what of any woman? The woman wants to shout: 'I can. He cannot take her. She may not know it but she's all I have.' If she did so, heads would turn, staring at her like the mad woman most of them suppose her to be. To her it would matter not, but she will not cast a blemish on her daughter's happiness. Happiness in a choice of partner is a rare commodity.

The woman gazes at the bride, her daughter, drinking hungrily of every detail of her fine wool dress, printed with rosebud sprigs, fabric cascading from a neat band at the waist, sleeves frilled at the elbow. The young woman stands slender and tall against all except her adoptive father, whose looks she favours. The woman has never understood how this could be, but at least over the years it has meant there have been no rumours.

Now her daughter will never know the truth. The constant ache in the woman's heart swells to a tide that is ready to burst from her breast, reforming as it ebbs into a wave of desperation like the salt water that scours her bathing pool. After today she will never again set eyes on her child, can never tell her who she is. For years she has hoped there will be a moment, perhaps after her daughter's adoptive parents' days, when she would no longer be bound by her promises and could come to her as a mother. Now even that smallest of dreams has been snatched away.

A surge of bitterness rises in her throat; a vileness that has no place at all at a marriage celebration. But this is deeper, darker, than anything she has imagined or known. It overtakes her, overwhelms her, and she sinks to her knees to pray. But not to her God, not to the Greater Glory to whom this house was built by her forebears.

In the still, quiet moment before the organ swells she swears to whoever may take it that her soul will not rest until the truth is out.

PART ONE: 2020

CHAPTER ONE

The moment I emerge from the woods the sea spreads in front of me, a never-ending green-blue swell in the morning sunshine. Leaving the scent of wild garlic behind, I take the footpath along the edge of the field before crossing the deserted road. I crane my head left and right, but there are no cars in sight.

The tiny National Trust car park above Basset's Cove is similarly deserted. So this is how it's going to be. A time of emptiness and peace, where modern life retreats.

I can imagine this lockdown will be terrible for many people, but when I woke this morning it was with an immense sense of freedom. Of space in my life. Space to do what I want, if only for a few weeks.

At school the head told us to be prepared for more than a slightly extended Easter break if Covid really gets a grip. Easy in some subjects, but my design technology students are part way through practical projects and it was a sad moment when I handed in the workshop keys, leaving all their hard work to gather dust for god knows how long.

Some of them, of course, do not want to learn any more than I want to teach. And not wanting to teach anymore is something I have found very hard to face. A slow realisation through the winter months — or was it just the lack of daylight getting to me? Ever since junior school, when anyone asked 'and what do you want to be, Carla?' I would reply 'a teacher'. After almost ten years, the gloss has definitely worn off.

I gaze down into the cove. The tide has left the damp sand exposed, so I can make out the rock ledges beneath the lace-edged waves as they roll over them. I stand in the gentle breeze, memorising the colour of the water so I can recreate it later in the tiny workshop attached to the back of my house. The alchemy of colour is everything.

The sea and the solitude entice me to stroll further. Where are the hikers, the dog walkers? At home, that's where. Everyone must stay at home. The empty car park bears witness to the fact they're doing as they're told, though I wonder how long the Cornish will listen. We're an independent-minded, headstrong nation. But no-one can escape the gravity of the situation. I am only outside because one exercise walk a day is allowed.

The path skirts the clifftops with flat farmland to my left where sheep graze and call to their lambs. Spring. Regeneration. New beginnings.

A lone fishing boat disturbs the sea, no doubt making for Portreath Harbour. Probably Kitto. It is too far away for me to tell the colours, but the shape is right. He'll have been after pollock last night. I'll give him the benefit of the doubt that he left before the lockdown was announced, but I wouldn't bet on it. He'll go crazy, staying at home. Ten to one he'll be asking to come around to mine by the end of the week. And the answer will be no. For so many reasons.

It is as the path is squeezed between the field and a crumbling stretch of cliff edge that I spy a runner approaching, a dark cloud of hair the only identifying feature. Typical. We're going to meet at the very narrowest part. There's nothing for it but to hop over the wall and startle the ewe lying in its lea. She's heavy with her unborn lamb and lumbers away in disgust.

As the figure approaches I see the runner is a man. Tall, long-legged, arms pumping in the loose sleeves of his top, he's making his pace look easy. When he is nearer I can tell what I took to be an unruly mass of dark hair is in fact close-cropped, and a shudder runs through me. I blink, and as I open my eyes he raises his palm in acknowledgement.

The roughness of the wall digs into my hand, the stones providing my anchor as nausea pitches and rolls. The man had an aura, throbbing black as night around his head. An aura I should not be able to see. But see them I do. Not often, but every time it happens it shakes me.

I had intended to go further, but instead I retrace my steps, waiting for my heart to stop pounding and my stomach to settle. The sea helps, with its ever-changing green to blue, stretching towards the horizon. Kitto's boat has disappeared around the far headland and into the harbour. Finally my breath becomes more even as the sunshine and gentle smash of the waves beneath the rocks below seep into my soul.

My positive frame of mind has reappeared by the time I turn into the farmyard. I wave at Mum through her kitchen window as I pass, then head around the corner to the Granary. I give the door a shove with my shoulder and, after shuddering a little, it comes free at the top where it sticks and I'm in.

I have lived at Koll Hendra Farm all my life and when I was small I remember Dad converting this building for my gran. That's where its name comes from. She christened it herself. And when she died four years ago I moved in. There had been talk of turning it into a holiday let, but it felt right for me to follow her here.

Gran and I were very close. Mum and Dad had so little time when I was small. Don't get me wrong, I grew up surrounded by love, but it's hard to make farming pay around here and they worked so hard, Mum always juggling some sort of job as well. These days she's an administrator at a commercial laundry. Thanks to the global pandemic, their work will fall off a cliff without the holiday trade and I suspect she's spent the morning writing a list of all the jobs she can do at home instead.

I throw my jacket on the back of the sofa then head into the kitchen. Sunlight streams through the picture window and beyond the small garden the tractor crawls along the far edge of the field. I'll just make a cup of tea then I'll get on with some work myself.

Some days Gran is closer to me than others, and today is one of them. Because it's a time of change, or because the runner on the cliffs had an aura as visible to me as his face? Gran used to say it was one of her gifts, being able to see what was hidden in people's souls, but it doesn't feel that way to me. I don't think I'll ever get used to it; even once I'm over the shock of seeing one, if it's someone I know it feels like an awful intrusion into their privacy.

I've always refused to learn what the different hues and shades mean; if I don't understand them then somehow I'm able to keep them at arm's length. But all the same, perhaps, deep down, it's where my fascination with colour comes from. My obsession with making colours in their purest form, rather than their murkiest. Colours where the light can pass through them and they ring and sing and dance with it. Colours in glass.

I take my tea through to the lean-to workshop, another room flooded with light, but this one built by Dad, my cousin Noel who works on the farm, and me. Gran left Noel and me five hundred pounds each in her will and I used mine to buy a second-hand kiln. So of course I needed somewhere to put it.

The room faces west to catch the evening sun, so in the summer it's at its best after I finish work. Except now I want this to become my full income, but how can I make glass art pay? I'll need a bigger kiln for a start. I attempted a business plan in January and reckon I need about £10,000 to get going. Right now I have £9,000 in my savings account. Almost enough. But am I sufficiently brave to take the plunge?

My workbench is in front of the window that all but fills one wall. Dad made it elbow height so I can work standing, but today I perch on the black leather stool we rescued from a skip when the beach bar at Porthnevek was being refurbished. My trusty tin of Caran d'Ache pencils lies open and I balance my sketchbook on my lap, rest back and close my eyes.

The green-blue of the ocean shimmers, stretching towards a deeper hue on the horizon, and like this morning it is sparkling. How to add sparkles without it looking naff? Capturing light, even in glass, is a perpetual challenge. Without it, it's featureless. I feel my forehead crease. But then … Kitto's boat appears. Red and blue paint. No, too many blues. Not right … just not right. But what is he catching? What's beneath? Pollock. Too boring. But svelte silver mackerel with their dark grey tiger stripes… I reach for a pencil and begin.

I work until a rap on the window disturbs me and I look up to see Noel, a grin filling his broad face beneath his mop of sandy hair.

"Fancy a bacon butty for lunch, Carla?" he calls through the glass.

I nod and slide off my stool, stretching, and he disappears across the yard. It's only as I'm washing my hands that I wonder if Noel is allowed in the farmhouse under these new rules. Am I? After all, I don't live there, but on the other hand, it's technically the same address. And it's not as though I'll be seeing anyone other than Mum and Dad. But Noel will go home to Lizzie and the twins. Then come back to us.

My parents are only in their late fifties, but Dad gets a bit wheezy sometimes and I don't want them put at risk. This morning's positivity is momentarily replaced by fear, but I can't let that happen. I can't let anything sap my creativity. This is what it is. We just have to get on with it.

I need not have worried as I find my father sitting at the rickety picnic table on the scrubby patch of grass at the side of the house, his collie Sam at his feet and Noel on a wooden chair a few paces away. The bench wobbles as I ease myself down next to Dad and take a mug of tea from the tray in front of me as the aroma of frying bacon drifts through the open kitchen door.

"So what have you two been up to this morning?" I ask.

"Ploughing the north field after the potatoes," Dad tells me.

"Catching that sodding billy goat," says Noel.

Dad raises his eyebrows. "Don't complain — the goats were your idea."

Noel's love of farming has been a godsend to me, because it took any pressure to follow my father into the business away before it had even begun. Koll Hendra has been in the Burgess family for over two hundred years since one of our less illustrious ancestors, the notorious smuggler William Burgess, somehow persuaded Lord de Dunstanville, the Baron of Tehidy to give it to him. I've always wondered what he had over the bloke for that to happen, but I'm glad it did.

Dad and Noel are bickering about whether to let the goats hoover up the remnants of the cabbages once the last batch is picked next week. Mum emerges from the house carrying a plate piled high with bacon sandwiches, her salt and pepper hair swept up in a ponytail.

"I don't think our cabbages should go to the wholesaler," she says. "Not with all the hoarding going on. I reckon we should keep a good stack in the barn for us and sell the rest to local people. Same with the eggs. I can put them on social media."

"I'm not sure it's allowed to have people trooping up here at the moment, and in any case, would you really want that?" Noel asks, and she looks a little crestfallen.

"Well ... only people we know."

Dad covers her hand with his. "Elaine. People we know could be carrying Covid too."

She bites her lip. "It's all so ... difficult."

"Don't worry, Mum. When I popped into the supermarket at lunchtime yesterday there was quite a lot of stuff on the shelves again. I think everyone's getting over the panic buying now. After all, we're not going to starve with all the multibuys you've stashed away in the freezer and the back of the cupboards over the years."

But I know this situation we're in is going to get to everyone sooner or later, and as I sit in the sun and munch my sandwich I feel all the more guilty for the opportunity I feel it's giving me.

This morning, sitting with my sketchbook, the ideas tumbled out one after another and I'm itching to get back to it. I look up at the flaking whitewash covering the walls and instead of thinking they'll need repainting soon and worrying how much it will cost, I see crackle glaze on the greys of sea-washed pebbles. I haven't felt this creative in nearly forever.

CHAPTER TWO

I take my exercise walk at the same time every morning, earlier than most people are up and about. A quick cup of tea with Dad before he starts work, then I'm away. Sam gazes after me with a doggy look of longing, but I know full well he would be racing back to his master before we'd gone a couple of hundred yards.

Today I'm planning quite a long walk through Tehidy Woods, out onto the cliffs then back via Portreath village store to pick up a box of teabags and maybe even some biscuits. It's a glorious morning and the sun is already burning away the sea fret that hung in wisps over the fields when I woke. Wild garlic, yet to flower, spreads under the trees and there is even the occasional bluebell. Above my head the fuzz of green is just beginning and I tuck the thought away in the creative corner of my mind.

I cut across the fields and into the woods.

As I skirt the deserted golf course I wonder if I'll see the runner. We raise hands in greeting now, and exchange smiles. His is wide and warm, completely at odds with the darkness of his aura. I'm over the shock of it now, that initial sickening fear, but all the same Gran always said, with people you never know what lies beneath.

There was a time when she tried to teach me, but I don't like what I don't understand, and anyway, how can you explain a weird band of light around someone's head? It simply shouldn't be there. Besides which, I was young and I was afraid that the more I learnt, the more auras I would see. She said it didn't work like that; she saw something around most people, but for me it just seemed to be when the colours were very intense.

The closer I get to the seaward side of the woods the more stunted the trees become, their bare branches twisted by years of onshore winds. Only in the protected valley below can they reach their full splendour but I love these hardy stalwarts. They remind me of the Cornish; stocky, dark and strong like my father. Men of the land. And the sea. Even Kitto is only the same height as me, although his hair is bleached blond by the sun.

Already Kitto is becoming a pain, pretending not to understand why he can't just drop by and lounge around on my sofa. And no doubt once he'd got through the front door, my bed. I've been telling myself for years that part of our relationship is over, but somehow it never quite happens that way. Then I tell myself sleeping with him is just scratching an itch, but it isn't quite that either.

The problem is that it's been too damn comfortable for us both. Too convenient. And if I'm honest with myself, up to a point, that point being Christmas, I kind of liked the familiarity of it. Until now, familiar has definitely been my friend, the unknown a frightening place. But I'm beginning to wonder if it's all rather drab, and I find myself raising the corner of a curtain to peep inside a world of colour. I have an uncomfortable feeling that starting my glass business is just the beginning.

When I emerge from the woods the sea is glistening ahead of me, and I take the track towards Basset's Cove. A lone figure stands near the cliff edge and I recognise him as the runner; tall, broad-shouldered, and still the intangible, barely describable, dark green non-glow around his head. I hope he will be on his way before I reach him, but instead he seems to be waiting for me.

"Excuse me, but could that possibly be a seal down on those rocks?" His voice is polite, his accent American. Not at all what I expected.

Standing the regulation two metres away — or maybe a little more — I follow his pointing finger towards the cove. "Yes, that would be a seal."

"Wow."

"Or perhaps a rather chubby mermaid in a wetsuit."

His laugh is as dazzling as his smile. "I suppose it was a rather stupid question."

He speaks with a hint of southern drawl, and I ask him where he's from.

"Sugar Land, Texas."

"You're a long way from home." Statement of the bleeding obvious.

"I arrived at the beginning of March on a year's contract so you could say my timing was unfortunate."

"Very."

We stand and gaze down at the motionless seal.

"It is OK, isn't it?" he ventures.

"Oh yes. It'll just be resting. We do see them along this part of the coast, although they're far from common."

He nods, then turns to me. "I'm Mani, by the way. I'd shake your hand but obviously under the circumstances…"

"And I'm Carla."

"Good to meet you, Carla."

"And you. But I really should be getting on."

"Me too. I have an online team meeting at ten. Have a nice day."

His footsteps drum away from me towards the woods as I set out along the cliff path in the direction of Portreath.

Mug of tea in my hand and a brand-new packet of chocolate digestives under my arm, I head for my studio. I've been sketching for days now, and my fingers are itching to actually make something, to see if some of my designs work. If I am going to take my glass seriously as a business, I'll need to be able to reproduce the same things again and again. And across different products too; coasters, small dishes and, if I had a bigger kiln, placemats … plates even, vases.

The need for a bigger kiln is my first stumbling block. Not so much the kiln, but somewhere to put it. There's a half empty hayloft next door but it would need so much work just to make it serviceable. Perhaps I'd be better finding somewhere with retail space where there'd be passing trade, but that would cost even more money I haven't budgeted for.

I can't let negative thoughts cloud my creativity. I select two sheets of glass; one of marbled blues and the other a clear green, and set to work measuring and scoring them, ready to break into strips. My hands find a comforting rhythm and my heart sings in anticipation of putting them together to recreate the ever-shifting patterns of the sea.

Glass cut, I place two kiln bricks at right angles and start assembling them. I'm going to make coasters first; the simplest of things, but good for testing designs. But as soon as I start to slot the strips together I realise there is something missing — that elusive sparkle. I crouch to thumb through my sheets of glass. Perhaps a clear iridescent with a hint of silver?

I place it on the cutter to score it, head bent low. A shadow falls on my workspace and I look up to see Kitto standing at the window.

He grins at me, displaying the uneven eye-tooth I found so cute when we were teenagers. "Can I come in?" he calls. Well, at least he asked.

"No."

"Why not?"

"Because you're not allowed. You're meant to be staying at home."

He shrugs. "Why worry? No-one around here's got it."

"You can't know that. Go away."

He hunches his shoulders. "But I'm lonely. And bored. It's no fun living on your own."

"Can't you take the boat out?"

"Would you come?"

"Kitto, it's not allowed. Everyone has to stay at home. But you can fish like Dad can farm — it's an essential industry."

"There's no point though, not with the hotels and restaurants closed. Maybe once a week for the locals but that barely pays. And we're coming up to Easter when it normally starts to get busy."

"I'm sorry, Kitto, I really am."

"Nothing you can do about it. But a cup of tea would cheer me up … just one cuppa can't hurt, can it?"

He's right. It probably wouldn't, but I know it would be the thin end of the wedge.

"Sorry. Look, just go home, will you? We can talk online later … this evening … over a beer, maybe?"

"It won't be the same."

"No, it won't be. But it's the best we can do at the moment."

"I never had you down as so … so … bloody toe-the-line conventional…"

"What the hell are you doing here?" Noel appears in the yard next to the low wall which divides it from my garden.

"Seeing Carla."

Reluctantly I edge the window open an inch so Noel can hear me. "And I'm telling him he should be at home."

"Too bloody right, he should." Noel folds his arms. He's bristling, but he and Kitto have never got on, and I wonder what might happen next, but then I hear my father's gentle voice.

"They're right lad, you'd best be getting off. If you get out in that boat of yours at all we'll have a few pollock and then you can deliver them, but otherwise just do as you're told. It's not for long in the grand scheme of things."

Finally Kitto nods. "OK, Bill. Will do." He sounds deflated but all the same winks at me before turning away from the window. And I know he'll be back. With or without his fish.

I continue to score and cut the iridescent glass and, after a while, my inner calm returns. Moving the strips around until they form the perfect pattern draws me in, and I have two batches of coasters from what will be the same set ready for the kiln before I hear my father's voice at the door.

"Carla, love, your mum's made a cake if you'd like a piece?"

I look at the clock on the wall to see it's gone four o'clock. No wonder my stomach feels a bit hollow. "Yes, please."

There is still some warmth in the sun so we sit at the table outside the kitchen door, even though Noel has gone home. As Mum fetches the old brown china teapot we've used ever since I can remember, Dad turns to me.

"Had a good afternoon? You're positively glowing."

"I've been working on some new designs and I think they're going to look really good. They're the colours of the sea and mackerel and if the first batch comes out of the kiln OK I'm going to try some with actual fish on."

"I don't think I've seen you as animated for ages. I reckon the extended break from school will do you good."

"It's been a tough term, but not as tough as some people are facing now." Although a part of me is dying to tell my parents about my plans for the business, I need to be just a little more certain first and I hope Dad won't push me.

Instead he looks away, and bends to pat Sam on the head. "Tough for the farm, truth be told. We were relying on the Easter income to pay for the work we had done to make the river field ready for the campers. Dave's been more than patient, but he needs the money too right now. It comes to something when even plumbers can't work."

"How much do you need, Dad?"

"No, Carla. I'm not having you bail out the farm again."

I put my hand over his. "You've always paid me back before."

"Yes, but this time I'm not sure when that will happen. What if this lockdown goes on and there's no summer season? Thank god your mum's still getting paid, that's all I can say."

Mum returns and pours the tea.

"What's going on here?" she asks.

"Dad won't tell me how much he needs to pay for Dave's work on the campsite and I want to help."

"And I say..."

Mum cuts across him. "It's four grand, near enough. And a couple more for the other suppliers. But don't feel you have to do it, darling. I hate the thought we keep using you as a bank."

"Call it rent for the Granary." I try to laugh, but that will be most of my savings gone and I'll be back to square one.

"No!" Dad thumps his fist on the table.

"Dad, please..."

23

"Oh come on, Bill, see sense. The government's promised to look into ways of helping the hospitality industry, so we should be able to pay it back soon."

"We're a farm." He folds his arms.

"We're hospitality too now. Diversification. It's Noel's favourite word," says Mum. "And he's right. It's just our timing was lousy."

The black circles under Mum's eyes are only half hidden by her tortoiseshell glasses. This whole Covid situation must be really getting to her and I kick myself for not having noticed before. But there's something I can do. I can transfer that money into their bank account right now and I reach for my phone. Family is family, after all.

CHAPTER THREE

I set up a messaging group with Kitto and our other friends so there is always someone around to chat. Perhaps, in some ways, lockdown might even bring us all closer together.

I am next to the path that runs along the edge of Tehidy Woods towards North Cliff, picking wild garlic, when I glimpse Mani running towards me through the trees. The green-black of his aura blurs into the shadows around him and for a moment his shape is as fluid as a wraith and my heart starts to thud. I feel myself back away, the scent of squashed garlic wreathing my ankles, but he stops a respectful distance from me.

"Good morning, Carla."

I clear my throat. "Hi, Mani. Good run?"

"Yeah. The air up here is so fresh … exhilarating. I just wish we were allowed out in it more." He points to the leaves in my hand. "So what are you picking?"

"There's some right next to you. Crush a bit and give it a sniff."

He does as I say, wrinkling his nose. "It smells like garlic, but it doesn't look…"

"It's wild garlic. And it's perfectly safe to eat."

"So how do you use it? I love messing around in the kitchen with new ingredients. And right at the moment, it fills some time."

"My favourite is pesto, but my mum makes a mean soup and it lends its flavour to most things. It's great with chicken, or used a bit like spinach but with more punch."

"Oh, right. I might experiment."

Already his aura has lightened and in the spirit of making a little time for everyone, it gives me an idea. "Why don't we have a virtual cook-off one night? OK, we'd only be eating our own food, but it would be fun to exchange recipes."

He grins. "Great idea. How do I contact you?"

"What's your email?"

He tells me and I type it into my phone, then as I step away from the path he raises his hand and runs past. It seems his surname is Dolcoath. Now that's a name with very local connections indeed and about the last one I was expecting.

Am I just being friendly, or have I asked Mani on a virtual date? Dating at a safe distance. I laugh to myself. I quite like that idea; it gives you the chance to get to know someone before you leap into bed with them. And do I want to leap into bed with Mani? I consider his physique and the answer is yes, but when I think of his aura, it's no.

I rest my laptop on Gran's largest mixing bowl to give it some height. This would be easier if I had more in the way of work surfaces, but there isn't the space, with the cooker and a floor-to-ceiling cupboard at one end, and the door to my workshop at the other. The long side, with the big picture window, is taken up with the sink, draining board, an old-fashioned butcher's block and the only worktop is chock-a-block with stuff.

Some people might call it a mess so I angle my laptop more definitely away from the kettle, mug tree, radio and mismatched storage jars, and set about putting everything I'll need on the table before pouring myself a glass of wine. Call time is seven o'clock, just ten minutes away, and Mani has sent me a link. I take my drink and gaze out across the fields. The clocks went forwards last weekend and the harrowed earth with its pinprick plants that will become cauliflowers is bathed in the rich evening light, and the sea a distant glimmer on the horizon. For about the millionth time I tell myself how lucky I am to live here. Even if the farm has just sucked up most of my savings.

At a minute to seven I click the link and Mani is waiting. He's wearing a dark green polo shirt and it's strange to see him in anything other than a slightly damp running vest, but there's something else, and it takes me a few moments to realise what it is. No aura. I breathe out a silent sigh of relief.

After we've completed the social niceties it's down to the business of the evening. I'm keeping it simple, cooking pasta with a wild garlic and walnut pesto, but he's gone all out and has decided to make spanakopita, a filo pie filled with feta cheese, using the wild garlic instead of spinach.

"Wow — you must be a good cook to attempt that."

"Not really, it's a little slice of home and all I've done is adapt Mom's recipe."

"Oh, OK."

"She's Greek, you see. Well, her parents were, but she's very proud of her heritage. It's where my name comes from; Mani is short for Manos, and my kid sister's Eleni, but she always calls herself Helen. She's braver than I am!"

"Is your mother that scary?"

He shakes his head. "Greek matriarchs are very strong, that's all, although they're loving with it. On the other hand, I didn't dare tell her I was messing with her spanakopita."

As I pound my pesto and he rolls out pastry I ask him about his Cornish surname.

"I guess it's part of the reason I chose to come here. Dad had always said his family emigrated to Tennessee as miners and as I'm a geologist, to return to be part of the resurgence of Cornish mining felt kind of neat, like coming full circle."

"You know Dolcoath is the name of a mine?"

"Yes, I looked it up. It wasn't too far from here either, was it?"

"I'm not really sure. My mining history is hazy to say the least, but I do know coal was brought in and ore exported through the harbour down at Portreath. Have you had the chance to go there?"

"I didn't have the chance to do anything much before lockdown. It took me a couple of weeks to find a place I could move into right away, and then it was a struggle to find the essentials to fill the kitchen cabinets, what with all the panic buying. I did seriously wonder what I was going to be able to eat and spent a whole lot of time going from store to store hunting for stuff. And *queuing*." He rolls his eyes. "I certainly learned how to queue."

"An essential British skill. But I'm so sorry you haven't seen Cornish people at their best."

"Do you know what? I think I have. My co-workers were amazing. They hardly knew me but they gave me all sorts of stuff to help me get by. I just wish I'd had the chance to get to know them better. Or even to meet my neighbours."

"It must be pretty lonely for you." Which if it's really getting to him could explain his aura.

"Oh, I get by. I speak to my family nearly every day and work is just one long series of online meetings. Anyway, this evening is meant to be fun. What's going into that bowl now?"

The evening does work out to be fun. A lot of fun. Mani is good company, chatty and entertaining. And he knows his food, knows about flavours. He tells me that once we're out of lockdown he'll cook for me 'for real'. I love his American turns of phrase and soft drawl of an accent. A taste of the different, the unknown.

We are saying our goodnights when my phone pings, but I don't look at it until I am shutting down my laptop.

Kitto. *I'm so lonely. Let me come up for an hour now it's dark. Your parents won't know.*

I perch on the edge of the table. *The answer is no. And it's nothing to do with my parents. It's the rules.*

But we're a couple. That changes stuff, doesn't it?

He is so bloody infuriating. Not to mention whiny. *Since when?*

The silence from my phone stretches on until I realise he isn't going to answer. Is he trying someone else, to see if they will break the rules for him? How dare he think we're a couple again all of a sudden, just because he's lonely? Or wants to get his end away. That's probably more like it.

I don't want sex with him anymore, I really don't. The last time was in that dead period between Christmas and New Year. We'd been drinking in The Tinners for most of the day, hitched a lift back to Portreath with some mates, ended up in his house, and then in his bed. It's not that I'm averse to a meaningless shag, they definitely have their place in this world, but there was something soul destroying, if not humiliating, about a fumble with your ex when he falls into a drunken stupor before you're properly finished. And I promised myself then. Never again.

After I've removed Kitto from my thoughts, Mani's words about his Cornish roots start me thinking about my own and I know Dad would be interested too. Although I think he's forgiven me for lending them the money, things have been a little scratchy between us since, and a project we could do together might help to put that right. I know he's curious because I remember him and Gran talking about it not long before she died.

I miss her, I really do, but I am glad she isn't having to live through Covid, with all the risks to a 94 year old that would have entailed. Not that we've heard of anyone locally catching it, Kitto was right about that at least, but you never know. There was a lot of fuss about second-homers bailing out of London at the start of lockdown, bringing infection with them, but we're almost three weeks in and there doesn't seem to have been a knock-on effect. Better safe than sorry, all the same.

I'd love to be able to talk to Gran about Mani's aura, and why I couldn't see it on the computer, but another side of me doubts that even she would know. It had certainly returned when we bumped into each other in the woods the other morning, but it's so weird; either he's denying his feelings, even to himself, or he is extremely good at hiding them, because he was as cheerful and positive as ever.

The next morning, I tackle Dad about the family tree as we carry kitchen scraps across the field to the goats, their distant bleating alerting us to the fact they've noticed our approach. He's given Noel a few days off, and I never mind helping out on the farm. There's a certain amount of love for the land in my blood, and it's saying this to Dad that points the conversation in the right direction.

"I've always thought you're more like your Gran, and her side of the family weren't farmers at all, although she herself loved it. She was a land girl during the war, you see, and even afterwards continued her involvement with the Young Farmers, and that's how she met my dad. They didn't exactly rush into anything though; it took him the best part of ten years to propose, apparently."

"Did she tell you much about her family?"

"Yes, it was quite interesting. Her father came here from Mexico in the 1920s. He was on a boat heading for London but they put into Falmouth and he fell in love with it so he stayed. Worked on the docks there most of his life. My Grannie Sarah was a maid in one of the hotels until they married, but it was her mother who was a bit of a character apparently; she lost her son and a brother to Spanish Flu in 1919 and became a medium. It's where your Gran got her aura reading from, I reckon."

I swing the bucket of scraps from one hand to the other. I didn't realise he knew about Gran, but why would he not? She never exactly kept it a secret. I wonder for a moment if she told him about me, but he doesn't mention it, and neither do I. Not just because he launches into telling me about the Burgesses.

"We've farmed Koll Hendra for more than two hundred years, but I've probably told you that loads of times. I'm a bit sketchy on the details, though. My dad always said his parents didn't get on terribly well, there was a lot of resentment between them for some reason, but maybe it was because farming was tough in the twenties and thirties. They were down-to-earth working folk who probably didn't think too much about family history, it's quite a modern thing, after all. I guess a place to start might be the Burgess who was a notorious smuggler. With the internet he might be the easiest to look up."

I nod. I'm better off looking into his side of the family because I'm not sure I want to go down Gran's side, where I might come across more mediums and the like, although how would I know from the historical record? "He was a William, wasn't he?"

Dad laughs. "Yes. There always seemed to be quite a lot of Williams knocking around in the Burgess clan. You were lucky we didn't christen you Wilhelmina!"

"You'd have to really hate a baby to do that."

He wraps me in a hug. "And we love you more than life itself. You know that, Carla, don't you? You're a daughter in a million."

And I glow in his arms because I know that everything's all right between us once again.

CHAPTER FOUR

By some miracle the good weather continues. Mum jokes that had it been any normal Easter holiday, with the tourists flooding in, it would be raining cats and dogs, but for now we have unremitting sunshine. It's as if Mother Nature is doing her best to cheer us all up and, in most cases, it seems to be working. I say most, because Kitto is still whingeing about being lonely and broke.

He rocked up here again the other afternoon, and although I hid in the farmhouse kitchen with Mum, I heard Dad tell him to get that boat of his on the water, because people will want fish for Good Friday and he could sell it off the quay. As I walk along the cliff on Thursday morning I am delighted to see *The Merlin* bouncing gently across the waves towards Godrevy Rocks. There's no doubting lockdown is tough for a social animal like Kitto, but keeping busy will surely help.

I watch him plough through the green-blue water for a while, trying to figure out how to depict the wake of a boat in my glass. It's a wondrous, fluid thing as it ripples and spreads; the shape will be easy but the nuance of colour created by the twisting and tumbling of the sea is perhaps beyond me. I comfort myself with the thought that nature will always have the upper hand and anything emerging from my kiln will only ever be the palest imitation.

I head inland towards the northern edges of Tehidy Woods. There is plenty of wild garlic in the dappled shade beneath the low, twisted trees, and their scent rises up to meet me. To my delight the first of the bluebells are coming into flower too, delicate heads dancing in the breeze. It will be a few weeks yet before their purple-blue haze covers the ground, but the next phase of spring is on its way, and I wonder, more than ever in this strangest of years, what it will bring.

I am on the wide track near the private estate that's been built where Tehidy House once stood when I hear running footsteps behind me and I step to one side. They stop.

"Good morning, Carla."

I turn and grin at Mani. "Hi, how are you doing?" His aura is black, black, black.

He grimaces. "Yeah, well. It's my sister Helen's birthday and she should have been flying in to join me today. Of course, now she can't do that. My mom always says you shouldn't waste time grieving over what you can't change, but it still feels a little tough."

"Oh, Mani, I'm sorry."

"I'm sorry too. I shouldn't be complaining, should I? Plenty of people are worse off than me."

But all the same, having to spend the four long days of the Easter break on your own, far away from family and friends… It isn't exactly something you'd look forward to, is it?

"Fancy another virtual cook-off?" I ask. "Maybe tomorrow or Saturday?"

"Hey, that's a great idea." He looks around him. "What shall we make this time? I really hope you're not going to tell me you can eat those pretty little pale yellow flowers over there."

"What, the primroses? Not as far as I know. But I'll think of something. I'll email you later."

"Cool."

We gaze at each other, smiling. His eyes are so dark, it must be his Greek heritage, and there is a shine in them that's captivating. I've done a good thing. I've made him happy. But I need to break this spell that has somehow bound us into stillness.

"You go first," I tell him. "I'm only dawdling along."

He nods, and sets off as I watch him. He has a nice arse as well. I tell myself to behave.

The answer to what we will cook is fish. It has to be really; it's Good Friday tomorrow and Kitto will need to sell every last bit he can.

I drop Kitto a message asking if he wants some help on the quay.

Sure it's allowed, Miss Goody 2-Shoes?

You'll need someone to make sure people social distance properly.

It is some hours later when I receive his reply. *Cheers, C. Sweet. 10ish.* I go online to let everyone local know, and then I email Mani, explaining where the boat will be, and that he'd better get there early.

I'm on the quay just before half past nine, in time to see *The Merlin* nose into the outer harbour. Gulls wheel around her deck, their wings glinting in the sunlight, but Kitto will have his catch safely stowed, well away from their greedy beaks. It occurs to me that life must be tough for these scavengers as well. Normally at Easter they can gorge on a diet of dropped chips and the odd bit of discarded pasty, with the promise of stolen ice cream for dessert.

Portreath Harbour as it is today was built to serve the tin industry a couple of hundred years ago. It's always had a reputation of being tough to navigate in bad weather, its sole approach being between a long protective mole and the jagged wall of the east cliffs that climb to the headland, with the stump of the old lighthouse perched so precariously on top it looks as though it's about to tumble into the sea itself.

I guess the outer harbour would have been the original one, with its irregular shape and beach below the wall to one side, the little white huer's hut perched above. The sight of it makes me wonder if there might be pilchards in Kitto's haul. There's a few things you can do with a pilchard, although it's a bit late in the season for them, but I have no time to think about it now because *The Merlin* has edged through the narrow gap into the seaward of the two deep, oblong tidal pools where the boats moor today. As it closes on the quay Kitto emerges from the wheelhouse and throws me a rope, which I wind around a metal post.

"Good start, C, here in time to be useful," he yells over the chug of the idling engine.

"I'm always useful."

He grimaces, for a moment looking like a stubbly elf, his wavy blond hair in sticky spikes from the salt in the spray.

"Good catch?"

"Me or the fish?"

Why, oh why, does he always have to be a smart-arse? But he's smiling and something of his normal spark has returned and that makes my heart sing. Perhaps, today, I can forgive him his irritating ways.

He jumps from the boat and reties the lines with proper knots, telling me my girly attempts won't do.

"Each to their own. Fancy teaching my class when the school reopens?"

He shudders. "You won't get me into that place, not for anything. Anyway, how about a kiss for the returning hunter?"

I blow him one, from a little more than two metres apart.

"That's not what I meant and you know it."

"It's all you're getting."

"Your loss."

I'm glad he took it so well. "Right, where are you setting up?"

"I thought direct from the boat. Keeps the fish cooler and away from the gulls."

"Good call. I'll mark two-metre strips along the quay for people to queue."

"Jeez, you're taking this seriously, aren't you?"

"Kitto, if this wasn't serious we wouldn't all be told to stay at home, would we? Nothing like this has happened during our lifetimes. Of course it's serious."

He rolls his eyes but jumps back onto *The Merlin* without further comment. I take a piece of chalk and my yardstick from my backpack and unfold it, measuring along the narrow concrete quay in both directions. Already people have seen the boat come in, but they hang back until I've finished.

"Good job, Carla," calls our friend Ray from The Tinners and I take a little bow. "Somebody's got to keep that one in line. Tara was worried it would be carnage down here."

The catch is mainly pollock, but there's the odd flounder as well, and a dozen or so mackerel, although it's early in the season for them. There are even a couple of dogfish, which Kitto reckons no-one will want, but I tell him not to chuck them just yet anyway. I pick three of the largest mackerel, trying not to wonder how to depict the blue-green skin beneath their stripes in glass, while Kitto wraps them in old newspaper and sets them to one side.

Trade begins steadily, but it's the most sociable queue I've had the pleasure to be involved with. This is a village, after all, and most of the people who drive into the car park next to the Waterfront Inn are our friends from a little further away. I just know this is going to cheer Kitto up massively, and I must encourage him to do it every week so he has something to look forward to, otherwise he's going to slide into another slump. Easter isn't only going to be tough for Mani, Kitto is on his own as well.

I collar Ray before he leaves. "You know you always have an Easter barbecue?"

"Not this year, hun. Obviously."

"Yes, but we could. Sort of. All in our own gardens. We could have a beer at least, virtually." It's hard to lower my voice at a safe distance but I mouth to him. "I'm worried about Kitto. He's not good at being on his own."

Ray nods. "I'll ask Tara, but I don't see the harm."

An SUV I don't recognise pulls into the car park and Mani steps out. Instinctively I move towards him but stop myself just in time, waving instead.

"You found us, then."

"No sweat. Say, this looks popular. Is there anything left?"

"If not you'll be buying a can of tuna from the shop."

He laughs, then strides across the concrete to the steps down to the quay while I lean on the railing to watch. I'm interested to see what he buys.

"Hey, what have you got?" he asks Kitto.

"This is for locals, pal." Kitto folds his arms. What's got into him all of a sudden? He was laughing with his neighbour Mabel two minutes ago.

"Mani is local," I call. "I gave him the heads up you'd be here."

Mani steps back. "Really, I don't want to tread on anyone's toes…" His politeness is in total contrast to Kitto's thinly veiled aggression. It's making him look a fool, and I wonder for a moment if that is Mani's intention, but there is no hint of sarcasm in his voice.

I sigh. "Just serve him, Kitto."

"There's not much left. Except…" Suddenly he grins. "There's a couple of dogfish."

"How big?" Mani asks, and when Kitto shows him he says he'll take the smaller one. I almost balk at the price, but he pays it without a murmur and retreats.

I wait at the bottom of the car park steps. "I am so sorry about that. He can be a total arse."

"No, he was right to question it. People aren't allowed to travel right now and he doesn't know me from Adam."

"There are ways of asking, though."

"Maybe." He grins and waves his newspaper package at me. "Anyway, I need to work out what the heck I'm going to do with this. See you at seven."

It's as Kitto sits on the deck gutting the remains of the fish, and I clean the chalk marks from the quay that he asks, "Who's the Yank then?"

I raise my voice a little so he can hear me above the cacophony of gulls circling the boat. "Poor guy moved here just before lockdown to work for that mine they're looking to reopen."

"So how come you know him?"

"I've seen him when I'm out exercising."

"Oh, so it's all right to talk to him, but not to me."

I stop scrubbing for a moment.

"We message every day. And we've had a few beers on FaceTime."

"Yeah, but you actually see him and I'd like to know what the difference is."

I stand up and wipe my hands down my jeans. "Listen to me, Kitto. There's a world of difference stopping — two metres apart at the very least — to say hi to someone for two minutes if you happen to bump into them, and actually arranging to meet and spend a significant amount of time together. People are respecting the rules, Kitto, and it's about time you did too." I realise I'm properly shouting now, my anger at his childishness spilling over. To stop myself saying something I'll really regret, I turn and start walking away.

I am twenty yards down the quay when he yells after me. "You forgot your fish." I turn, ready to tell him where he can shove it, when a newspaper parcel wings its way through the air, splitting apart as it does so, mackerel flying to the four winds. The gulls perched on the rail swoop within seconds.

"You stupid, stupid, bastard!" I yell, before stomping off towards the village shop. One of these days, I really am going to give him what for.

CHAPTER FIVE

Later, I return from my exercise walk to see Mum crossing the yard in my direction, holding a plastic bag.

"I saw Kitto leave this on your doorstep. It smells a bit fishy so I thought I'd better take it in."

There's a note attached to the bag, which simply says 'sorry' and for some inexplicable reason I almost well up.

"What's he done now?" Mum asks.

"He was such an arse this morning and we ended up having a row." I choke out a laugh. "He actually threw our fish at me so I guess this is a replacement."

She gives me a hug. "Pop it in your fridge then come and have a cuppa."

Mum and Dad's kitchen is the most comforting place I know. The Aga is built into the massive old fireplace, the stonework behind it exposed, not to look good, but just because no-one has ever bothered to plaster it over. Above it is a wooden airing rack, which most of the winter — and a good part of the summer, this being Cornwall — is covered with clothes, but at the moment is weighed down with nothing more than a couple of tea towels.

A solid oak table stands in the centre of the room, scarred by generations of knife marks and stains. Every so often Mum or I will treat it with proper beeswax polish and I can get completely lost tracing the knots and lines that give it its character, like the wrinkled skin on a wise old woman.

Dad is at the table, mug in front of him and his phone about eight inches from his face, which tells me he's catching up with the news or sport. Lockdown is the latest in a string of excuses for him not to go to the optician and I don't pass up the opportunity to tease him about it again.

His normal defence is to change the topic of conversation and he doesn't disappoint.

"Noel and I were looking at the old hayloft earlier. Half of it's just full of junk and it would be a great place to put that new kiln you were talking about. Bit of retail space too."

I don't have the heart to tell him my kiln money's gone into the farm.

"She's not going to get much passing trade though, is she?" Mum points out.

"Noel's campers? Walkers?" he shoots back.

I sit down opposite him. "It's a great idea, Dad, but it would cost a fortune to do up."

"Maybe not as much as you think, because we could do a lot of the work ourselves. There's power in there anyway, and it wouldn't take much to run the water from the Granary."

I can't tell him that up to a couple of weeks ago I was thinking along those lines myself, but there's no point handing in my notice if I don't have the money. I'd been rather hoping that even with my half a term's notice, under present circumstances I wouldn't have to go back, but now I don't have a choice. I have to begin saving all over again.

To make matters worse there was an email from the headmistress yesterday, suggesting lockdown is going to be extended, and that we need to start teaching remotely, and open the school for key workers' kids and vulnerable children. I have absolutely no enthusiasm for trying to fathom out how to teach such a practical subject as mine long distance. Most of the students hate the theory side anyway and trying to get all but the minority to sit at home and study will be well-nigh impossible.

"Why so glum, love?" Mum says, squeezing my shoulder. "Not that row with Kitto still bothering you?"

"No, of course not. It's par for the course. But it's so lonely for him on his own with no family and he isn't the only one. We're so lucky to have each other."

"I know, darling, and I count our blessings every day. But come on, haven't you got that online cook-off thing tonight with your friends?"

Friend. Singular. So why don't I correct her? "Yes, and now I have some real fish to cook I need to think what to do with it. I was going to make Stargazey Pie with tinned pilchards as a bit of a joke."

Mum frowns. "But they don't have heads…"

Dad roars with laughter. "Come on, Elaine, that's the point."

I feel better once I've finished my tea and I head back across the yard to the Granary. I've raided Mum's fridge for some mushrooms and I'm going to make a fish pie. Two, in fact, so I can pop the first one across to my parents for their supper. Dad was already hunting in the back of the pantry for a bottle of Muscadet so I think they're probably going to have a date night if I'm cooking for them. I love the thought they're still doing that in their fifties.

My evening with Mani is definitely not a date, but all the same I figure a shower will freshen me up. Afterwards, I put on my pea-green cotton jumper. At least I'll look respectable and feel better. Adding a splash of perfume reenforces the idea that I'm doing this for me.

We log on punctually at seven o'clock and Mani is wearing a blue and red checked shirt and, he tells me, cowboy boots.

"Really?"

"No, not really. I didn't have space to pack them." He laughs. "Seriously, I don't even possess a pair, but tonight, Carla, I'm taking you to Texas."

I exaggerate a sigh. "If only."

"Yeah, if only." He looks a little wistful for a moment then says, "In a culinary sense anyway. I'm making fish tacos with slaw and my mom's special salsa. Without the black beans. I think I covered every aisle in the supermarket and I couldn't find any. It was getting to closing time and they almost had to throw me out."

"I appreciate your efforts. Big time. I have to admit I didn't go any further than my mum's fridge for extra ingredients, but then I'm only making a fish pie. And I also need to confess I've made one already this afternoon." And I tell him about my parents' date night.

"That's real sweet. I can't imagine my mom and dad doing that."

"Tell me about them." I set to work chopping mushrooms while he dices a tomato for his salsa with neat strokes of the knife.

"Mom, she's very traditional, Greek. So proud of her heritage and she definitely rules the roost. I don't think my dad's ever done even a bit of housework in his life and she doesn't get why I love cooking so much. I know her views are outdated but I wouldn't dare tell her. For all that though, she's got a lot of love for Helen and me, but she still thinks she knows best about what we should do with our lives. Don't get me wrong, I miss her like crazy, but I kind of had to escape. Do you ever feel that with your folks?"

"No. But then I have my own space. I live in a cottage across the farmyard from them and it's the perfect arrangement. They never, ever intrude. Well, Dad will open the door and call around it, but Mum always knocks. They let me live my own life. Even when I might be ballsing it up, they don't say a word, but if I want advice I know where I'll get it."

"They sound amazing. I could never get away with Mom not having a key to my apartment and at first she used to come over at all sorts of times. It caused one hell of a fight when I asked her not to."

"So how does she feel about you coming here?"

He rolls his eyes. "Let's just say I'm pleased she doesn't hold grudges. It was the usual big blow up and then it was over and done with."

"And have you inherited that trait?"

"If I'm honest, a little, but it takes a helluva lot more to get me riled and I can usually control it when I do."

I angle my phone towards the cooker as I start to fry the mushrooms. The black aura. I did actually unbend my principles and look it up. It can mean built-up anger and grief. This guy may as well have a flashing warning sign around his head, yet he has only just shown how self-aware he is. That has to count for something.

"You didn't get riled with Kitto today. Not at all."

"Like I said, he had every right to question me and he was quite civil once you put him straight."

"Except he palmed you off with the dogfish."

"Well that's OK, Mom has a recipe for almost everything. How it tastes, well, we'll find that out shortly. Or at least I will. That's kind of the oddest thing about this. We're sharing dinner but we're not. Once we can, I'd like to change that."

I smile. "Me too."

Now that did sound more like date territory, but why am I so keen? Apart from the obvious; he's a good looking guy who seems really nice. I need to ignore that aura rubbish. If I try hard enough I might be able to teach myself not to see it. But imagine kissing him, knowing it's there... No, I can't think about kissing Mani for any number of reasons. Except right at this moment, I can't quite work out what those other reasons could be.

PART TWO: 1809

CHAPTER SIX

Harriet Lemon followed Lady Susanna de Dunstanville and her female guests out of Tehidy's great dining room and across the panelled entrance hall. A fire was burning brightly in its marble surround, a page boy wearing the Basset family's red and gold livery standing by ready to load more logs should the flames dare to lose one iota of their light or warmth.

In the drawing room the deep pink velvet curtains were drawn against the November night. The dancing light from the oil lamps bathed the fronds of wisteria that decorated the wallpaper, making them appear to ripple in an imaginary breeze. And it certainly was imaginary, for indeed nothing so much as the tiniest draft rattled the windows or crept under the door.

As usual, the silver samovar was set on a small table next to the fireplace, the fine Spode tea set, with its delicate pink cabbage rose pattern and gilded edges ready at its side.

Lady de Dunstanville turned to Harriet. "My dear, would you?" She handed her the key to a rosewood tea caddy before sitting on a sofa a comfortable distance from the fire and continuing her conversation with Elizabeth Daniell and Frances Vivian.

In most families the important job of preparing the ladies' tea would fall to the daughter, but it would be pointless asking Franny to do so, even if she was here. Which rather begged the question; where was she? She had left the dining table a full half hour ago to give her precious horse, Selkie, an apple. Not the most ladylike behaviour, to simply grab the piece of fruit and walk out, especially when there was company, but she did it every night and was nothing if not a creature of habit.

The problem was that Franny understood so little of society. At the age of twenty-eight and the daughter of a baron, one would have expected her to be well-versed in its rituals and customs, but it had proved an impossible task to teach her even the most basic etiquette. Not because she was being deliberately difficult (although at times earlier in their acquaintance Harriet had wondered), it was because the very ideas made no sense at all to her rather literal brain.

Even the phrase 'coming out' had caused a problem. "Why is it called that, when the events it encompasses are all held inside, and I have been spending time outside all of my life?" she had asked. And even worse, when Franny had heard someone refer to Harriet, who was four years her senior, as an old maid, she had chosen to ponder it in public with her friend who, as far as she could see, was really quite young and very much a lady.

Being called an old maid had felt like a slur on her character, but truth was, Harriet had no desire to marry. She was more than content here at Tehidy as Franny's companion, ready to interpret the world for her as best she could. And, of course, her position allowed her to take advantage of the unusual freedoms granted to a single woman assumed to be beyond marriageable age. Not to mention the extensive library to which she had access, and every creature comfort she could wish for.

Besides, four of her sisters were married and although they had their own households she could scarce see any advantage to the state. Shackled to some man, being taken to his bed at will. Harriet shuddered. That would be the worst thing of all. She was glad her father, Sir William, and her mother, the gentle

49

Jane, had never pushed her into matrimony. Here, with Franny, she could indulge her own particular passions, not to mention devote time to the study of philosophy and the arts, to music and sketching, and now and then in the evenings, lively conversation.

It was simply not true that women left the dining room for the men to talk about the important issues of the day. Not with a mistress like Lady de Dunstanville at Tehidy, and intelligent guests such as those who graced her sofas this evening. As she passed tea to the assembled company their topic of discussion was not frippery and lace, but the fear of cheap copper from overseas and the impact it might have on the Cornish mining community; whether the government should intervene to tax the imports and what poor relief measures might need to be put in place, should the worst happen.

Although enjoying the different points of view and politely presenting her own, Harriet had half an ear open for Franny's return from the stables. She really had been gone far longer than was necessary. Of course it was always possible she had fallen into conversation with one of the grooms about a particular horse and had lost all track of time, but then Harriet heard the scuffling of rapid footsteps on the stairs and the slamming of a door somewhere above.

After waiting for an appropriate pause in the conversation, she pleaded a slight headache and left the room. The lamps' glow cast a fluttering shadow on the polished wooden panels as she climbed the staircase and crossed the landing above, the low heels of her silk evening shoes making not a sound on the Axminster carpet.

Franny's room was on the left-hand side, with its view over the elaborately styled roof of the chapel pavilion and up the slope to the woods beyond. There was no sound from within, and no answer when Harriet knocked. Nor did she wait for one, turning the handle in almost the same motion and slipping inside. The fire burnt brightly, Franny's nightdress set to warm in front of it by her maid, Ann, and the lamps were lit. Franny herself stood by the window, apparently gazing at the heavily-swagged dark green curtains that blocked the view beyond.

"Franny?"

"He was going to ride his horse and it was lame."

"Who was?"

"H-him."

Harriet quickly distilled the possibilities, coming to the conclusion that the likely culprit was Lord de Dunstanville's cousin and former political rival, Sir Christopher Hawkins, who had quite rudely left the dining room before the ladies, claiming a long ride home. The man was barely tolerated at Tehidy, but out of civility invited to hunt once or twice a season, and seemed to relish being as awkward as possible while he was here.

"Sir Christopher?"

Franny nodded, and Harriet stepped closer, laying her hand on Franny's shoulder. To her surprise, she leapt away, wrapping her arms tightly around her chest.

"My dear … what happened?"

"Do not touch me, do not touch me." The words flew from her lips in a forceful staccato.

"Very well. But you must still tell me. I assume you tried to persuade him otherwise than to ride?"

Franny nodded again, her knuckles white where she gripped her upper arms. It was then Harriet noticed the grazing on her hands.

Trying to keep her voice steady, she asked, "And he refused?"

"I even offered him a loan of one of our horses, but he said … he said…" Franny frowned, as if trying to remember the exact words. "That it was no matter, because he would ride me instead. But of course that made no sense so I asked him what he meant."

Franny was not a woman prone to hysterics, but she was shaking from head to toe.

"Perhaps you should lie on the bed, or at very least sit down," Harriet suggested.

The idea that Franny had suffered some sort of violence at Sir Christopher's hands was beginning to take hold. It was all too possible; the man had a thinly veiled hatred for his Basset cousins and had been well in his cups.

Franny nodded. "My knees … they feel very strange … and they burn so. I think my stockings must be holed from rubbing against the floor of Selkie's stall."

Oh lord, what had he done to her? Had he really forced her to all fours and sat astride her back? Poor, poor Franny, the awful indignity of it. Harriet felt close to tears, yet the anger building within her burnt more bright. She stretched out her hand. "Come, lie down and let me look. Perhaps we should bathe them with warm water."

Franny's hand was cold in hers as Harriet led her to the bed. Harriet's instinct was to lie next to her, hold her, but she forced herself to concentrate on the task in hand, settling Franny on her pillows then removing herself gently down the covers to lift the silk hem of Franny's evening gown. Straw was caught in the chenille trim at the bottom, and there was a tear in the fabric almost six inches long.

Franny was right, her stockings were badly torn around the knees, already sticking to the bloody grazes. Harriet's first thought was to ring the bell for Ann to bring warm water, but some deeper instinct told her to keep this a secret for now, at least until she understood the full extent of what had happened. She fetched the ewer herself and lifted Franny's chemise, stifling a cry. Her pantalettes were bloodied and torn as well.

Franny's eyes were closed, her face a sheen of sweat, no doubt remembering and trying to understand what had happened. Harriet knew it would be beyond her to process it even, and for that small mercy she was glad. She herself was vaguely aware of such matters, having married sisters, and she was shrewd enough to guess what Sir Christopher had done. It was beyond belief, sickening her to the core and filling her with impotent fury. She would wager he would not have been so bold with any other gentlewoman, and she was shaking with rage as she realised how badly he'd taken advantage of Franny's vulnerability.

Pulling herself together she exclaimed rather too brightly, "Oh your poor knees, and you were right about your stockings too. What a horrid trick to play, to ride you like a horse. Well, not to worry. I will wash them and ready you for bed, then ring for a soothing tisane. By morning you will have forgotten all about it."

But Harriet would never forget. What that man had done was unforgivable. No-one else should touch Franny's most sacred places, places only she was permitted to share.

If it took her a lifetime, Harriet would have her revenge.

CHAPTER SEVEN

For the first time in weeks the sea two hundred feet below in Scradjick Cove was clear and calm, the waves caressing the rocks with a whimper, rather than a roar. It was time, William Burgess thought, more than time. Portreath's preventative men had been dealt with, having been sent on some fools' errand to Hell's Mouth where a local farmer in his pay would detain them with rumour, while here the cargo from *Sweet Emily* would be spirited ashore.

He turned his cloak inside out to show its red lining and spurred Liberty into a gallop. Here on the cliffs he felt the freedom that had given his mount her name; the sea melting azure towards where his ship was anchored, the salt air making the skin on his face burn. Although he was riding with a definite purpose, his heart pumped with joy as Liberty's hooves thundered over the soft grass.

Above Red Head Cove he reined her in and lifted his eyeglass towards his ship. Already the first boat was lowered, so they had seen the signal. Tom Nance was waiting in the cave at Scradjick, ready to load the barrels onto the ropes that would be dropped from the top of the cliffs. All was set for a successful day's business. Lord knows, his crew needed it after all this time.

The excited whinny of a horse behind him alerted him to the fact he was not alone and he swung around, dropping his eyeglass into his pocket.

"Franny! What brings you here?"

His childhood friend brought her mount to a halt with an elegant swerve. She really was the most accomplished horsewoman he had ever known.

"The same as you, I wager. This glorious February weather. Harriet tells me I have been like a caged bear, kept inside, but in truth I do not know how she can say it because she has never seen such a creature in her life."

How typical of Franny, William thought, but he was used to her particular way of seeing the world.

"I have seen one," he told her. "Not caged, but tied to a post at Illogan Fair. I thought it right cruel to keep captive such a fine animal for human entertainment."

Franny shuddered. "Then I am glad I did not see it too. Tell me, how are Brutus and Belle?"

William smiled. She would ask about the dogs above his family, but he could not complain because it was over a love of animals they had bonded, an unlikely pairing of the Tehidy steward's son and the daughter of a lord; he at nine years old and she just four. When first she had come into his orbit she could barely speak, but she had trotted after him all the same, from stables to kennels and back again, already handling her first Dartmoor pony with aplomb.

Their friendship had proved enduring, and had even survived the turmoil he'd experienced during his later teenage years over his slow recognition that they shared a father. He had always wondered why his running away from grammar school and other transgressions had been so well tolerated by both Thomas Burgess, his adoptive parent, and his employer, and why he had been offered work as a groom when perhaps he should have been cast out into the world.

There had been no single moment of realisation, but as he had grown he had come to resemble Lord de Dunstanville more and more. On a rare visit indoors, invited on great tolerance to entertain Franny who had sprained her ankle, he had spied a portrait of his father as a young man. Yes, he may have been wigged and dressed in finery, but there was no escaping that the long narrow face, rather hooded eyes and in particular the small, full lips were his own.

The question had been how to profit from this information and it was one he had mulled over for quite some time. Much as he loved the horses, he didn't want to spend the rest of his life in the service of others, and already he had been lured to the fringes of smuggling by dint of his ability as a horseman. He wanted to become a man of business on his own account, but how best to approach the matter?

His opportunity had come on a crisp hunting day some twelve years before. Franny's relatively new horse had taken a tumble over a hedge, leaving its rider caught up in the brambles and greatly out of sorts. It was William who had stopped to free and appease her, and later Lord de Dunstanville had sought him out to thank him.

Alone in the stables, he had seized his moment. Looking the man in the eye he had said, "Of course I would help her, my lord. She is my half-sister, is she not?"

He had expected his employer to at least flinch, but he did not. Instead he had nodded. "I will not deny it, William, out of respect for your dear mother who died in childbirth. But I would ask that this matter goes no further."

His cool acceptance had been almost worse than denial, and William had clenched his fingers tightly into his palms as he had asked, "And who was my mother to you? An unfortunate dalliance?"

"Emily was the sweetest of girls, but I was young and she was not of my class. Had she lived, I would have looked after you both. As I have done you."

William had lowered his eyes and nodded, thinking fast. "You have indeed, my lord, but I must think to my future."

"You are not happy here?"

"I would rather be able to set up on my own account, make something more of my life, than remain a servant in my father's household."

"Then let me think what can be done."

William had been about to say that it needed to be enough to buy his silence, but looking into his father's face he knew he did not need to. They understood each other very well.

Franny's eager voice brought him back to the present. "Shall we race?"

He shook his head. "I am afraid I cannot this morning. I have business to attend to."

"Business? But you are a farmer."

"I have fingers in many pies."

Franny frowned. "You have become a baker too?"

William laughed. "No, it is simply a turn of phrase. What I mean is that I have many different lines of business to occupy my time."

"Then I will not keep you. But it would have been entertaining, all the same."

"And you would have won and taken a good wager from me." He looked out to sea, down the coast towards St Ives where dark grey clouds were threatening the clear blue sky around them. "Enjoy the sunshine while you can, Franny. I think it may rain later."

She followed his gaze. "You are right and I must waste no more time in conversation." She bent to pat Selkie's neck then urged him into an easy canter.

As William turned his mount back along the coast towards Scradjick Cove and Selkie's hoofbeats faded behind him, he pondered their unexpected meeting. It wasn't their words that exercised his interest; so much was normal for Franny and he understood her well, better than most, he would guess, but it was the way she had looked. Even given her sallow complexion her face had a pasty hue, her grey eyes smaller than ever under their heavy lids. He shrugged. She had been cheerful enough — it was probably that, like all of them, she had been cooped up inside for far too long.

It was several hours later when William turned onto the track leading to Koll Hendra Farm, followed by Tom Nance who was leading a trio of ponies with barrels strapped to their backs. Normally such an undertaking would be carried out at night, but given the vagaries of the weather and his ruse to keep the preventative men occupied elsewhere, William had reasoned that the best thing was to get the contraband stowed away as quickly as possible.

There were several hiding places around the yard, but today he chose the hayrick behind the granite barn as the goods would be moving inland tonight. He thanked Tom for his trouble, pressing a crown into his hand. This was, in reality, little more than a tip, because he would get his share of the proceeds in due course. But it was the hungry time, and even with a small farm of his own further up the valley, he knew his friend was finding it hard to put food on the table.

As was his wont, William entered through the scullery door. Koll Hendra was a fair to middling sort of house with a large kitchen where the fire was always lit, a chilly front parlour and a small room to the left of it that was notionally called the library but in fact the only book it contained was a bible, and that was seldom read. Above were two sizeable bedrooms and a room in the attic where Alice, their maid of all work, slept.

Mary was in the kitchen, pounding pastry, her figure made all the more generous by the advanced stage of her pregnancy. To William she was luscious as a ripe apple, but with the baby almost due he knew he should push lascivious thoughts from his mind. Last year they had lost a girl, stillborn just a few weeks before her time, and neither of them could bear for that to happen again.

She looked up at him and spoke sharply, pushing a stray lock of her red-brown hair back under her crisp mob cap. "Did I see barrels, William? In broad daylight and at this, of all times."

He bent to scoop his toddler son from the hearth rug where he was playing with his building blocks.

"Dada!" the child called in delight as he swung him around.

"And do not think to distract yourself with Young Will," Mary continued. "Answer my question."

"The barrels will be moved tonight. I am sorry my dear, but now the storms have abated I had to act. Families are hungry and the brandy cannot be sold in *Sweet Emily*'s hulls."

With a sweep of her hand she indicated the apples on the table, stored in the hayloft since the previous autumn, the pot of stew on the stove, filling the kitchen with the enticing aroma of onions and beef. "Then perhaps they do not manage their affairs as well as we do."

Inwardly William sighed. This was not his normally caring and charitable wife, but the worry of their child's impending birth was testing her sorely. He set Will on the mat and came to stand behind her, rubbing her back.

"We have more than most anyway. As well as the farm, the rope-making business turns a pretty penny…"

"Then why must you free trade as well? It is irresponsible to put yourself at risk when you have a family. What would we do if something happened to you?"

"Firstly, you would be well provided for and secondly, it will not."

"You cannot be sure, William." There were tears in her eyes and he held her to him, wrapping his arms gently around her stomach and feeling the baby kick. It would not be long. It could not be long. If he were to admit it, he was as frightened as she was about her confinement.

"All right," he promised her. "No more contraband at the farm until the baby is safely delivered." After all, there must be other places he could hide it.

Harriet sat in the window seat in her bedroom and watched Franny emerge from the walled garden, no doubt having deposited Selkie in the stable yard. The first thing her friend did was look up and wave, and Harriet raised her hand in reply, as Franny strode across the gravel towards the portico and thence into the house.

Harriet bit her lip. Could she put it off much longer? She had received a reply to her letter to her eldest sister Anne three days ago and held it in her hand with a heavy heart. Pretending she had suspicions about a maid, she had asked about the early signs of pregnancy, and the answer had not pleased her at all.

The one thing that gave her even the tiniest sliver of hope was the complete absence of morning sickness, as Franny's appetite was as robust as ever. In fact, she insisted on boiled eggs for breakfast every day, when she had never so much as looked at one before. On the other hand, given her sister had noted she had suffered from a strange desire for mackerel, Harriet was worried indeed.

It had been the tenderness of Franny's breasts that had first alerted Harriet to the possibility that Sir Christopher's attack had had the worst possible outcome. As they lay together one afternoon she had begged to be touched more, yet more gently, and had cried out in ecstasy as her fingers had traced her newly darkened nipples. Later Harriet had remembered her sister Louisa complaining how strange and sore her bosom had felt when she was first expecting a happy event and she'd felt sick to her soul.

The final tell-tale sign on Anne's list was currently exercising Harriet's mind. Had Franny's monthly courses stopped? It was impossible for her to know without asking, but all the same she could not remember the last time Franny had sent her away, as was generally her wont at such times. Harriet threw the letter down. For her own peace of mind, she had to know the truth. Even though the answer would have the power to rip her world in two.

The one good thing was, that indelicate as the question might sound, once asked Franny would answer it honestly. It was this trait in her personality that had worried Harriet most when their friendship had moved beyond what was strictly conventional between women, and at first she had proceeded cautiously.

She could no longer remember what had driven her to kiss Franny for the first time. Curiosity, a yearning for a little excitement, or desire? Perhaps all three, although the latter had been at the forefront of her mind, but desire for what? To be different, to be daring? Or to sate the restlessness that had always been in her, yet do so in a manner that would keep her social position secure.

They had been sitting outside the temple folly in Tehidy's grounds, their backs to its classical columns to sketch the view inland towards the rugged outline of Carn Brea as it rose through the smoke from the mine chimneys. However, when she had glanced over at Franny's work she had seen not the view in front of them, but her own face with its pointed nose and chin and almond-shaped eyes.

"Why Franny," she'd said, "you have made me quite beautiful."

"Because you are beautiful."

Harriet had known there could be no guile or teasing in Franny's reply and it had given her the confidence that perhaps her advances would not be rebuffed. Closing her eyes, she had leant forwards to kiss Franny on the lips.

Although once started she could not stop the kiss, Harriet had been gripped by fear over how Franny would respond, but then she'd felt Franny's mouth begin to move in time with her own; wondering, exploring. And when they'd pulled away Franny had grinned at her and said, "That was nice."

"It was."

They had both returned to their sketching, Harriet's mind in turmoil. How could she make Franny understand not to tell? If she did — and she was believed — Harriet would surely be sent back to her cloistered spinster existence at her family home of Carclew, and isolation and social shame would follow.

She'd swallowed hard. "It was so nice that one day I would like to do it again, but it must be our secret."

"Why?"

Of course, it had been the question she'd expected, but still Harriet was uncertain how to answer. In the end she'd said, "Because I ask it. Is that answer enough?"

Looking a little unsure, Franny had nodded. She had kept her word as she always did, although it had been several weeks before Franny herself had taken the initiative and they'd kissed again.

But now Harriet must put such happy memories out of her mind. After they had breakfasted she would suggest another trip with their watercolours, this time to paint the daffodils which were appearing at the edge of the wood. There she would have to pluck up the courage to ask the question she dreaded the answer to most.

CHAPTER EIGHT

"Lady de Dunstanville, may I speak with you privately?" Harriet quietly edged into the morning room.

The baroness put down her embroidery and smiled encouragingly. "I might say, my dear, that sounds a little ominous. Come take a seat on the sofa next to me."

The morning room at Tehidy was at the front corner of the house, in order to take best advantage of the light. Here, as well as in the drawing room, the walls were covered with patterned paper, this time flocked with tiny green and blue birds, and the elegant furniture was upholstered in pale blue silk. But today it did not feel like the calm oasis that Harriet had always found it to be.

She folded her skirts under her and turned at an angle to face Lady de Dunstanville. "I can find no way to soften this blow, my lady, however hard I try, but I have reason to believe Franny is with child."

Lady de Dunstanville's face was white as chalk, and she gripped the hard arm of the camelback sofa. "I pray you are mistaken, for I do not see how that can be."

Harriet could not look at her. "It was last November, after one of the hunts. She went to the stables as usual but Sir Christopher Hawkins found her there and…"

Lady de Dunstanville spoke unsteadily. "Even him … surely he wouldn't…"

"At the time I hoped against hope I was wrong. There was some sort of argument, with Franny wishing to dissuade him from riding his lame horse, and she told me … she told me…" Oh, how Harriet wished she could spare a mother the man's cruel words. "That he would ride her instead," she finally whispered.

"Oh." The sound was a tiny one and for a moment Harriet thought Lady de Dunstanville would call for her salts, but instead she took a deep breath, high spots of colour appearing on her cheeks.

"The one small blessing is that Franny does not understand what actually happened to her," Harriet said.

"Then how do you know?"

"When she came back I heard her bedroom door slam and excused myself to find her. She was upset because her stockings were torn and her knees were bleeding, but oh, my lady, there was blood on her undergarments as well."

Such was the pent up fear and anger inside her, Harriet could no longer prevent herself from letting out a sob, and within a moment she felt Lady de Dunstanville's ice-cold hand on her own.

"There, there, Harriet. I know this must be distressing for you as well, but why did you not tell me at the time?"

"I did not wish to concern you with it when I was perhaps denying the full gravity of the situation myself."

"And does anyone else know of the incident?"

"I sent Ann away when she knocked that night and later excused the blood by saying Franny had slipped and taken a fall."

"Very sensible. But you are above all sensible, dear Harriet, which is why you make such an excellent companion for my daughter. But what I am wondering is how, as an unmarried woman yourself, you are able to draw your conclusions about my daughter's condition?"

"I was worried about what might be so I wrote to my sister, Lady Davie, on the pretence I had suspicions about a maid. I finally spoke to Franny about it yesterday and she tells me that now she thinks of it, she has not been visited by her courses since well before Christmas."

"Oh." Lady de Dunstanville was swaying slightly now.

"Your salts?" Harriet asked.

"No, no, I must keep a clear head if I can. This is no time to be swooning like some silly schoolgirl."

Harriet nodded, glad that Franny's mother benefited from a rod of iron beneath her pretty manners and comely appearance. "I do not believe Franny understands the import of this," she added.

Lady de Dunstanville clasped and unclasped her hands. "I am sure she does not. She is such an innocent, even more so because of the manner in which she sees the world. I was so afraid, when she was young, that a suitable match would present itself but that he would turn out to be cruel in certain ways. I was almost relieved when it didn't."

"But what are we going to do, my lady? It will have to be explained what is happening to her body."

Franny's mother shuddered. "I do not know which is more terrifying; that or telling Lord de Dunstanville. But clearly both need to be done."

"May I take it that, given what you have just said, you would not seek to force her into an unwelcome marriage?" Harriet held her breath. For her, this was the most important question of all.

But Lady de Dunstanville could give her no comfort. "That, my dear, must be her father's decision."

Harriet's darkest nightmares and sweetest dreams had been filled with vengeful thoughts about Sir Christopher, but if Lord de Dunstanville was to force him into marriage with his daughter she felt sure she would actually kill the man, rather

66

than let that happen. With her own bare hands, if necessary, but satisfying as it was to imagine them around his neck while his bulbous eyes popped and he struggled for breath, she knew she had not the strength.

How could a woman of gentle birth affect such a thing? She lacked the skill to run a sword through his chest. Neither could she shoot. And her horse was far too meek to gallop him into the ground, although perhaps Selkie … but she did not share Franny's skill as a horsewoman to handle such a beast.

No, although she could plan so many forms of revenge she would need a man to carry them out, and the thought made her angrier than ever. Hopefully Lord de Dunstanville would no more countenance a forced marriage than his wife, so she would not need to actually kill Sir Christopher, and she could go back to her favourite pastime of thinking up a thousand more subtle ways he could pay for what he had done.

Even choosing the right words to explain the fact of her pregnancy to Franny was never going to be easy, Harriet knew. The word itself would be unfamiliar to her, and the terms more often used in polite society would simply make no sense. Telling her she was in 'an interesting condition' might be true, but said absolutely nothing unless you understood the code, which Fanny surely did not, and as for 'expecting a happy event', well, nothing could be further from the truth.

Knowing her daughter well, Lady de Dunstanville had decided to use the simplest of words and break the news while the three of them were walking in the formal gardens, a distance from the house so as not to be overheard, yet close enough not to have a footman accompany them. The pale sunlight flooding the gravel paths and symmetrical flowerbeds gave little warmth, and Harriet wrapped her cloak more firmly around her.

"Harriet and I believe you will give birth to a baby in the summer."

A crease appeared between Franny's eyebrows. "But how can that be? I have no husband."

"It seems Sir Christopher is the child's father, following your um … er … altercation with him in the stables."

"Well, I certainly won't marry him. Or any man who rides his horses lame."

"Indeed," replied her mother. "Neither your father nor I would consider him a suitable match."

In fact, Harriet knew that Lord de Dunstanville had been wild with rage at the news. Normally a well-humoured, logical man, he had been overcome by a fit of fury that Harriet could empathise with only too well. It had taken all of his wife's powers of persuasion to stop him riding immediately to Sir Christopher's seat at Trewithen with his pistols. Even now he was still muttering about a duel, but every time he did so, Lady de Dunstanville reminded him what possible reason could he have for challenging the man, without bringing shame upon his daughter?

Harriet's principal emotion at Franny's lack of comprehension was one of relief. She had been right; Franny had no idea what Sir Christopher had done to her in the stables; that most heinous and wicked of acts that no man should ever commit. It was a tiny straw of consolation, in that now the event itself was over it could not further harm her by remembrance or shame. But quite how she would cope with the reality of being with child, and the necessary secrecy that must surround it, was Harriet's main concern now.

They walked a little further, the crunch of their footsteps on the path and the birds singing in the neat hedgerow border the only sound. On the edge of the woods above them daffodils swayed in the breeze, but Harriet took no joy in them. She and Franny were about to be jolted from their comfortable existence here at Tehidy and the damage that might do to her friend was incalculable. Franny hated being away from the regular pattern of her days here for whatever reason. And she, Harriet, would be the one who had to navigate her through it.

But that news was for another day, and as it seemed Franny was incurious about her condition, Lady de Dunstanville let the matter drop, and they discussed instead the progress of the tramline being built to link the harbour at Portreath with Dolcoath mine, and if the weather continued to improve, when the bathing cottage at Carvannel Cove might be reopened for the summer. This, at least, would prove a distraction for Franny, so Harriet joined her in expressing a wish that it could be affected earlier than usual, so long as the storms did not return.

CHAPTER NINE

William rocked the wooden crib in front of the kitchen fire with his foot. His younger son, Henry, was almost a month old and had been baptised at Illogan Church that Sunday past. It had been a relatively straightforward birth, thank God, but Henry seemed to be a colicky baby and the constant rocking was something of a necessity if William wanted to think while Mary was putting Young Will to bed.

Think he certainly needed to — and fast. Rumour had reached him that for some inexplicable reason his natural father had challenged his cousin and political rival, Sir Christopher Hawkins, to a duel. William's informant had told him it was due to the bribery charges brought against Sir Christopher in the course of his borough-mongering, but his acquittal at Bodmin Court had been almost two years before, so in William's view there had to be something else behind this.

The whys and wherefores were not William's main concern, however, although perchance he might be able to make some capital of them later should the truth of the matter come to his attention. Generous as Lord de Dunstanville was, he could never be sure that his goodwill would not dry up, so a few additional levers to press matters should the need arise were always useful.

The real problem, however, was that if Lord de Dunstanville died, this useful extra source of income would stop. As a woman, Franny would never truly be in charge of her own financial affairs, even once she inherited, and neither could he go to her cap-in-hand. He had his pride, after all, and he had faithfully sworn to their father he would never reveal himself to be her kin.

The thought of his father's untimely demise had never bothered him before; although in his fifties Lord de Dunstanville appeared to be in rude health, but a duel was an entirely different matter. Particularly when the only thing the two participants generally shot were pheasant or deer. Anything could go awry, and when gentlemen took to their pistols against each other, quite often it did.

William would not leave anything to chance if he could possibly help it. His informant had told him the carriage would leave Tehidy House at around four in the morning, and he would be waiting to follow. Of its destination he was uncertain, but it would no doubt be some lonely stretch of moorland that could be reached by dawn. Hopefully not so bleak there was no boulder or patch of gorse behind which he could stay hidden and observe, ready to act if he had to.

Mary returned to the kitchen, her reddish-brown hair escaping from her mob cap in the way that still made his heart twist, even after the five years they had been together. In truth, he had never seriously looked at another woman since chancing upon her in the street in St Ives one summer afternoon. With the sunlight setting those tendrils of hair aglow, he had been lost.

Of course her parents had disapproved; about the port he was known as a free trader and although he knew for certain that Mary's father had quite a taste for smuggled rum, marrying his daughter into the business providing it was quite another matter. No amount of explanation that he was a farmer and rope manufacturer of no small means as well would bring the man around, although it had impressed young Mary, and been enough to persuade her to elope.

He had installed her with a respectable widow in Illogan until the banns had been read three times, and married her the day after. And their happiness together had been bountiful and blessed. Apart from the times when she shared her father's disapproval of his business activities, when the temper hinted at by the hue of her tresses came to the fore. He very much feared he was about to light that particular fuse now.

It had been a long few hours trying to sleep in the wooden chair in front of the banked down fire, but William had considered it wiser not to attempt to join Mary in their bed, only to have woken her at this ungodly hour and risk another outpouring of venom. God, she could be a vixen when she chose, but a part of him took a guilty pleasure in her anger, knowing how much in other ways he positively relished her passionate nature.

But as he waited in the darkness under the trees opposite Tehidy's East Lodge he was sorry he had not been able to tell her the truth. For once her fury had been misplaced, and yet he had encouraged this misplacement, letting her think he had smuggling business to attend to. But how could he otherwise explain his absence when she had no idea of his true parentage? In the small hours of the night, he had doubted the sanity of this enterprise.

He was not long to his contemplations before he heard the clatter of hooves and the squeak of carriage wheels. He reined Liberty further into the thicket until they became nothing more than shadows as it passed. It was the post chaise pulled by a pair, with the driver riding postillion, and one of the grooms, who William knew to be a former sharp-shooter in the army, on the bench seat up front. Lord de Dunstanville was wise to take such precautions — who knew what felons lurked beneath the trees alongside the road during the hours of darkness.

It was an unusual experience for William to be the hunter and not the hunted. More often than not on his nocturnal journeys across the county his principal concern was keeping ahead of any preventative men who might have taken chase behind him, the skill and guile he needed to do so filling his veins with a heady sort of blood that enriched his pleasure beyond most things. All that was required of him now was to stay as close as he could to the carriage without being seen himself. It was a poor game by comparison.

The moonless night was his friend and his thick cloak protected him well from the mizzling rain. Passing through Illogan village they were quickly on the road that Sir Francis had himself caused to be built across Treleigh Downs, linking the estate to the highway that ran up the spine of the county towards Bodmin.

William followed not by sight but by sound. The horses were running at a fast trot, the post chaise's metal frame creaking as it bumped along the road. The noise meant it was safe to hang back, as long as he did not miss the point it turned down some lane or other towards its final destination.

As they continued east the drizzle lifted a little and as they crossed the high ground around Chiverton the cloud cleared for a moment and William caught a glimpse of the coach before it began its descent of the hill. In the distance ahead of him the faintest band of light on the horizon tinged the darkness so he knew they could not be far from their destination. For a duel, the appointed hour was always dawn.

It was not long before they left the road to follow a rough track towards Allet Common. William hoped that bleak and featureless land was not where the morning's drama would be played out, for there was no hope of hiding rider and horse there, and with every mile he found himself becoming more nervous for the man who was sitting in the carriage ahead.

What nonsense was this! It was not as though there had ever been affection or anything like it between them, and although Lord de Dunstanville had spoken of the mother he had never known with sorrow, it was clear he would not have married her. So she would have lived in servitude, her reputation sullied by his pleasure, alongside the boy who was a bastard. Normally that thought made him angry, and want to lash out at his father, for all his generosity towards him. But this morning he could summon up not so much as a flicker of ire. Damn it — it was important to him and his family's future that the man lived.

William had to hang back as they crossed the common, so once the hedgerows had been regained on either side he urged Liberty forwards, only to round a bend and be confronted by the sight of the post chaise at the side of the road, along with a brougham. It was too late to do anything other than bury his face into his cloak and canter past, observing as he did so Lord de Dunstanville and a tall, stooping man in military uniform who must be his second, heading along a footpath that led to the bottom of the valley.

That there was enough light to see them meant the time and place were near. Above the woods on the opposite side of the River Allen the dark grey sky was smudged with pink and birdsong began to drift in the air. Holding hard to the hedge line of the next field William led Liberty to the river's edge to drink, thankful the soft ground had silenced her hooves. He waited until the combatants had crossed the plank bridge just upstream then tied her to a sapling ash and primed his pistol before following them.

For once in his life, he did not have a plan. He had vowed only to intervene if he had to, but by then his father could be either mortally wounded or dead. He would need to trust his instincts. Comforted by the fact they had served him well during his thirty-three years on God's earth, he continued to move as quietly as possible through the woods.

At the top of the rise was a clearing some forty yards across where an ancient fort was rumoured to have stood. A man in a muddy brown greatcoat and beaver hat strode into the middle of the grassy area and Lord de Dunstanville's second approached him. While remaining in the cover of a sturdy oak, William crept as close as he dared to where his father was standing.

Despite the chirruping of the birds as the light increased, he was near enough to overhear the conversation when the second returned.

"Sir Christopher refuses to back down so you, as challenger, will have first fire and at thirty paces."

"Very well, Temple. The gentler part of me had hoped to avoid this, but the insult is so heinous, that man has left me with no choice. Have them prepare the ground."

Alternate shots. That at least gave William a chance to intervene if things looked close first time around. It also gave Lord de Dunstanville the opportunity to wound or kill Sir Christopher Hawkins — provided he was a good enough shot. William could do so in a trice; his aim was exceptional. Should he position himself with a clear view of Sir Christopher, so he could fire a fraction before his official challenger?

But that would give him away and incur his father's wrath to boot. Though he was no gentleman himself, he knew enough about their code to understand that sort of behaviour was beyond the pale. And if he was caught he would likely be locked up in Bodmin gaol for his trouble. All the same, he crept between the trees until he was both close to Sir Christopher's party and had a clear route of escape back to his horse.

The combatants stepped from the shadows into the cold grey light in the clearing. Stripped to their breaches and shirts, the pinkness of the dawn made the latter appear washed with the palest blood and despite himself, William shuddered. He had no truck with premonitions or superstition, but somehow he could not help it. He told himself it was only because his family's financial security depended on what happened in the next few minutes.

Sir Christopher's narrow face was gaunt and grey, his expression haughty as he faced his opponent.

Lord de Dunstanville called across the clearing, "You know the true reason for calling you out, Hawkins?"

"Indeed I do. And I assure you, it was not worth the trouble."

Lord de Dunstanville's face twisted with fury, but his rage at the further slur caused him to misfire, the bullet doing no more than disturbing the ground six inches from his opponent's foot.

William cursed beneath his breath for he was sure that had been Sir Christopher's intention. The man was a cheat, nothing was more certain, but what could be done? Now his father would have to stand as target for him to return the shot.

The time he took to take aim seemed endless but Lord de Dunstanville was as immobile as granite, the faint puce tinge to his skin the only outward sign of his anger. Sir Christopher raised his gun, pointing it obviously and deliberately at his challenger's head. William gripped the handle of his pistol tightly and pulled it from the capacious pocket of his cloak. If that coward killed his father he would not leave the field alive himself.

A shot rang out, a puff of white smoke from the muzzle. Lord de Dunstanville remained upright as the bullet passed a hair's breadth above his wig. Sir Christopher's intention must be to the death.

Lord de Dunstanville gathered himself, calmer this time, and took aim. At the first shot the birdsong had ceased and there was absolute silence in the clearing, save for Sir Christopher's second's laboured breathing as he stood, sweating profusely, just yards away from where William was hiding.

If anything, Lord de Dunstanville's bullet was even closer. So close it seemed to shake his opponent's wig upon his head, and when William looked again he could see it was slightly askew. A near miss, or a deliberate hit? How long could he allow this to go on? With every exchange of fire death circled ever closer.

Deep inside he knew he was but a bystander. He had to let this dreadful theatre play out. If he intervened, even so much as to shoot Sir Christopher Hawkins' gun from his hand, the duel could be voided and they would have to meet again for Lord de Dunstanville to have his satisfaction. And as the light of day became clearer and cooler, William knew he would not risk his own neck by killing Sir Christopher himself. He wanted to see his boys grow up; and it came to him that in most ways that mattered Mary was right — being a good father should above all be his guiding light. A father like he himself had never had. If he killed Hawkins it would only be to protect a source of income; there was certainly no affection between Lord de Dunstanville and himself, and to take a man's life in return for money was something he would not do.

He slipped his pistol back into his pocket and crept a little further away, in most part proud of his cool head, but with a small, uncomfortable nagging corner of his brain asking where was his honour. Honour? He had none, except perhaps the honour that was found amongst free traders. Certainly not a gentleman's honour, which had, along with a title and lands, been denied him by the side of the blanket on which he'd been born. Which made him all the more determined his own sons should have every advantage.

But walk away from his father he could not, so he turned as Sir Christopher raised his gun to chest level. This time he meant it, and William's blood turned to ice. Yet as he watched the path of the gun, it continued upwards in a slow, swinging arc, until it was discharged harmlessly into the air.

"You have your satisfaction, Basset," he said, "but your blood I will not spill."

William let out the breath he'd been holding then ran silently down the slope between the trees to the bridge, and across to the hedgerow where Liberty was quietly waiting. He untied her bridle from the sapling ash then turned for home at a canter.

CHAPTER TEN

It being the day following the Easter celebrations, Harriet knew Franny would consider that whatever the weather, bathing season had finally begun. Up until now Lady de Dunstanville had prevaricated over opening the cottage, but had admitted to Harriet a few days before she could do so no longer. As she gazed from the morning room window, where she waited for the Basset ladies to come down for breakfast, she was relieved to see that at least the sun was shining and the trees were motionless under a clear blue sky.

There was nothing clear about Harriet's mood, however, as she woke each day full of anger towards Sir Christopher and frustration at her own feminine weakness. A part of her wished it was not so; that she could rid herself of at least some of the bitterness and enjoy the life she had once loved so much. But clocks went only forwards, and nothing would ever be the same again.

Breakfast at Tehidy was always an informal affair, as Lord de Dunstanville rarely partook unless there were guests in the house, spending the mornings in his study, or around the estate about his business. So it was a time when the ladies could be alone, as once the coffee and toast had been served Lady de Dunstanville generally dismissed the head housemaid so they could talk in private.

The table in front of the window had been laid for three, the silverware gleaming in the sunlight. To lose all this, to be cast out into a more modest household, even for a relatively short while, was going to be so very hard. Hard on Franny in particular, Harriet reminded herself, for she had never known anything else. Even to Harriet, whose own father was a wealthy baronet, life at Tehidy was exceedingly comfortable.

And how would they make Franny understand what had to happen? Never mind persuade her to play her part in the subterfuge they would need to concoct. Harriet's head ached just to think of it and she rested her forehead against the cool glass. It would not be long before they had to go away; already she could see the changes in Franny's body and she could no longer shut her eyes to it, no longer keep telling herself she could wait just one more day before broaching the matter with Lady de Dunstanville.

For how would she tell of such intimate matters without revealing the secret she held most dear? For if it was known that she and Franny were lovers she would most surely be sent away, and not just for a matter of months, but never to return. She knew too well how that would play out; an estrangement between the friends, Franny removed from the area for her nerves to recover, society's finger firmly pointed in Harriet's direction for being so cruel.

She heard the door open behind her and turned, rapidly picking up her embroidery.

"Good morning, Harriet dear. I hope I have not kept you waiting; I have been busy with my correspondence."

"Good morning, Lady de Dunstanville, I was just using the light to find the loose thread in my embroidery."

"That is a most skilled piece of work, Harriet." Lady de Dunstanville took the green and gold reticule from her. "A most life-like horse's head."

"Thank you. But I must put it away now because it's a surprise for Franny and I believe she will join us soon. She came back from her ride some full forty minutes ago and I am sure she will wish to bathe later."

Lady de Dunstanville perched on the edge of the chaise longue. "I do wish she would not go bathing in her condition, but it would be like it is with the riding, just that gaze of incomprehension while she asserts she is perfectly well. Which of course she is, and I am glad of it for more than just the usual reasons."

Harriet nodded. "The fact that Franny is doing as she always does should allay any rumours that might arise from this matter. If we can manage that she is away from Tehidy for the shortest possible time..."

"But Harriet, it is inevitable her condition will start to show itself soon and already I am concerned that Ann will notice something amiss before we do." She tapped her finger against the pale blue silk of the upholstery. "But perhaps a bathing expedition could play into our hands. If you do not mind, my dear, perhaps you could suggest that you go without your maids, so in helping Franny to change you could make the necessary observations yourself. A wet bathing dress does cling so, does it not?"

"An excellent notion, my lady." Why had she herself not thought of it? And yet as Franny breezed into the room, demanding toast, butter and hard boiled eggs because she was famished after her ride, her relief turned to dread at what was to come.

It was some hours later they rode through the woods onto the North Cliffs then followed the track into the valley where Portreath lay, the sea dressed in the simple blue of spring to their left. A footman had gone ahead on the dog cart to light the fires and provision the Basset's cottage in Carvannel Cove. Although it was a secluded spot on the very edge of the village, while Franny was bathing it would be his job to keep prying eyes away, and although he did not know it, now for reasons more important than simple propriety.

As they descended the cliff, Harriet could see the harbour opposite was crammed with all types of ships, their masts swaying in the breeze. Smoke rose from the low mounds of the lime kilns on the flat land behind the sandy beach and the people hurrying hither and thither looked no more than ants from this height. It always surprised her that such great industrial endeavour was so close to the rugged beauty of the clifftops, but it was so often the way in this part of Cornwall; you could not leave Tehidy in any direction without running up against mining, stamping, or some other heavy work.

The footman was standing stiff and formal outside the low wooden door to the cottage, his liveried uniform at odds with the humble dwelling behind him. But dwelling was perhaps the wrong word, Harriet thought. Dwelling implied someone lived here, but these days this was little more than a toy house, visited only for pleasure, with a cosy parlour and informal dining room on the ground floor, and upstairs where there should be bedrooms were dressing rooms for those who wished to bathe.

And it was in the perfect position for bathing, tucked into the corner of a small valley just off the main beach, the western cliffs curving around in front of it, a natural shelter from the prevailing wind. Franny loved it here so much that her father had caused three bathing pools to be cut into the rock, where the sea could swirl in and delight his daughter without her courting any danger from the unreliable currents that scoured Portreath Bay.

They went inside and Franny removed her bonnet with a sigh, inhaling the scent of beeswax. "The first time we visit in spring is like coming home after a long trip away. Everything smells so polished and fresh, and today it is even better because it is just you and I to share it."

Harriet took her by the hand. "Come, let us sit on the chaise for a while and enjoy the view from the window. It is so clear I swear we will be able to see the tip of St Piran's Head."

"No. We will go straight upstairs and you can help me to undress."

"You want to swim now?"

Franny frowned. "That is not what I said."

So often, when here alone, they indulged in what Franny called 'playing house'. It sounded as innocent as a childhood game but the ways that pleased them most were far from it. This was the place they could enjoy their passion for each other more freely than anywhere else, but for once Harriet's heart was heavy as she followed her up the wooden staircase.

Much as Franny's physical desires had blossomed with her pregnancy, Harriet's had all but dwindled away. Oh, not because she did not find the changes in her lover's body attractive, it was rather something deep inside herself, something she barely understood. But all the same she would not refuse Franny's attentions, leastways not this particular time, because it occurred to her that enhancing her pleasure could make her more amenable to their going away from Tehidy.

Afterwards, as she helped Franny into the blue flannel dress she wore for bathing, she decided the moment was ripe to broach the subject. Tentatively, cautiously, in a way that would seem unplanned, she simply sighed and said, "Oh, Franny, would it not be marvellous to live like this, together and close to the sea."

Franny's grey eyes sparkled even more, making her almost beautiful. "Then I could swim every day."

"And do whatever you wished, my love."

"What a strange thing to say, Harriet, when I can already do everything I please."

Which was a situation Harriet knew could not continue for very much longer and although she smiled at her lover, her heart felt leaden at the thought of what was to come.

Harriet had, in the end, asked Lady de Dunstanville just one request; that when she found a place for her and Franny to spend the coming months it could be by the sea. The older woman had thought for a moment, head on one side, before telling her she knew of somewhere that might do, and she would make enquiries.

And so it came, on a wet Wednesday in early May, when the rain was streaming down Tehidy's windows like tears and the trees in the park bending their backs against the wind, that it fell to Harriet to tell Franny the plans. Perhaps 'fell to' was setting a slur against Lady de Dunstanville's otherwise unblemished conduct in the matter, for Harriet had been quite insistent that she would do it.

She and Franny were lying together on Franny's bed, enjoying each other's comfort and talking, as they often did before the hour came to dress for dinner. They had closed the curtains around them to keep out the draft that rattled through Tehidy's normally reliable windows, so it was as though through dusk they watched each other's expressions.

"Your mother has found a place for us to go, a place by the sea."

"To go?" There was more of a question in Franny's tone than Harriet had anticipated.

"We spoke of it in the cottage, a place where we can live together simply until your baby is born."

"We did not speak of it in terms of the baby."

"No, but it is the baby that makes it possible. Already I can see your stomach is becoming more rounded and before it is noticeable in normal dress we must leave."

There was a long silence before Franny spoke again. "I do not understand why."

"To protect your reputation, of course."

"But as I am not to marry, why does it matter?"

"Because after your father's day you will be baroness in your own right and carry the family name. I am sure you would not wish for people to speak ill of it."

Franny sat up, hugging her knees. "But I have done nothing wrong!"

"Of course you have not, my love. It was Sir Christopher who…" Just speaking his name left a vile taste in her mouth.

"Then why hide?"

Harriet thought carefully before answering. "It is not fair, it is perhaps not right, but it is certainly what is expected. And it will be easier to find an adoptive home for the baby away from Cornwall where you are not known."

"You did not say we would be leaving Cornwall."

"Not far. To Devon, a place called Torquay. It is but a fishing village although it is said the waters there have health-giving properties. The cottage is close by the shore and, I understand, comfortably furnished." Harriet sat up too, and held her friend's hands. "Dearest Franny, I believe we will have a most pleasant stay. We will, of course, take Ann, because we can trust her, and a small local staff has been employed for when we arrive. We will be able to live simply, as we wish, without the rigours of society to bind us."

Franny huffed. "Then I will think about it."

It would be pointless to tell her she had no choice.

PART THREE: 2020

CHAPTER ELEVEN

A week after Easter the weather breaks and I wake to thick drizzle sweeping from the sea. It crept in so silently it surprises me when I open the curtains; there was no tell-tale patter on the window, it is simply there, beading the cobweb so carefully spun against the pane overnight and obscuring the landscape, the distant strip of shimmering blue I have begun to take for granted invisible.

To be fair it suits my mood. Next week I will have to face going back to work. Admittedly it will be part-time, and for now it will be mainly working from home. Some students need to get back to school because they're vulnerable or their parents are key workers, and the head's preparing a rota for teaching them. All the other kids will be expected to work via a virtual classroom, so I'll have to be available in the mornings for that. Which will be fine. What I don't want is to be back in the school itself, where there's every chance I could bring infection home to Mum and Dad.

I sit on the low windowsill, hugging my knees. Lockdown has been extended too, by at least another three weeks, and this is really beginning to bite. In the village the community is pulling together to care for and protect our own, even those who are too proud to ask for help.

My creativity is starting to feel sapped. Another day wasted and I'm fast running out of them. This is so not like me. I'm a doer, not a navel-gazer. Maybe this is my penance for enjoying those first few weeks of lockdown so much. And not quite achieving enough from them. I tell myself to get a grip, but all I can think about, staring into the mist that coats the cauliflower field, is that once I'm back in the classroom I won't be able to go into Mum and Dad's house. I've kind of taken their hugs for granted, and it hits home again how terrible this must be for Kitto, and Mani, and everyone else on their own.

Quite frankly, it makes me want to weep. What the hell's got into me this morning? I ponder going for my walk to stir myself, but I know in this mizzle I'd be soaked through before I got to the end of the lane. So, instead, I lounge around in my dressing gown, drinking tea and beating myself up for not being in the studio, until Dad peers around the door.

"No point spraying the top field today so I thought I'd start on the hayloft. Want to join me?" He makes no comment about my state of undress at half past nine in the morning and I'm grateful.

"Sure," I tell him. "Just as soon as I've had a shower."

"I wouldn't bother, love. It's pretty filthy in there."

He isn't wrong. By the time I've hauled on some leggings and a sweatshirt from the wash basket he's opened the double doors that lead onto the yard, the greyish daylight illuminating years of grime. The workbench at the furthest end from the Granary is the only part of the space that's even remotely clean and I dread to think what lurks in the corners and up the ladders to what an estate agent would call a mezzanine floor, but in reality is little more than planks of wood.

I gaze around me. "This is going to take a lot of work, Dad."

"And you'd rather be actually making your glass, I know."

"It isn't that…"

"Then what?"

"What if … what if it's all a waste of time? What if I can't get the business off the ground? What if no-one wants to buy my stuff?" I'm aware I'm tracing a square in the dirt with the toe of my trainer, just like I used to when I was a child.

I expect Dad to say something like 'of course they will, love', but he doesn't. Instead he fixes me with an uncharacteristically hard stare that reminds me so much of Gran.

"Carla, what you need to work out is how much you want this. Nobody else can make that decision for you. If you want it enough, you'll move heaven and earth to make it happen, like you did to become a teacher. I know you. And if you're really thinking it's pointless because you lent all your money to the farm then you can think again. There's going to be some government cash for hospitality businesses so we can pay it back sooner than you think." Suddenly he grins, and throws the rubber gloves he's been holding at me. "In the meantime, it won't hurt to get this place cleaned up, whatever happens."

We start by removing the layer of dust that covers everything — and I mean everything — Dad with his broom attacking the floor with enthusiasm, and me with a damp rag wiping every other surface; cupboards and shelves, and all the detritus on them, the old treadle sewing machine from way back when, the tin bath hanging from a nail on the wall. The list is endless and most of the stuff in the hayloft should have been chucked out decades ago.

Now the worst of the grime has been removed the job doesn't seem quite so daunting. I'm loath to be far away from even the misty grey daylight so I start with the old kitchen cupboard that's just inside the doors while Dad disappears into the darkest corner of the interior, Sam following him, nose to the floor.

The cupboard contains a stash of old newspapers from the 1970s and I haul them out, calling to ask Dad what we're going to do with stuff like this. The council tips are closed at the moment so we decide to burn anything we can, and bag and stack everything else near the door so it's easy to load into the farm Land Rover at a later date.

It isn't very long afterwards that Dad calls me over to show me an old travelling trunk he's found. It's huge and utilitarian, but seems to be made of reddish-brown leather with the initials MST stamped on it in large black letters.

"I think this was my grandfather's," he tells me, "the one he brought from Mexico. I have a vague memory of your gran bringing it here after he died." He pats it fondly. "He was a nice old boy. Always had penny sweets for your Uncle Howard and me, and he used to tell us funny stories."

"I wonder if there's anything of his in there?" I ask.

"I doubt it. Your gran used it as a sort of ottoman at the bottom of her bed for a while, but I can't remember what happened to it before she brought it in here."

He eases the dull metal catches with his thumbs and they open with a pleasing snap. I am disappointed to see the trunk is almost empty, except for a brass fireside set in various stages of disintegration, and a wooden box that appears to be covered in coal dust. It's quite solid, almost half a metre long, with a doorknob handle at each end. As Dad lifts it out I can see it has four little round feet to match.

"Do you think there's anything in it?" I ask.

"It's hard to tell. It's heavy, but that could just be the wood." He shakes it gently. "There's something moving though."

He carries it over to the workbench and switches on the light before wiping a corner with his finger. "Run and get a clean cloth, will you, love? A soft one. I want to go careful with this."

I do as I'm told then watch as he gently rubs the duster across the lid. The wood he reveals has a beautiful patina, rich with age, but even better there's some sort of design on top, with curving leaves and an empty cartouche in the middle.

"I know what this is," Dad says. "I reckon it's an old tea caddy. I've seen them on those antiques programmes your mum watches. Give her a yell and see what she thinks."

As it happens, when I go to find her, Mum is halfway across the yard with a tray of tea and biscuits. She exclaims over the caddy, then all but rips the duster from Dad's hand and sets about cleaning it herself.

"How on earth did it get into this state?" she asks. "It's covered with coal dust of all things, but it's really beautiful underneath. You're right too, Bill, it is a tea caddy. It has a lock, and that probably means it's Georgian." She laughs a bit self-consciously. "Hark at me, like I'm some sort of expert. But tea was very valuable then so they had to take care of it." She tries to lift the lid. "It's locked now as well. Is there a key?"

I scrabble around in the trunk but I can't find one.

"That's a disappointment," Dad says. "I want to know what's inside."

"Probably more boxes," Mum tells him, "the ones they kept the tea in. And if we're really lucky a little bowl to mix the leaves. I'll need to read up on how to clean it properly. It might even be worth a couple of hundred quid."

Dad grins. "Well if it is we'll put it into Carla's new business account."

"What new business account?"

"The one you're going to open for your glass art. When you're ready, of course," he adds hurriedly.

"That's a great idea," Mum agrees, patting the box. "Whatever this is worth, it's yours, Carla. Every little helps."

I smile at her ruefully. "Thank you. It's going to need quite a lot to lick this place into shape. I mean, I was thinking just now

91

… even the lights. We'd need so much in here to show off the glass properly if it's going to be a selling space. LEDs are perfect for the displays, but daylight too." I shake my head. "I just keep thinking of the cost, and if I'm going to give up work I need to keep some money aside to live on."

"Want some advice?" Mum asks.

"Go on then."

"Don't think about the money. Not at the moment. Allow yourself to dream, find what you really want. I hated it last term, seeing you come back from school all weighed down and miserable. I know you've fallen out of love with teaching and life's too short. You're most likely going to be working for at least the next thirty years, so you'd better find something you enjoy."

"I didn't know it was that obvious."

Dad gives me a hug, tea slopping from his mug. "You're our daughter."

At lunchtime we decide to call it a day. The water running from my shower is filthy, and as I shampoo my hair for a second time, I think about what Mum said. With my savings tied up I haven't dared to even go there in recent weeks, but now seems as good a time as any to explore the rather alien idea that if money was no object, what would I do with my life?

These are big and scary questions I don't often allow myself to think about, because they mean I have to face up to the fact that I hate the unknown. I'm thirty-one, I probably should have some answers, and not just about work. Do I want to find a permanent partner, have children? Has my on-off relationship with Kitto been as convenient to me as it has been to him, obscuring the need to think this through? I certainly didn't feel used until after Christmas, or cheated on when he's been seeing someone else, for a very long time.

I did when I was younger though, and because he was my best friend too it bloody hurt. By the time I went away to university we were properly a couple and had been for a few years, although we'd been mates for far, far longer. Probably since we were about seven, although when we turned sixteen it was as if someone flicked a switch and we couldn't keep our hands off each other. We learnt everything we needed to know about sex together, and as a result got really good at it. Even out of bed we liked doing the same things and we had the same friends. We're both only children and it felt good to be part of a pair.

When I went away to university I stayed true to that. For the whole first year. But Kitto didn't. I came home to find him snogging some redhead tourist outside The Tinners and my world imploded. He didn't even apologise; told me it was my fault for going away, and what did I expect him to do? I had the loneliest summer of my life, but as Gran said at the time, it taught me to be pretty self-sufficient.

With the same circle of friends, once again we gravitated towards each other, especially when I came back to Cornwall to work. Except this time I knew the rules. We've both seen other people, but we keep drifting back to one another. Only now I'm beginning to realise it's not enough.

Is it because I do want to 'settle down'? But I am settled, here in my little cottage. I don't feel as though I need anyone to complete my life. And children? I don't know. Being a teacher I see the results of both good and bad parenting. It's the toughest job in the world and I don't think I'm up for it. And yet, perhaps, with the right person...

Most of my friends, the ones I was at university with certainly, seem to have their lives sorted, so why don't I know what I want? I suppose the cold, harsh reality is I don't have that many choices, so whatever Mum says about dreaming, it would probably be a waste of time. What happens when the farm runs out of money again, and I don't have any either? Maybe one day all Noel's bright ideas for the farm will pay off, and that will be the time to change things.

Yet there is no doubt I'm at my happiest when I'm in my little workshop cutting and forming glass, or outside watching the sea from the cliffs, or in the woods, letting nature inspire my new designs. Even the thought of it lifts my mood, as does the sunshine slanting across the floorboards as I cross the landing to my bedroom to get dressed. The natural light will be fantastic in the workshop this afternoon, so that's the rest of my day sorted. Even if I have to nail myself to the bench. I've wasted far too much time already moping around.

As I pick up my phone a notification flashes onto the screen. It's an email from Mani and that broadens my smile even more.

Hi Carla, missed you the last couple of mornings. Hope everything's OK with you. Anyway, I've been digging into my family tree and have found out something exciting. Would you like to not meet up for a beer at five? Mani.

I'm sure I can adjust my plans to fit him in.

CHAPTER TWELVE

This time as we chat online Mani is sitting at a glass bistro table in a conservatory with an irregular stone wall behind him that I take to be the original exterior of the house. I ask him about it.

"I really lucked out with this place; it's part of Tehidy's converted stables so in all the ways that matter it's pretty modern, but it still has so many fantastic old elements, like a little round window in my study and this amazing black granite mounting block outside the front door. And now, well, you may think I'm crazy, but I honestly reckon this was meant to be."

"What have you found out?"

He leans forwards towards the screen, grinning wildly. "You know I said I've been looking into the history of Dolcoath mine? Well, the family that owned it for about three hundred years were the Bassets. And they owned Tehidy too. Isn't that amazing? They might even have walked into what is now my living room to see to their horses."

I laugh. "Or to watch someone else seeing to them. They would have been super-wealthy; hot and cold running servants everywhere. Don't you have *Downton Abbey* in the States?"

"Of course we do, just not really on my radar."

"To be fair, the period when the mines were in their heyday was more *Poldark*, a hundred or so years before, but if you want a flavour of big country houses in that era then check out *Pride and Prejudice*. It's bound to be on Netflix or something."

"Helen will know. She majored in English Lit."

"Well when you get bored, watch it."

"What do you mean, when?" But he's laughing too. In fact he's looking quite relaxed, which is great to see. "Anyway," he continues, "that's not the only coincidence. Reading on I discovered that about ninety years ago what was left of Dolcoath was bought up by South Crofty, and that's where I'm working. Isn't that neat?"

"That is very neat, as you say. Any luck tracing potential Dolcoath relatives?"

"Nope. Not one other person with my last name, which is really weird. Plenty of street names, a garage business, even a vacation rental."

"That is odd."

"I guess the next step is to work back through my family tree to see if I can find the connection with Cornwall. Have you ever done anything like that?"

I take a sip of wine. "Not really. Dad made a few notes before my gran died and he's always meant to do it, but farmers don't have a lot of free time. And I'm back to work on Monday." It strikes me again how many of these strange, but to me golden, days I've wasted. At the beginning of lockdown I had planned to do so much, a new beginning, almost. Where has the time gone?

"Hey, Carla, what's wrong?"

Oh my god, was it that obvious? What can I say? "I'm pretty nervous about going back. I mean, next week will be OK because I'm on the rota to work from home, but after that I'll probably have to go in."

He nods. "I can understand why you're anxious about going back. I mean, anyone would be, but you could be in contact with what … a hundred or so people?"

"Not so many as that. We'll be working in what they call bubbles… Still, it is what it is and nobody made me become a teacher, after all."

"Well I think it's a fine career. When I recall the good teaching that shaped me … and I certainly wouldn't have the patience to do it myself."

After we end the call I sit at my kitchen table with another glass of wine, looking out into the dusk and feeling restless. I haven't been for the one walk I'm allowed yet today and there's just about time before it gets dark. Not my normal large loop around Tehidy, but I could head out across the cliffs for a while. Better than sitting here getting drunk.

I take the footpath that skirts the holiday lodge park, normally buzzing at this time of year but now silent and empty, the furniture on the terraces wrapped in tarpaulin. Of course, the visitors who come here might buy my glass and they'd probably let me put a leaflet in their guest information folders. It's something to think about, anyway. Then I realise I am still thinking … no, dreaming, about it. Or am I planning? A frisson of excitement runs through me. Planning sounds good. Planning will make it real.

The distant strip of sea is washed by a faint pinky-orange glow that spreads from the horizon. This really can't be a long walk or I'll be stumbling around in the dark on my way back. But it's good to be out in the air, the landscape fresh-washed from this morning's rain, the loamy scent of damp earth drifting into my nose. I cross the road that leads down to the village and take a farm track towards the cliffs, the ankle-high shoots of dark green wheat to either side. Not a bird chirps and in the distance the soothing rhythm of the waves thuds gently against the rocks.

My thoughts turn to Mani. There's so much about him that, even on our brief acquaintance, I really like. And so much I don't understand. There's no doubt I fancy the guy; I mean, who wouldn't? He has the body of a Greek god, and I giggle to myself at the thought of him getting it from his mother. And now his unflattering crew cut is beginning to grow out I can tell his black hair is naturally thick and luxurious, perfect for running my fingers through…

I have to stop this. He's just lonely, in need of a friend. He's only here for a year so it would be crazy to fall for him. Is that what I'm doing? If I'm honest I suppose I am a little, but what would be the harm in dating once lockdown ends? As long as we didn't let it get serious. It would certainly send all the right messages to Kitto, if nothing else.

The glow on the horizon has faded to orange-grey as the breeze picks up, rustling the grass-like wheat, and the night clouds scud in. I wish I'd taken some pictures of the sunset now, to try to recreate the colours in glass. Normally I'm working with greens and blues but I need to extend my palette, create a full range…

A couple of hundred yards ahead of me I see a light bouncing along the clifftop path. Someone else out walking, or more likely cycling or even riding a horse, given the height, except they've had the sense to bring a torch. Time I was heading back. But as I turn, in the corner of my eye the light appears to leap and twist, high above the hedge-line.

I blink, and it's gone. I wonder for a moment if the person has taken a tumble, their torch spinning into the air, but as I peer into the gloom the light reappears further along the cliff. I exhale. They're OK.

But as I walk home the strangeness of the pattern lodges in my mind. Something about it wasn't right at all. I just can't quite put my finger on what.

CHAPTER THIRTEEN

I am so not in the mood for Kitto right now. My first two mornings in the virtual classroom have been a veritable hell of unreliable IT, panicky emails from GCSE students about their projects and quite frankly stupid questions from some of the others about the theory I've set them to study. It's going to be fun marking that lot. Not.

So when Kitto rocks up in the farmyard just as I'm going for my walk I almost blow a fuse.

"What are you doing here?" I hiss. Hiss, rather than yell, because Noel is in the workshop and if he comes out god knows how far this will escalate.

Kitto stuffs his hands into his jeans' pockets. "To see you, of course."

"Which isn't allowed."

"Come off it, Carla. You're back at work now, you'll be seeing loads of people, one more won't hurt."

"But it's against the rules."

"Sod the rules! C, I'm climbing the walls on my own. Please." And there are tears in his eyes. Real tears.

I heave a sigh. "I'm heading out for a walk on the cliffs. You can tag along if you like. Two metres distance, mind."

"I've already walked up here," he grumbles.

I don't have the heart to say 'take it or leave it' so instead I tell him I'll walk with him back home.

I lead him down the field opposite the farmyard towards the woods that enclose the riverside path that runs from Illogan into Portreath. Once we are in the shelter of the trees I stop. "Tell me what's wrong."

"You know what's wrong. I'm not cut out for all this being on my own. I … I don't know how to deal with it — it's like when I lost Dad all over again. There's nothing to get out of bed for, so I don't. But there's nothing to stay there for either so I get up. Then I go down to *The Merlin*, but she's in the best shape she's ever been. There's nothing to do apart from go to the shop and buy some beers. But even that isn't helping anymore."

He is in a bad way and this is really, really tough. He's such a social animal normally, he's never at home.

"And there's nothing needs doing in the house? Your garden's a permanent dump. You could maybe tidy that up."

"C, it's company I need. I'm fed up with video chats. It's never the same."

"It's better than nothing."

"Is it, is it really? It just makes me remember what I'm missing. I'm throwing in the towel with it all. If you won't help me I'm just going to stock the house with beers and stay in bed drinking until this is over. At least with the money the government's promised us I can afford it."

And he'll do it. I know he will. "Come on, Kitto…" But what can I say?

"Come on what?"

"I don't know… There must be someone worse off than you in the village, someone you can help? One of the old boys, maybe?"

"Community group's got it covered," he mutters.

"Look, if there's anything I can do…" I correct myself. "Anything legal, that is."

"Let me move in with you, then it would be all right."

I don't know why I didn't expect this, but it isn't happening. "My sofa's not that comfortable."

"I didn't mean the sofa, C, and you know it." He rams his fists into his pockets again but the rims around his eyes are red. "What do you want me to say? That I've missed you more than anyone, that this whole thing has made me appreciate what we've got?"

"You don't have to go that far." I raise an eyebrow in an attempt to make him smile, but all he does is grab my hand.

"But it would be true, you know." And he sobs. He's trying not to, and it comes out as a sort of hiccupping sound, but I know genuine distress when I see it. I was with him the night his father died, the days afterwards, the funeral.

After a few minutes he pulls himself together. "Sorry. I didn't mean for that to happen."

"It's a shit situation, especially when you live alone. I get that. I really do."

"So you'll think about it?"

Eventually I nod. "But only if you try to turn yourself around too. I know it's so much easier said than done, but if you could keep off the booze during the day and do something else at least. I mean, I know it's not exciting, but when was the last time you cleaned your kitchen?"

"And we can meet, you know, like this, where no-one can see? And I promise you, faithfully promise you, I won't go near anyone else, so your mum and dad will be safe."

It might be enough to get him through this. It just might. Surely, surely, lockdown can't go on for much longer. "OK, if you really need to see me, then OK."

"Thanks." He moves in to hug me, but I step away, finally dropping his hand. I should never have let him get close enough to touch me, but what's done is done.

"Let's get you home."

It's only half past eight the next morning when I stroll back into the yard after my walk. I'm not due online first thing because I'll be marking all afternoon, and I want to make the most of my time. Plus, I hadn't seen Mani for a few days and going out early means I normally do. I was right, and we stopped to exchange a few words on the track out to North Cliff. He'd seen the seals again and was pretty excited, but by the time I reached Basset's Cove they had slipped back into the sea and away.

Dad strolls across the yard to greet me, Sam at his heels.

"Fancy spending a couple of hours in the hayloft?"

I really want to carry on designing my sunset collection, but if I make much more without selling anything — or having somewhere to keep it — I won't be able to get into my living room at all.

"OK then, why not?"

Of course by my own rules I shouldn't be inside with him, but when I told Mum and Dad that I couldn't come into their house anymore because Kitto held my hand, Mum's response was to hug me so tight I couldn't wriggle away. Next week that will need to change and I'll need to have a will of iron to impose it, but for the moment, well, I know how lucky I am.

In fact my luck improves even more when I log into my emails at lunchtime and see one from the head saying that I won't be required to go into school unless one of the other teachers is sick. Apparently she's decided that continuity will be better for the students than swapping about. Honestly, I could have told her that, and saved myself a whole load of worry at the same time.

Once I've finished my marking I wander across to tell my parents the good news. Mum's on her own in the kitchen, rubbing some sort of liquid into the foot of the tea caddy we found in the barn with an old T-shirt.

I wrinkle my nose at the smell. "What's that?"

"Part linseed oil and part white spirit. It said on the internet it's the best thing to use, but it took almost a week for the oil to arrive from Amazon. This poor old box is filthy with coal dust and it deserves better."

"Coal dust?"

"All your dad could think of was that it was in the old gorse cupboard next to the fire, before your gran had it all knocked in to make space for the Aga. But it's a puzzle, because only really rich people could afford tea at that time, not farmers. I guess when these caddies went out of fashion they were passed down. Perhaps a daughter of the house was in service and was given it or something."

I nod, and drift over to the Aga and lift the kettle. As usual it's half full so I set it on the hob to boil. "Talking of tea…"

"Yes please, love. You finished for the day?"

"Uh huh. And I have some really good news. I'm not going to have to go into school after all, not unless someone gets ill. I could kick myself for going for that walk with Kitto and getting so close to him."

Mum looks at me, pushing her glasses back up her nose with her little finger. "Carla, you did the right thing. You couldn't have refused him. It would have been wrong, and it wouldn't have been you. How's he getting on, anyway?"

"Pushing me for an answer about moving in. But he's fishing today, so at least I'm having a respite and he'll be happy out there."

"You really do need to tell him. Unless, of course, you're genuinely considering it."

"No!"

"I have to say I'm relieved. I mean, there's absolutely nothing wrong with Kitto, but I know you don't love him."

I slide onto the chair opposite her. "I'm comfortable with him though. I know him inside-out, warts and all."

"Carla, that isn't love, not the sort that keeps a relationship alive. Before committing to someone you need to think. Not only if you want to wake up next to this person tomorrow morning, next week, next month, but in ten years' time. Will you still be able to look at them sometimes and get that gorgeous squirmy feeling in the pit of your stomach because you're just so damn happy to have found them?"

I laugh. "Not everyone's like you and Dad."

"But it's what I want for you. I know how precious it is."

I nod. "And to be honest, unless and until I find something like it, I'm perfectly happy on my own. It would take someone really special for me to want to change that."

"Perhaps that's how you need to explain it to Kitto."

"Yes, but I keep thinking … if I can hold off just a few more days, perhaps things will change, perhaps the government will give a hint about how much longer all this is going to last…"

"Well of course it's up to you, love."

The kettle begins to whistle and I fetch the mugs from the cupboard. I know she thinks I'm wrong but there's a part of me believes that as long as Kitto has hope of a light at the end of the tunnel then he'll be OK.

CHAPTER FOURTEEN

Already there is a glorious greenness to the woods, well beyond the fuzz of new growth that started just a few weeks ago, bursting into every conceivable bright hue of the colour. At this rate I'll need some new glass and my mouth waters at the creative possibilities of leaf shapes and greens.

Unbelievably we've been locked down for just over five weeks now and if it wasn't for this worry over Kitto I would be quite enjoying it again. Even working part-time isn't too bad and it occurs to me it might be an option going forwards; a blurring of the transition, rather than leaping off a financial precipice.

I am meant to be giving serious thought to how it might work as I wander through Tehidy Woods, but I find myself distracted by nature. Not just the lambs on the pasture behind the gated development where the old house used to be, but the small things, the simple things; the glossy dark leaves of the rhododendrons, perfect foil for the deep pink hearts of bud just waiting to burst. The fresh brightness of the maples above the fuzz of bluebells. Colours fairly spinning in my head, my fingers itching for my Caran d'Ache pencils and sketchpad.

There will be time when I get home. I'm early this morning and as I turn to walk up the path next to the lake, the sun dazzles between the trunks of the trees. I look up into an oak — a different green again — bright, lime, without the maple's hint of gold, but most fascinating are what look like ribbons of fuzzy beads dangling from its branches. I gaze at them, trying to focus, but it's hard to make out exactly what they are with the sunlight behind them.

As I look away something distracts me, something bright jerking about in the corner of my vision. I spin around but it's gone. The imprint of the oak leaves is on my eyelids as I close them and I shake my head from side to side. But when I open them the unnatural dancing brightness is there again; right next to the old stable block where Mani told me he's living.

I feel a sudden sense of foreboding and want to run, but my legs won't let me. I stumble to a fallen tree trunk at the side of the path and collapse onto it, breathing hard and trying to focus on the feel of the bark beneath my gripping fingers.

"Carla, are you OK?" I hadn't even heard Mani approach. I look up to see him gazing down at me, a lot closer than two metres and with concern written all over his face. "You look real pale."

"Y-yes. I'm fine. I just tripped, that's all. On a loose stone." I bend down to rub my ankle. "It's all right now though. Just needed a moment."

I stand, but I still feel wobbly.

"Can I help you?" he asks. "I know it's not allowed, but I live close so you could lean on me to get to the stable yard then I'll run you home in my car."

"Thanks but I'll be OK, I can walk it off."

We progress slowly up the path, Mani behind, ready to run forward and catch me if I stumble.

"I'm spoiling your run," I tell him.

"No you're not, I was just about done anyway. You gave me a bit of a fright, you know, but your colour's coming back now."

"I'm afraid I was making a silly fuss over nothing. I can barely feel it now."

"Well that's just great. Anyway, I've got something to tell you. I was going to email to ask if you wanted to talk online, but there's no time like the present."

I look up at him. "Go on."

"Well I thought I'd try to find out a bit more about Dolcoath mine, but you know how it is when you're on the internet with nothing much else to do; one click kind of leads to another." He laughs. "Anyway, I soon moved on to the Basset family who built Tehidy. I was interested to read that it burned down. It was a hospital by that time — in fact, it had only just opened — and it had been sold out of the family to pay the last guy's gambling debts."

"Talk about clogs to clogs…"

"Pardon me?"

"Sorry, it's an English phrase. A northern one, really, when a family goes from poverty to riches to poverty again."

"Oh no, the Basset family had always been seriously wealthy, but it all started to go wrong about eighty years before, when an unmarried daughter inherited. Of course she had no children so it passed to her cousin, but he didn't have any kids either so it went first to one of his brothers, then the other, until finally there was an heir, but he gambled the whole fortune away. It just amazes me how fast it all fell apart. I mean, the father of the unmarried daughter was a baron who backed Trevithick's steam engine, ran a bank, did all sorts of stuff, as well as owning the mine and the estate. Then eighty years after he dies — nothing but a pile of debt."

"So when was that? 1830s? I wonder why the daughter didn't marry? She would have been hugely eligible."

"Maybe she didn't want to."

"I don't expect she would have had much choice in the matter. She'd have come out into society and a suitable alliance would have been made within a couple of years at most."

"That's harsh."

I shrug. "It was the way things were back then. I suppose it was the downside of having such a privileged existence, and once there was an heir and a few spares a couple could pretty much lead their own lives as long as neither of them caused a scandal."

"I guess we're lucky nowadays. Parents may have their opinions about our choice of partners — my mom certainly does — but at the end of the day it's up to us who we marry. Or not, as the case may be." He says it with a smile, but there's a hardening in his voice, something almost imperceptible and I wonder if I've imagined it.

"And if we choose not to marry, or be in any sort of relationship at all, then that's our choice as well," I tell him.

"Exactly."

We've reached the road that leads back into the housing and he glances at his watch. "Are you OK now, Carla?" I nod. "Sure?"

"Of course."

"Then I'll get a move on. I have some stuff to read through before my first meeting and I need to shower."

"Have a good day, Mani. And thank you for looking after me."

"My genuine pleasure."

At least our conversation has taken my mind off the dancing lights. I decide to chew on a more practical problem. Kitto. Tell him my decision or let him hope for a little bit longer? According to the news, the number of deaths from Covid are beginning to fall, thank goodness, but the daily briefings scream continued vigilance. For how long? How long until the pubs and restaurants reopen so Kitto can get back to work properly? And, almost more importantly, socialise again. How long before we see normal?

Back at home I take a mug of tea through to the workshop, open my sketchpad and try to settle to recreating the colours and shapes of the leaves from my morning walk, but it just isn't happening. Every time I half close my eyes to remember I see the lights, diving and spinning against the dark foliage.

I return to the kitchen and gaze across the fields, taking a sip of my tea. It's cold and I gag. I seriously need to sort myself out. But what I really want is Mani's reassuring presence. There was something about him this morning; solid, reliable, real.

He'll be in the middle of his working day but the need to connect is strong. Maybe he's on social media? I'm not the greatest of users, but it might be an idea to check in on how my old university friends are doing during the pandemic anyway. But that's an excuse. I want to find Mani.

With a name like his he isn't hard to find. In his profile picture you can't see his face too well because he has a baseball cap rammed onto his head, and he hasn't bothered to put up a background. His profile is locked down too, but there, almost at the top, is a public post he was tagged in from last August; his engagement to one Eloise Price. And there they are, arms wrapped around each other, her glossy dark hair cut in a neat bob around her pretty oval face.

Why had I assumed he was single? Because he's here, alone? Because although he's mentioned his family plenty of times, he's never mentioned a fiancée. It feels a little dishonest in a way, but what business is it of mine? Maybe being apart in these circumstances is a little too painful to talk about to a virtual stranger? My finger hovers over the friend request button but I change my mind. At least I know where I stand, and I've found out before there's any damage done.

The thing is, I could have fallen for Mani and as the initial stab of disappointment fades it's replaced by something that's almost relief. If he'd been single we could have had some fun, become close, and then he would have gone back to the States. And would it have been worth it? No. That kind of fun isn't what I want anymore. What I want now is all or nothing. Why risk my cosy existence for less?

Just before I log out I notice I have a message request from a woman I was at school with, but haven't seen for ages. Not for any particular reason, it's just our paths didn't cross once I came back from university and she'd had a couple of children. But it looks as though Kitto might have kept in touch with her.

Hi Carla, I hope you don't mind me messaging but Kitto's been on my doorstep again and he's doing my head in. We had a fling a year or so back and now he's acting like it never ended and begging to move in with me. I know you two stayed close — anything you can say to call him off? It's upsetting my kids. Thanks, Tina x

Oh, yes. There's plenty I can think of to say to Kitto right now. On both of our behalfs. And I don't think I'll be pulling any punches.

We meet in the woods below the farm again. I want this to be private and it needs to be face-to-face. I've been wondering if Kitto will even bother to turn up, because not only does he obviously have several female irons in the fire, but yesterday the national daily briefing had better news; we're past the peak of infection. The inference being, it's all going to be all right. Maybe one of the women he's been playing on a string will take him up now, but it certainly won't be me.

He's lounging against a tree. I'm gathering myself to say my piece when he says, "Honestly, C, I was beginning to think this Covid shit would be over before you made up your mind."

I fold my arms. "Then seeing as this shit is, apparently, not as deep as it was, you won't mind too much that my answer is no. One of your other women is bound to say yes, but it won't be Tina either, because she's asked me to call you off. She's sick to death of you as well."

"Hey, don't be like that. Tina don't mean anything." He looks genuinely puzzled, pathetic bastard that he is.

"And neither do I, apparently. But that isn't what's riling me, Kitto. What's riling me is that you promised me — *promised me* — if I was to carry on meeting you then you wouldn't see anyone else to keep Mum and Dad safe."

"Did I?" He sounds so bloody nonchalant, although he won't look me in the eye.

"You know you damn well did."

"Sorry, I forgot."

"I'll need a better apology than that."

"To do what?"

"How about to ever speak to you again?"

"Oh, well … if it's that important then I really am very sorry I forgot."

I feel so betrayed. And so bloody stupid I fell for his tricks in the first place. I can hardly bear to look at him, let alone find something appropriate to say.

He walks towards me, arms open. "How about a snog to make amends?"

He is absolutely unbelievable and I feel as though I'm going to burst. "You must be joking."

"Aw, c'mon C, don't go all frigid on me…"

More than anything I want to slap him around the face but instead I step back and hiss, "I don't expect you to have heard of No Means No, Kitto, but I'm sure you know what get the fuck away from me means. You must have heard that a few times before."

I take a deep breath and walk away. He doesn't even bother to call after me.

So much for best friends.

I knew the conversation would be hard so the sunset colours of glass I ordered are already set out on my workbench. I slide onto my stool and survey them, but even though I move them this way and that they're refusing to sing. It's hopeless, and I'm wasting a precious Saturday afternoon because Kitto bloody won't grow up. On top of all the times I haven't been able to focus because I've been so damned worried about him. Bitter? You bet I am.

I wander into the living room and thread my way through the boxes of coasters, diminutive handkerchief vases and dream catchers I've been making, to the photo of Gran I keep on the bookshelf. She must have been about seventy when it was taken, her hair equal parts salt and pepper, straying from its bun, her red and blue checked shirt open at the neck. But she doesn't look old, she looks strong. She damn well had to be, widowed with Dad just seventeen and Uncle Howard at university. And a farm to run on her own. I bet she never wasted time on bitterness. What's got into me?

Thinking of her now, tall, straight-backed, but never straight-laced, tough on the outside but full of love, brings a tear to my eye. Dad says I'm like her and I desperately want it to be true. Yes, there are elements inherited from her that I hate, but she bore them with fortitude, embraced them even. But what I need most of all right now is some of her strength so I can forget this last humiliation at Kitto's hands — and it will be the last — and find my creative mojo again.

She always used to say to me, 'Carla, you're stronger than you think. All women are, because we have to survive.' And she knew all about survival. She lived on for thirty-seven years without my grandad, yet when she was close to death she told me she missed him every day.

If I want love at all, which right at this moment I am damn sure I don't, I would want it to be like that, not with some idiot like Kitto messing me around. And if I don't find it I'm better on my own. Like that unmarried Basset heiress Mani told me about. I can understand if it was what she wanted — I certainly relate to that right now. But how the hell, in that day and age, did she get away with it?

I rack my brains for her name but I'm not even sure Mani mentioned it, so I drop him a message and he comes back almost straight away.

Frances. Her father was Francis. Confusing or what?

Like Dad's family — all Henrys and Williams.

Such imagination ;-) Want a beer later?

Do I? No, I'm not in the mood. *Tomorrow?*

Cool.

CHAPTER FIFTEEN

Mani is sitting in his conservatory, beer in hand when I join the video call. After politely asking about my ankle, the conversation turns to whether I discovered anything about Frances Basset.

I sip my wine. "I lucked out there. Mum had a book on the history of Portreath she bought in a charity shop and it had a bit more than the basics I could find on the internet. Some tantalising glimpses, in fact."

"Like what?"

"Let's just say it doesn't seem she was blessed with her mother's good looks, but that wouldn't have been enough to put off the suitors, not with her wealth and position. The house alone sounded absolutely fabulous; art everywhere, liveried servants, all mod cons like oil lamps and even wallpaper in the best room."

Mani sighed. "I wish more of it had survived the fire. It would have been quite something."

"In normal times I could have taken you somewhere like Trelissick, so you could get the idea."

"Well maybe once this is over you can. Living here I could get quite into history. It's all around us."

"I know. Even that leat you run along…"

"That what?"

"You know, the little stream…"

"OK."

"Well I'd always assumed it was to do with industry, but apparently it was part of a system built so that pleasure barges from the lake could reach the river and then the sea. These

Bassets had serious, serious money. Even the dogs were treated by the family doctors."

"Maybe it was all just a bit remote for Frances to find a husband."

I laugh. "You really must read your Jane Austen, young man. Young ladies like Frances would have had a London season where they went to lots of balls and parties with the express intention of doing just that. It would have normally been when they were about sixteen or seventeen and so far I can't find anything about Frances at that sort of age, but it was when her father was given a second baronetcy, one that would pass down through the female line. It strikes me perhaps he knew there needed to be an extra incentive."

"For a husband?"

"Or maybe to persuade Frances to marry so her children would carry the title. As it was, it died with her, as we know."

Mani leans forwards. "Unless there was a scandal somewhere along the line, and that's why no-one would marry her. Perhaps there's a lost heir somewhere in the woodwork."

I laugh. "It's always possible I suppose. It would have been a huge matter of shame, although I'm damn sure it would have been hushed up. But something else I read made me think there might have been more to it than that, although perhaps I'm putting two and two together to make five."

"Go on."

"There's an account of a visit to the estate by an antiquarian, and he implies that Frances was lacking in the social graces, and that would have been a far more important reason not to marry than just her looks. In Regency society you had to know how to play the game, and clearly she didn't. Then somewhere else I read that her cousin was in an asylum for years. It made me wonder if perhaps she may have had a disability or something?"

"And however much money was at stake, potential husbands would have been hard to find, especially in those days when mental illness and physical and learning disabilities weren't well understood."

"Exactly."

"So no lost heir. That's a pity. I'll just have to get back to trying to track down the Dolcoaths."

I raise my glass and he raises his back. "Good luck with it!"

He's grinning at me through the screen and a ball of contentment settles in my stomach. We can be friends. Just friends. It's all I want right now, and it will be good.

PART FOUR: 1810

CHAPTER SIXTEEN

As the hired barouche crested the hill above Torquay, Harriet watched Franny crane excitedly from the carriage to better see the view. In deference to the good weather they were travelling with the roof pushed back, and after a hearty meal at a roadside inn along the way, she sensed her friend beginning to enjoy the adventure. Not so Ann, who was looking slightly green in the seat opposite.

Harriet smiled at her kindly. "Almost there, and then you can rest."

The young woman shook her head. "Oh no, Miss Harriet, I will need to unpack your dresses and arrange…"

"There is no urgency in the matter. We will be less formal here, I hope. Remember, your mistress is supposed to be from a more middling sort of family."

Ann bit her lip. "It is very hard to call her Mrs Coxe and not my lady, although I have been practising. I would do nothing to jeopardise her honour, Miss Harriet, you do know that."

"Of course. Which is why Lady de Dunstanville has taken you into our confidence. We all know we can rely on your discretion and devotion."

"Look, Harriet," Franny exclaimed. "This is quite the village, so unlike Portreath, settled as it is snugly amongst gentler hills."

"I believe Fern Cottage is on the far side of the harbour where the landscape is most green, and quite secluded, being a little way from other habitation."

"It is a shame there is no stabling so I will not be able to ride." Which, as Harriet well knew, was a deliberate choice on Lady de Dunstanville's part.

Resisting the urge to squeeze Franny's hand she replied, "You won't need to when you can swim. And we can walk out to sketch every day too — all these new places."

Franny turned to look at Harriet. "And keep no company but our own. Indeed, I can see there are singular advantages to this plan."

The road brought them past the crenelated walls and ivy-clad gatehouse of a venerable old house before coming out on the harbour front. A mole reached into the centre of the sheltered bay, a half dozen fishing ketches unloading their catch into baskets, the shouts of the men as they worked filling the air. On the landward side was a terrace of humble dwellings, where children played and old women sat outside mending nets. Some looked curiously at the carriage as it passed, and two small girls close to the end of the row stopped their game to wave. Much to Harriet's surprise, Franny set down the green and gold reticule she had embroidered for her and waved back.

At the most inland corner of the harbour the road met a small square with two comfortable-looking inns and a number of shops. Still hugging the side of the bay, the barouche climbed the gentle slope for a distance of some five hundred yards, before they spied a thatched cottage, standing alone in a walled garden with a gate leading directly onto a small sandy beach.

Franny clapped her hands together. "This is absolutely charming. I do not know what to do first; bathe or fetch my watercolours."

"There will be time enough for both tomorrow," Harriet replied. "The brightness of the day is already fading so I think perhaps a light supper before we retire, but nothing more. Poor Ann needs to rest as well — she has suffered so throughout the journey."

No doubt alerted by the sound of the carriage, a stocky middle-aged woman wearing a mob cap and whose stiff white pinafore seemed to cover her whole dress, emerged from the front door, followed by no more than a child in maid's uniform.

The older woman stepped forwards to greet them as the hired groom helped them to descend the barouche.

"Good day to you, ladies. I am Mrs Whitney, housekeeper-cook, and this is my niece Phoebe who will serve as general maid."

Phoebe bobbed a curtsey almost to the floor.

"Such pretty manners," Harriet observed, "but we hope not to stand on too much ceremony here. This is Mrs Coxe," she indicated Franny, who was gazing at the sea, "and I am Miss Buller. Perhaps Phoebe could show our maid Ann and the groom where our trunks should be stowed? Mrs Coxe is to have the best room."

"Very well," said Mrs Whitney.

Harriet tapped Franny on the shoulder. "My dear, perhaps you can continue your enjoyment of the view from inside the house."

"Just one moment longer. I want to stay until that tiny boat has rounded the headland."

Harriet drew Mrs Whitney to one side. "You have been made aware of Mrs Coxe's delicate condition?"

"Yes, Miss Buller."

"I am afraid that losing her dear husband at this time has turned her head a little, and makes her forgetful of the world around her. It is why her mother decided that sea air and the waters here would be so beneficial. May I rely on your and Phoebe's patience?"

There was genuine sadness in Mrs Whitney's eyes. "Of course, Miss Buller. Do I understand that, given the circumstances, I am to take my instructions from you?"

"I think that would be best, for the moment at least."

"Then on the matter of supper?"

"A cold collation and a dish of tea will suffice for Mrs Coxe and me, perhaps served within the hour? And if you have some broth for Ann, I am sure that would be welcome as she has not travelled well."

"I will see to it directly."

Installing Franny on the window seat in the modest yet comfortable parlour where she could continue gazing at the sea, Harriet followed Mrs Whitney on a brief tour of the house. And brief it was indeed, for the house was small; smaller, in fact, than even the lodges at Tehidy, although she had to admit it was reasonably well furnished, aired, and spotlessly clean.

On the opposite side of the hall to the parlour was a dining room, with a table that would seat no more than six people. But as they would not be entertaining it would be perfectly suited to their needs. It just looked so impossibly tiny, the beamed ceiling low, the walls but plaster painted with distemper. It was almost as though this house was to be a punishment, yet Franny had done nothing wrong.

It was Sir Christopher who should suffer, and the thought was never far from Harriet's mind. She had come to accept that she could not harm his body, but what of his reputation? Although there was little of that intact, if truth be known; he had already been removed from parliament for his bribery and borough mongering, indeed his name had been erased from the House, but he seemed not to care. Now his main concerns were making money from his mining interests and pretending to be a gentleman, which he certainly was not.

But how to expose him, without also revealing Franny's shame? She doubted he even knew of the child, and that was as well because who could guess what he might have tried to insist on? The only thing of which he seemed to be inordinately proud were the gardens which surrounded his house. Oh, if she could she would uproot every plant and hack down every tree. But it was impossible. She clenched her fists in rage.

Mrs Whitney coughed quietly, interrupting her malicious thoughts.

"I do apologise," said Harriet, "I was just thinking what a charming room this is."

And with a heavy heart she followed the housekeeper up the highly polished yet rather narrow staircase to whatever cramped conditions lay above.

CHAPTER SEVENTEEN

As William rode Liberty into the stable yard at Tehidy he found himself surrounded by the familiar sights, sounds and most of all, smells of his youth; warm horses and leather, barrows of steaming dung ready to be carted off to the far corner of the walled garden. Never one for schooling, he had run away from the classroom so many times his adoptive parents had at first been angry and then despaired, so he had sought solace amongst the horses and dogs instead.

Here, for a while, he had found his place. Certainly long enough for the boy to become a man; to learn about the proper husbandry of horses and to ride better than any other hunt servant. And be sufficiently tolerated by the old head groom to be given time to learn to read and write and do arithmetic from Franny as their friendship blossomed over the years.

Franny was the reason he was here today, although he would admit it to no man. A rumour had reached him that she had gone away, yet to do so without telling him, without coming to the farm to say goodbye, was unlike her and it made him curious, if not a little concerned. She may not have understood society's strictures and mores, but her treatment of those she esteemed was nothing if not consistent.

Simon, the current head groom, walked across the yard to greet him. "It is good to see you, William. How is young Henry?"

William swung down from his horse, attaching her reins to an iron ring in the wall near the water butt. "Three month old already — it is scarce believable that time moves so quickly. Your father is keeping well?"

"As can be expected."

William nodded. "I would converse with you privately, Simon, if we may."

Simon looked around the yard bustling with activity as horses were led to and fro to the blacksmith, whose hammer blows rang out from the far corner. "Then you have picked a difficult time."

"In Selkie's stall, perchance, as I understand it is empty."

Simon frowned. "Then you understand wrongly, my friend. But come, it is as good a place as any and in any case I would wish to assure myself she has been shod correctly in Lady Frances' absence."

They walked together past the shining granite mounting block Lord de Dunstanville had commissioned for his daughter, to Selkie's stable door below the oriel window. William followed Simon inside.

"I felt sure Lady Frances would not have travelled without Selkie," he said.

"It is indeed a little strange, but I understand she has gone to take the waters so perhaps has no need of her mount."

"She has been ill?"

Simon shrugged. "That I cannot answer. I was simply told to take Lady Frances, Miss Harriet and her maid as far as the coaching inn at St Keyne, where arrangements had been made for their onward travel. I suspect they plan to be away a goodly while, given the number of trunks, but perhaps that is simply women for you. Anyway, of what do you wish to speak?"

"In truth, I was expecting to find an empty stall, where perhaps I could beg your forbearance with regard to housing a couple of barrels for a week or so, but I can see I was mistaken."

"And when would these barrels arrive?" Simon asked.

"Day after tomorrow, should the weather remain fair and the preventative men otherwise occupied."

"Then I will think on it and send word with one of the boys if it can be done."

William clapped Simon on the back. "Thank you, my friend. You will not go unrewarded." And although it was nought but a ruse to hide the true nature of his business, at least it would mean no barrels needed to be taken to Koll Hendra for the time being, and Mary's current good humour would remain intact.

As William rode through the woods his thoughts turned from his wife to his half-sister and childhood friend. There were aspects of the story Simon had told him that did not ring true. As well as Franny's lack of farewell, and the fact she had travelled without Selkie, which was puzzling in itself, the decline in her health must have been rapid indeed. Unfeasibly so, because he had spoken at length to her in this very wood when they had both been riding out and there was nothing wrong with her then. Indeed he had remarked to Mary afterwards how her complexion had lacked its normal sallow cast, and how much her eyes had been sparkling.

He remembered the conversation particularly because Mary had wondered if Franny was in love. William had scoffed at the idea; joking that could only be true if a new horse or hound had entered the stables, and she had said nothing of either. Franny had successfully avoided marriage up until now and had never, as far as he was aware, even had a beau. She was unlikely to undertake that particular adventure as she approached her thirtieth year, having shown absolutely no interest in it before.

All the same, as he thought on it now, there had been something about her that had put him in mind of Mary in the first months of their marriage. There had been a kind of glow about Franny, a softening of her features which led her angular face to appear a little rounder. Perhaps his wife was right after all, and she had been sent away to avoid an unsuitable liaison.

William reigned Liberty in beneath the shade of a plane tree on the eastern edge of the park. He knew exactly when he'd seen that undefinable glow before; he'd seen it about Mary when she had been carrying Young Will. Now perhaps it had been love that had caused it, or perhaps it had been her condition.

But Franny? It simply was not possible. She was watched over, cosseted, protected — by Harriet Lemon in particular — how could such a thing have happened? And how would Franny have understood it if it had? She had been kept so removed from the ways of nature even, that when any of the dogs were in whelp or horses about to foal she was removed from the stables by her governess until the deed was done.

And of course with Franny there was more than the simple protection of a gentlewoman, there was the unusual way in which she saw the world. William knew that had she been of lower birth she might even have been shut away in an asylum for her awkward manner and at what at times might appear as rudeness or lack of understanding. But Franny would be a baroness one day, a gifted one at that, although only those closest to her would ever understand her own particular brand of quick-wittedness.

But that was in the future, it was the present conundrum that exercised his mind now. How could he find out the truth?

Certainly that would depend on finding Franny. But why was the truth important to him? What possible use could it be to his furtherance? He would never, ever, use it as a lever with Lord de Dunstanville because he would never expose his half-sister to ridicule and scorn. Yet their father did not know that was the case, so perhaps…

In William's experience, information, often carefully garnered, meant power. And power meant wealth and security. Even if it had no value now, it could be stored away as insurance. Like the time he had taken a wrong turn in an inn, and found one of the Truro Vean gaolers lying with another man. Like the vicar's son at Gwithian whose thieving ways he'd exposed, then neatly covered up again. Up and down the county were men who owed him allegiance through a secret shared. And one more secret never hurt.

St Keyne lay conveniently on the road to Polperro, the largest free trading port in southern Cornwall; could he invent some business there? Legitimate business, if possible, he decided as he rode into the yard and saw Mary pegging out the washing. Young Will was beside her and ran towards him calling, "Dada, Dada," and for a moment he thought his heart would burst with pride at the sturdy little boy who was his flesh and blood.

He jumped down from Liberty and scooped him up by the arms, swinging him around as he laughed.

"Fly like birdy, fly like birdy," Will called, giggling, and contentment settled over William like a cloak.

In the garden he kissed Mary on the cheek.

She nodded in Will's direction. "He waits for you, you know, almost from the moment you leave."

William nodded. "If I did not have to provide, I would not leave."

"I think you would. You enjoy adventure too much." She was laughing, but there was a flash of pain in her eyes.

"You understand me too well, Mary Burgess. But perhaps … in moments like this, I wish I did not and I wonder, could the farm and the rope business be enough?"

She put her head on one side, her brown eyes both serious and sparkling, making her more beautiful than ever. "For our coffers or for your heart?"

He took both her hands. "My heart is yours. I promised you before God and those promises I will not break." He smiled. "But perhaps it is my restless soul that is the problem. Or perhaps it is fear. When you have had so little as I had, Mary, you wish beyond all for your family to be secure."

"Little, William Burgess? Little? I do not suppose you know what hunger is. Your father was steward at Tehidy, a man of position and not some small income, I'll be bound."

For a moment William wanted to tell her the truth, but quickly dismissed the thought. Why court trouble when he did not need to? "You are right, of course, but I think perhaps I am only now learning what family is, having more or less grown up in the stables." He laughed. "If only because I would not go to school."

"Which should show you that money is not everything, and besides, you know as well as I do there is plenty of coin hidden in the gorse cupboard next to the fireplace."

He looked around, relieved to see none of his workers was in earshot, but all the same it was time to bring this conversation to its end. "Come, let us not fall out over this. On such a glorious day perhaps we should take the dog cart to Carvannel Cove and picnic there with the boys. It would give you occasion to wear your new bonnet, and the tide is falling back so I could teach Young Will how to fish the rock pools."

Mary was grinning as she said, "Now tell me you are not a gentleman of leisure, to be able to do such things while others work."

William was serious when he replied, "Never that, my darling, but I am my own master and always intend to be."

Could his safe, lawful business be enough?

CHAPTER EIGHTEEN

Franny and Harriet, sketchbooks under their arms, strolled away from Fern Cottage towards Beacon Cove. It was a fine June day with a warm breeze that caught the ribbons of their bonnets and filled the sails of the distant fishing boats. Bees buzzed in the gorse on either side as their skirts swished along the path that was really little more than a fox or rabbit run, and ahead of them the sea sparkled the prettiest blue.

"You should bathe with me, Harriet," Franny said. "It is quite warm enough, you know."

Harriet shuddered. "And if a wave were to come and knock me over?"

"I would not let you drown. I would be perfectly lonely without you."

The words 'and I without you' were on Harriet's lips but she did not utter them, for somehow she found she could not. Why, when that true and kind response would doubtless make Franny happy, she did not know, but Harriet had become unused to kind thoughts since her waking hours had been filled with plotting against Sir Christopher.

Oh, but it was pointless, pointless. Why could she not be more like Franny, whose hurt it was after all, and put events behind her? Her lover seemed to be taking a genuine joy in the situation they found themselves in, happily inhabiting the fantasy world that her condition had forced them to adopt.

At first, Harriet had doubted Franny could live with such duplicity without giving herself away, but she had taken to heart what she called 'our little theatre of playing house' and had stuck to the simple part Harriet had set out for her before they arrived. So much so, that Harriet sometimes wondered if she was coming to believe she actually was Mrs Coxe from Shropshire, widowed some months before when her husband met with an unfortunate accident while riding to hounds.

Theirs was now a simple life, but of course not without comfort. Should anything be required, Harriet had only to write to Lady de Dunstanville and it would be arranged, although of course she had been provided with some money herself. In truth they spent little. They had once ventured into the village to visit a tea shop to try the waters, but they had tasted so horrid they had not returned, explaining to Mrs Whitney that bathing in the sea itself was doing Mrs Coxe so much more good.

The benefits were apparent from the glow on Franny's skin and in her eyes. Harriet had always found a certain handsomeness in the sharp angles of her jaw, but now her full lips and breasts added a lusciousness to her that at times was almost irresistible. But even during those hours together, when they could be their true selves, she could not banish her thoughts of Sir Christopher. Afterwards, when she was alone, it made her weep bitterly; he should have no place in their bed and yet he was stealing their joy away from her.

They settled themselves on a crumbling wall overlooking the sheltered waters of Beacon Cove. The low wooded cliffs ran along to their left, the rich greenery spilling over their tops in unruly clouds. At the far end of the beach was a huge rock just off the shore, topped with two cusps which were reminiscent of a recumbent crescent moon. Mrs Whitney had told them it was called Saddle Rock, due to its shape, and it was this they had agreed to sketch today.

The sun was warm and Harriet was glad of her bonnet as she applied herself to her task. She did not have a natural eye like

Franny and the need to concentrate was a very good thing. Even so, she too had benefited from the tutelage of the Flemish artist Mr Ruythson, who had spent several summers at Tehidy teaching Franny to make the most of her God-given abilities, and the initial results of Harriet's labours were not displeasing.

Having sketched the rock and finding it difficult to create the correct perspective for the cliffs, Harriet glanced at Franny's work and let out a small gasp. Her friend was not drawing the view at all, but rather Harriet's own face peered up at her, her bony nose and pointed chin, framed not only by her wispy blonde hair, but below by her breasts, her nipples pert and dark.

She put her hand to her mouth. "Franny! You can't!"

Franny barely paused in her recreation of Harriet's favourite lapis lazuli drop earrings. "Why ever not?"

"Because … because … you are not meant to have seen my bosoms, for one."

"But I have and they are beautiful. I take great pleasure both in them, and in the fact that mine have become of almost equal girth."

Harriet blushed. "But our pleasure is our secret too, Franny, it always has been and needs to remain so. You understand that, don't you?"

Franny stopped drawing and flicked her pencil back and forth between her long fingers. "But here it is different, my dear. This simple life you promised me; I like it. In fact, if Selkie were here and I could ride him, it would be perfect."

Harriet took her hand. "I like it too, but we must remember it is but for a short while."

"Again, why? Can we not stay and live as we please? It is most welcome that you can come to me once Ann is asleep, and leave with the dawn. It gives me great comfort to have you near."

"Because, Franny darling, you have your duties as a baroness to consider."

Franny smiled. "I am not a baroness yet and I pray I will not be so for many years. Until then, this is the life I desire and I am minded to write to Mama and tell her. I am sure she will be pleased I am so happy here."

Harriet clasped her hand tighter. "And I am happy too, so let us not cause problems until we have to. In the meantime we must remain discreet. Do you trust me?"

"Of course."

"Well then." Alone as they were on the headland, Harriet felt brave enough to silence Franny with a kiss.

CHAPTER NINETEEN

The inn at St Keyne was long and low, situated opposite the church at a fork where the road led either to the crossing point of the river or to the coast. Which way had Franny travelled when she left here? This business was exceeding strange; why not undertake the whole journey in the Basset's own carriage? Could she be staying with the Oliver family at nearby Great Trethew?

Now William was here he wondered how he was going to find out, but as stables were his natural habitation he rode through the open gates and into the courtyard, the sound of Liberty's hooves echoing to the low eaves.

A groom wearing a none-too-clean shirt and dusty breeches came forwards. "Can I help you, sir?"

William swung himself from the saddle. "My horse could do with a rub down and some feed after our journey." He patted his pocket where a few small coins chinked just loud enough for the man to hear. "Do it well and you will be rewarded."

"Of course, sir."

William watched as Liberty was led away, but the man had a soothing manner with her, and he could tell he was good around horses; poor or not, he knew his business. So he went inside to refresh himself with a jug of ale.

The interior of the inn was comfortably furnished and the maid serving him presentably dressed. Apart from an old man sucking on a clay pipe in the corner he was the only guest, so there could be no gossip to be had here. A direct question seemed indelicate and perhaps even unwise. He attempted to strike up a conversation with the maid, but she only stuttered and blushed so he left her to her work and returned to the yard.

He leant on the stable door with his ale and watched the groom carefully rub Liberty down with a handful of straw.

"I'll wager you are like me, my friend," he told him, "in that you prefer the company of horses to people."

"Indeed I do, sir. And this beast is a particularly fine one."

"She is. Her parentage lies in the stables at Tehidy, a great house to the north-west of the county, beyond Truro. They are famed for the quality of their breeding."

"I know of it, sir. Their coach stopped here not a few weeks back, carrying the ladies of the house, and I noted particularly what fine beasts drew it. A pleasure to stable."

"It was their groom told me of this place. They changed horses here?"

The man picked up a fresh handful of straw from the pile in the corner. "And carriage, sir. They took one of ours with my brother as groom."

William ran his fingers through the coins in his pocket. "Are they still in the area? I would wish to pay my respects if it is the case."

"That, sir, I do not know. My brother has but taken the cart to Looe for provisions, though, so I can ask him on his return."

"Thank you. Now when my horse is ready I will go about my business, but I will come back tomorrow for your answer."

As the man handed him Liberty's bridle William pressed two silver sixpences into his palm, then went on his way.

The long evenings of early summer played in William's favour and there was still good light as he crested Talland Hill and looked down onto Polperro Harbour. So this was Cornwall's most famous free trading enclave, the village hugged tight into its rocky cove. He knew there would be opportunities to do business here, but he had promised Mary that he would undertake lawful commerce only, and he intended to stand by his vow. If only to prove to her — and to himself — that he could reduce their reliance on smuggling.

Besides, there was too much risk, even for him, to be involved in any free trading here. The notoriety of the area must surely bring its own problems, and he could not believe the preventative men were ever far away. Not knowing the terrain, melting into the landscape when he needed to would not be as easy as it was on the county's northern coast where he knew every cave, every thicket and every disused mine shaft that could hide man, beast or booty.

The port below him was at the end of a long inlet, a hillock to the right cutting off almost half its channel to the sea like a protective fist, keeping it safe from the prevalent westerlies that plagued the Cornish coastline. A little further inland was a mole, nothing to rival Portreath's in length, but sturdy enough, protecting the innermost harbour. The left-hand side of the bay rose too steeply for there to be much in the way of habitation and most of the houses clung to the hillside opposite, a sensible few of the better type half-hidden behind the sea wall, or on the road that disappeared from his view along the bottom of the valley.

One man controlled the trade at Polperro, and one man only. A man born in St Pirans, an hour's ride from Portreath, who had left to find his fortune. A man by the name of Zephaniah Job, and it was he who William desired to see, but perhaps he had left it a little late in the day. Maybe he would find an inn first and enquire as to his whereabouts for the morrow.

He urged Liberty into a trot, descending Talland Hill into the village proper. The Three Pilchards was one of the buildings above the sea wall, but to find its stable yard William needed to thread his way through the narrow backstreets where women sat outside their doors gutting fish and gossiping. They apparently paid a stranger no heed, but William knew in such a place news of his arrival would surely spread fast.

He left his horse with a stable lad who could be no more than eight or nine years old and went into the inn through a side door. Fishermen clustered around the empty fireplace in the low-beamed room, their clothing bringing inside the stale smells of the harbour; rotting seaweed, fish and the tang of salt air.

The innkeeper stood next to a row of barrels and bade him welcome, although he spoke in a guarded manner and did not look him in the eye.

"Do you have a room for the night?" William asked.

"That depends."

"On who wants it or how deep his pockets are? I am no friend of the preventative men, if that is your concern."

The innkeeper shrugged, no doubt unwilling to commit himself either way.

"My name is William Burgess and I come from Portreath on the north coast. I make ropes and would do business in the town so desire to speak with Zephaniah Job to present my credentials."

"I will send a boy to ask him. Then we will know whether or not you have need of a room."

William took a jug of ale and sat in a window seat as far from the fishermen as possible; not on account of the smell but so they would feel they could continue their conversation. He knew all about strangers at inns; he had a part share in one such establishment in Pool, but there the landlord made it his business to be friendly to all, including preventatives, and many a time his guile had worked to William's advantage.

After a while the boy returned and whispered something to the innkeeper. The man called across the room. "Mr Burgess, Mr Job asks if you would take a dish of tea with him while I make ready your room. Will you be requiring supper on your return?"

William stood. "Thank you. I will." He had been accepted, after a fashion. Perhaps his name carried a little weight here after all, at least with a former St Pirans' man.

The sun had dipped below the headland and already dusk was creeping into the narrow streets. The boy seemed to be taking him away from the village, but stopped in front of a fine new double fronted house with elegant pillars on either side of the door.

"Shall I wait, sir?" he asked.

William nodded and pressed a penny into his hand.

He gauged Job to be a man some twenty or so years older than himself, dressed in a plain velvet tailcoat with an old-fashioned ruffled shirt beneath. He greeted William in his study, a room which looked out onto the street with the opposite wall lined with bookshelves. There was a chair on either side of the fireplace, and a globe rested in its mahogany stand next to an impressively large desk.

Job stood to greet him when his manservant showed him in. "Your reputation travels before you, sir."

"As a rope maker?" William asked, raising an eyebrow.

Job laughed. "As a free trader."

"Then I hope the purpose of my visit will not disappoint you, because I come to ply my, shall we say more regular, trade. I am sure there must be call for it in this village."

"It is possible, depending on the outcome of our discussions. There is great need of rope for the boats, if nothing else."

"My ropes are made long enough to stretch down mines. And cliffs."

"We have no mines here." Job folded his hands in his lap. "But as for the other … let us say that I will only do business with men I can trust."

William shrugged. "I run my own organisation. I still walk free."

"Ah, but sometimes in order to do so, men take the king's gold."

"Not this man, but it is hard to see how I could prove it. And anyway, I do not need to know to what use the rope is put, merely the length and girth required."

"I accept your point, and of course there could be rich pickings for you here, in so many ways. Although I do not know you there is a straightforward manner about you I find quite pleasing, and if you could but deliver a letter for me as a sign of the goodwill between us… Where do you travel from here?"

"Back to St Keyne, and after that my onward journey will become clearer."

"Then that is perfect. The letter is for the sailmaker at Looe, which is but a modest detour. You will do it?"

William bowed his head, although with some degree of misgiving, for the content of the letter he would not know. But trust had to start somewhere. "The pleasure will be mine."

It was only afterwards William wondered if Job had perhaps known the direction of his travel, or whether he had so many contacts with whom he needed to correspond, he could have chosen someone in any of the villages hereabouts. But if Job had known, perhaps he would also know the nature of his questioning at the inn, and that might bring its own perils. Job was a trader by nature, it had made him a wealthy man. He was bound to know that information meant power.

Delivering the letter might be risky as well, and in most circumstances William would have had no compunction in opening and resealing it to find out. But this was a test of trust he sensed he must not fail; indeed, it might be perilous to fail, particularly if Job knew he was looking for Franny. A shiver ran up his spine, yet it was a not unpleasurable one. Mary was right; there was something deep within his soul that would make it hard for him to live without risk, and he both welcomed and cursed it.

Since he had witnessed his own father fighting the duel against Hawkins, a feeling had settled on William that it was all the more important to be a good father himself. Certainly not a father who was absent more than could be helped and definitely not a dead one. A man who provided for his family, yes, but one who was there to keep company with his wife and teach his boys the ways of the world. The sort of father he himself had never had.

Once again it was a fine summer's morning and he settled Liberty into an easy canter for the ride across the cliffs. The sea sparkled something of a different blue here; brighter and less green, and the land around him was formed of softer curves like a woman's body, most of it down to pasture where sheep and cattle grazed. It was beautiful in its own right, but he missed the rugged toughness of the north.

Arriving in the bustling port of Looe he found the sail loft easily enough with its position near the outer harbour, filling the sharp angle between the road that led inland to the east and the quay. He secured Liberty to the wooden staircase that ran up the outside of the building and climbed the steps.

The sailmaker was at his business in a large room with windows on every side to give the best of the light. He ceased his stitching when he saw William, and stood and stretched. "Can I be of assistance?" he asked.

"Tom Potter?" The man nodded. "I bring a letter from Zephaniah Job. I was passing close by so he pressed me into service."

"Then can I offer you a jug of ale and perhaps some small victuals before you continue your journey?"

"That would be most welcome."

The man disappeared to the far reaches of the loft and called down what William presumed to be another staircase. "Florence! I have a guest. Bring some bread and mackerel, along with two jugs of ale."

Returning to the main part of the loft, Tom Potter slit the letter open with a round fingernail, scanning its contents. He grinned. "You did not say the letter was to your advantage, man."

"I did not know."

Potter handed the piece of paper to him. It was a simple note of introduction for William Burgess, rope maker, that he might do business in the town. Curiouser and curiouser. Perhaps there was some sort of code hidden within, but certainly Potter seemed to have taken it at face value, for they spent a pleasant, if slightly tedious, half hour discussing the percentages that might be available to the sailmaker should he recommend a certain purveyor of ropes.

William was still puzzling on it as he rode away. Knowing Job's reputation, there was most likely more to this than met the eye. But one thing was certain; had he been stopped by the preventative men on his journey, they would have had no reason to doubt the letter and he would have been sent on his way. Job had said something about goodwill; maybe that was what it had been — goodwill on his part. Would William now be somehow in his debt?

But he had other fish to fry this fine morning and once he was away from the village he urged Liberty into a canter and headed up the river valley to St Keyne.

At first he thought the inn yard deserted, but after a few minutes he spied the groom climbing down from the hayloft. To make their conversation a little more private, William stepped into the cool shade of the building, the sweet scent of fresh fodder filling his nose.

The man wasted no time on niceties. "My brother does remember, sir. He took the ladies to Torquay. To a cottage beyond the village square. He says if you follow the coastal track around from the harbour you cannot miss it, because it is the last before the headland."

"Thank you, that is most kind." William felt in his pocket. "And your kindness will be rewarded."

The man inspected the coins. "You pay a good price for information, sir."

William shook his head. "I pay men well who care for horses, that is all."

Should he go on to Torquay now? In truth he was more than half way there, but he did not want Mary to be worried by his extended absence. Nevertheless he returned the direction he had come, back into the valley and across the other side towards the turnpike road. It was senseless to go home, when he would only need to return another time. If he could reach the market town of Totnes by nightfall he would be early in Torquay the next day, ready to pay a morning call on Franny.

CHAPTER TWENTY

The church clock was striking nine as William rode through Torquay's town square, but otherwise all was quiet. The tide was high and he was sure the boats would have left the harbour some hours since, making this seem a sleepy place. Despite its supposedly curative waters, it was a quiet and out of the way place, if you wanted to hide away for some reason.

He followed the track along the water's edge, and just as he was coming to the house he assumed to be the last, he spotted a figure in a dark blue dress emerging from the sea. As he stopped to take a closer look it started waving, then strode up the beach with a strange waddling gait.

"William! Can it really be you? Well, how stupid, of course it is. How delightful to see you and Liberty. I am missing Selkie so much. Tell me, have you paid him a visit and given him an apple from me?"

William dismounted with a grin, trying not to gaze at the way the wet fabric clung to Franny's body, revealing without any shadow of a doubt her condition. "I have visited Selkie and he had just been shod, but I am sorry to say I did not give him an apple. Something I will remedy as soon as I get home."

"Thank you, William. I am sure he must miss me, as I him."

"Indeed, but you can be reassured Simon is taking good care of him."

"When you go, William, will you ride him for me? Take him through the woods and onto the cliffs? He does so love it there and I know you will handle him gently."

"Of course, whatever you wish."

"Thank you. Now come to the house, do. You are in time for breakfast, although for a man it will probably not prove a hearty one." She opened the garden gate and set off up the path at a lick, calling to Harriet as she went, while William tethered Liberty to the post.

He turned just in time to see the look on Harriet's face when she opened the door. Shock and horror were characterised by a brief pulling together of her narrow mouth before she composed herself and did her best to smile.

"Why William, what a delightful surprise. Come, I will show you a shadier spot to leave your horse while Franny changes into more appropriate attire for receiving guests."

She advanced down the path and led William along the outside of the hedge that sheltered the garden from the sea. "There is a small orchard," she said curtly. "You can leave your mount to graze there."

"Thank you."

They walked on in silence, and it was only when they were amongst the apple and plum trees that Harriet spoke again. "You have doubtless marked Franny's condition?"

"Indeed."

"Then you will of course understand we are here under assumed names. Franny is Mrs Coxe from Shropshire, who has recently been widowed, and I am her companion Miss Buller. I suggest you are a cousin of some sort."

"Or perhaps Franny's brother?" There was something about her coolness that brought out the devil in him.

"Cousin is quite close enough a relation, I feel."

Oh, it would have been tempting to tell her, but of course he held his tongue. "As you wish."

"And may I ask why you are here in the first place?"

"In reality, or in your imaginary world?"

146

She blushed a little at that. "An answer to both would be useful."

"The answer to both is that I had business but a little distance away."

"How did you know we were here?"

"A businessman never reveals his sources, Miss Buller."

"But why did you come?" There were high spots of colour on her cheeks and genuine anguish in her voice.

"I think you are not so concerned about why I am here, but what tales I might take back with me. But you have my assurance I would say or do nothing to harm Franny. Ours may be an unlikely friendship, and one of which I have always sensed you do not approve, but our bonds were formed in childhood and remain strong."

Harriet had the good grace to look down. "I am sorry, William. I suppose I should have known better than to doubt you, but our being here was meant to be a secret. Your visit has quite unsettled me."

"For which I apologise. However my intentions are true enough."

She nodded. "Come inside. I need to tell our housekeeper we have company for breakfast."

"After which, I will be on my way. But tell me, is Franny well? She certainly appears to be in the rudest of health."

"Indeed she is, and that is a great comfort to me."

"And her comprehension of her position?"

She looked at him sharply. As if she did not know he understood the peculiar way Franny's mind worked as well as anyone. "She recognises she will give birth to a child and give it up."

"And the father?" He had been in two minds whether to ask such a question, and the black look he was given in return told him he would have been wiser to keep his own counsel.

As her pregnancy advanced it was becoming usual for Franny to rest for a while after breakfast, particularly with the weather so warm. It was therefore Harriet's duty as hostess to accompany their guest back through the orchard to retrieve his horse and see him on his way.

Harriet had watched William carefully over their repast, weighing up the possibilities. There was no doubt Franny trusted him completely, and his enquiry after her welfare had seemed genuine enough. But more than that, as a somewhat notorious free trader, he would no doubt have access to the kind of ruffians who could wreck some revenge on Sir Christopher. He may even want to do it himself, if he knew the truth.

As she followed him up the garden, she put aside all thoughts of how trustworthy he might or might not be. This could be her one chance to enlist William's help, and she could think of no other man whose fondness for Franny might persuade him to act. With any luck he would be so enraged he would choose to do so of his own accord. After all, he was in a position to. As a woman, she certainly was not.

She stopped beneath a plum tree, already heavy with fruit. "William." He turned to look at her. "You asked about the baby's father and if you are prepared to be sworn to secrecy, I will answer."

He nodded curtly. "I am prepared."

"It is Sir Christopher Hawkins." She gazed at the hem of her gown in what she hoped he would take as modesty. "He took her by force," she whispered. Looking up, Harriet had expected anger to suffuse his features, but instead he nodded again, this time slowly.

"Now that, at least, makes sense of the duel."

"Duel? What are you talking about?"

"Did you not know? Perhaps our positions are reversed and it is I who need your assurances our conversation will go no further."

"Which, of course, you have."

"Very well. Back in March Lord de Dunstanville challenged Sir Christopher to a duel. Ostensibly it was over matters of parliament, but I, for one, never believed it. It seemed such a small thing, a matter that had been settled years ago. Besides, I was there and I overheard my lord say the insult was too great to ignore."

"I know when Lord de Dunstanville first heard of Sir Christopher's vile behaviour he flew into so wild a rage he threatened such action, but I thought his wife had persuaded him otherwise."

"Then perhaps she does not know. But honour was satisfied, Miss Buller. After Lord de Dunstanville disturbed his wig with a close shot Sir Christopher stood down. The man's a coward and no mistake, but I, for one, was glad it went no further."

Harriet brushed an imaginary mote of dust from her sleeve. "You think a duel sufficient punishment for what he has done?"

He pursed his lips. "Under the gentlemen's code, honour has been satisfied."

"And your code, William?"

"Because I am no gentleman? What of your code, as the daughter of a baronet?"

"I am … undecided. I must admit, the duel puts a different complexion on the subject. It is the right way to settle matters of honour, I know, but are you not angry? I find that I am. Or perhaps, because you are a man, you see these things in a different light?"

"Now *that* I do consider a slur upon my character. No man should ever take a woman by force, or injure her in any way. It is abhorrent to every natural law. But while you are right and I am angry with Sir Christopher Hawkins, revenge is not mine to take. That is up to Lord de Dunstanville and he has done what he considered best."

Harriet drew herself up to her full height. "I never believed you to be without courage, William."

"It is not a lack of courage that drives me, but an abundance of common sense. I cannot feed my family from the confines of Bodmin gaol, and I doubt you would be able to do it for me." He tipped his hat in her direction. "Good day to you, Miss Buller. There is no need to accompany me further."

He had dismissed her. That low-born upstart steward's son, who for some reason known best to herself, Franny worshipped. He should have had more respect, he should not be permitted… But Harriet was wasting her time berating him, even to herself. If he would not help her, he was nothing. And anyway, she was in no worse position than when she had woken up this morning.

Except, except … the news of the duel. In that respect alone, Burgess could have been right. Gentlemen's honour had been satisfied over the matter so perhaps there was nothing to be done. For a single moment she felt a cleansing relief run through her, but then she remembered the dangers her darling would face during childbirth and the simmering anger reappeared.

She picked up her skirts, and turning her back on William, swept through the orchard towards the house.

After William took his leave it was too hot to go out sketching, so they remained in the cool of the parlour, Franny dozing on the chaise longue while Harriet calmed herself by stitching a tiny bonnet for the baby. The task of preparing a layette for a child who was to be given away felt pointless to her, but it would have seemed strange to Mrs Whitney had nothing been done, and after all, the baby would be close by with a wet nurse for a few weeks while Franny recovered from the birth.

Despite her energies for bathing and walking, Franny was frequently tired as her confinement approached, sleeping more by day and less at night. Her wakefulness was a good excuse, should Ann find them together in her bedroom in the morning. The maid now seemed accustomed to it, but Harriet sometimes wondered if she had guessed their secret.

Franny was right when she said there was much to recommend their life here, and Harriet wished she could be free of the heavy bitterness she felt to enjoy the days of summer that her friend found so halcyon. Again she asked herself if the duel had been enough. Her head told her yes, but her heart felt differently, and she was still infuriated by William's response. Surely such a man would have wanted to entrap Sir Christopher into some dark alley and beat him senseless? That would have satisfied Harriet far more than any polite duel over Franny's honour.

Gazing at Franny's sleeping form, Harriet's heart twisted in an unaccustomed manner and she had to catch her breath. What was she doing, letting herself be so completely consumed with vengeful thoughts that spoilt her days and wormed their way into their nights? She needed to start to think more like Franny before it was too late; now that honour had been satisfied, accept these unexpected days here together as a gift.

Oh, why was she so consumed by bitterness when Franny apparently cared little about what had happened? In this respect it was truly a blessing that Franny's mind worked differently to other people's; because of it she had no real concept of honour, or shame, and in her mind Sir Christopher's real crime had been to ride his horse lame. It was almost as though she barely connected him to her condition at all.

Neither did she fully connect it to their stay in Torquay. Although she had been told several times that once the baby was born they would need to go home, she remained positive that her mother would relent and they could remain at Fern Cottage indefinitely. It was as though she had extended the fantasy they were living out to suit herself, or had even come to believe it.

But whatever Franny wanted, staying here was one thing that would not happen. As soon as she was recovered from the birth they would leave for Tehidy, taking the baby with them as far as Plymouth, where Lady de Dunstanville had made arrangements for its adoption. Back at Tehidy Franny would be reunited with Selkie and would very quickly forget that she wanted to stay in this tiny cottage as the arms of familiarity closed comfortingly around them again. Perhaps this summer would be remembered as a dream, although Harriet knew as Franny's time approached it could still turn into a nightmare.

Alongside her anger, Harriet knew very real fear, particularly in the small, grey hours of the morning when she lay next to Franny, watching the moon's passage through the window. Fear that childbirth could take her darling from her, as could so very easily happen. Fear that she would be left with nothing but an ache in her soul that was impossible to fill. It was then she bargained with herself that she would do anything, agree to anything, for Franny to survive.

As she watched, her lover's eyelids fluttered open and returned her gaze.

"Why are you looking at me?" she asked, her voice husky with sleep.

"Because you are beautiful, like a ripe peach."

"I am not at all beautiful, with this huge ball of baby filling me up."

"Well I think you are."

Franny rolled her eyes and struggled to sit upright. "How much longer can it be, do you think?"

"Did not the doctor say another three or four weeks when he called?"

"That man did nothing but ask impertinent questions I did not wish to answer. What does he know? I am more interested to meet the midwife. At least she has given birth herself so will be familiar with what happens, and I am minded to ask her."

Harriet's stomach turned at the thought, and she must have failed to keep her pained expression from her face because Franny carried on. "Really, Harriet, we both should listen to what she says, otherwise how will we know when the baby is coming?"

"I believe there are pains," Harriet muttered. "At least, that's what my sister Louisa told me."

"Pains? This whole adventure becomes worse with every minute. I wish it to be over, and soon. Why ever does it take so long? It is far too hot to be inconvenienced in this manner. Whatever was God thinking when He made it so?"

"God is not a woman," said Harriet sourly, and it occurred to her that any number of the gentler sex's ills could be put down to that fact.

CHAPTER TWENTY-ONE

When Franny's pains started, despite it being a hot and humid July morning, Mrs Whitney immediately lit the fire in her bedroom, which was to serve as birthing chamber in so modest a house, and closed the windows. Franny protested vociferously but the housekeeper insisted this had to be done to prevent her or the baby catching a chill, and as Harriet helped her to change into the chemise and underskirt the midwife had told her to wear, they were both sweating copiously, the stuffy atmosphere making Harriet's head spin.

"Harriet, open the window," Franny commanded. "I can bear the pain, but not the temperature."

"Mrs Whitney must have done this for a reason. Perhaps if you lie still it will not feel so intense?"

"I do not want to lie anywhere. The pains are not so bad; they come in pulses and between them I would prefer to be occupied."

"Shall I read to you?"

"You know I have no interest in books, least of all now."

"Perhaps a few items from the *Sherborne Mercury*?"

Franny jumped from the bed and strode to the window, flinging wide the curtains. "Now, at least I can see to sketch."

Harriet took a deep breath. "Then I will fetch your paper and graphite. As long as you promise not to open the casement."

Franny cast her a murderous look, but nodded. Her acquiescence was a sign of how nervous she was about the whole process, and Harriet could not blame her. She herself was gripped by a quiet terror too. In the drawing room she picked up the bible that was kept on the bookshelf and, holding it in her hands, said a silent prayer for the child's safe delivery.

The next few hours passed off peacefully enough as Franny sketched and Harriet read the newspaper, both as close to the window and as far from the fire as possible. Mrs Whitney tutted when she came with a dish of tea for Harriet and jug of barley water for Franny, but she said nothing, banking the fire a little higher. Franny was already looking rather flushed, and when Harriet reached to comfort her when the pains came, her chemise was cold and damp to the touch while her flesh burned beneath.

She called on Ann to sit with Franny a while and went downstairs.

"I think the midwife is needed, Mrs Whitney. The pains are becoming more frequent." She would have preferred to have sent for the doctor, but having taken a dislike to him at their first meeting, Franny would not have him in the house.

Mrs Whitney turned to Phoebe, who was shelling peas at the table. "Go for Mrs Carson immediately."

The girl nodded, and removing her apron, ran from the room.

Just after Harriet returned to the birthing chamber, Franny's pains came on so strongly she yelped in anguish and shock, and once the worst was past Harriet and Ann helped her into bed. Instructing Ann to fetch a clean chemise and make sure a fresh supply was laundered and ready, Harriet perched on the edge of the mattress and held Franny's hand.

"It will not be long now, my love, then it will be over."

There was terror in Franny's eyes, which Harriet hoped was not reflected in her own. "You will not leave me, will you?"

"I promise." Harriet leant forwards and kissed Franny on the lips, but a few moments later the sound of the front door opening and closing beneath them made her pull away.

When Mrs Whitney led the midwife into the room, the woman looked around her, aghast.

"Goodness me, it's like an oven in here. Open the windows at once and quench the fire." Mrs Whitney started to argue but Mrs Carson silenced her with an icy look. "Yes," she said, "I agree it was once the way these things were done, but now the medical profession consider fresh air is more important to keep infection away. And look how flushed Mrs Coxe is already, and her hardly started at that."

"Hardly started?" Franny's eyes held that look of terror again, and the midwife patted her hand.

"There, there, my dear. It will be done before you know it, and when you hold your baby in your arms you will forget all about the pain."

Standing at the open window, Harriet's nails dug into her palms. She feared that the pain was the very thing that Franny would remember.

In the early hours of the morning the midwife's words came back to haunt them. Harriet felt as though she had been in this room forever, watching her darling Franny alternately writhe in torment then collapse into a fitful sleep, only to be woken by her own anguished cries.

Despite her calm manner it seemed the midwife was becoming concerned. Apparently the baby was not lying in quite the right position, and her attempts to turn it had accomplished little and only made Franny scream even more. Moreover it was obvious that she had a fever, not so high to be dangerous, Mrs Carson assured Harriet, but her kind words did little to allay her concerns.

"If I cannot see the head by an hour after sunrise we will need to send for the doctor," she told Harriet after drawing her to one side.

"But what can he do that you can't?" Harriet whispered.

"I appreciate your confidence, Miss Buller, but when a confinement proves difficult two heads are better than one."

"Then why not send for him now?"

"I am still hopeful that with each contraction the baby is turning."

"And if it does not?"

"The doctor will know what to do. Why not try to sleep a little?"

"I promised I would not leave her."

Harriet returned to Franny's bedside, sitting on the hard chair that had been brought up from the dining room. She wanted nothing more than to lie beside her, but with the midwife present that was not possible. Nor could she kiss her, and it came to her mind that the kiss they had shared yesterday morning could be their last and tears welled in her eyes. She wiped them away with her sleeve. It would not do for Franny to wake and see them.

Another contraction gripped Franny and Harriet ran a cloth dipped in cool water over her forehead while the midwife tried to hold Franny's trembling legs in place. She was so exhausted that what had been screams now came out as piteous mews, and Harriet thought her heart would break. She was going to lose her; lose the love of her life, and all she could do was mop her brow and pray. And as prayer seemed increasingly ineffective, she knew without doubt she would sell her very

157

soul to the devil, or to Sir Christopher Hawkins himself, to have Franny survive this.

Mrs Carson looked up at her. "Wake your maid and tell her to go for the doctor. She is becoming too weak to risk waiting any longer."

The following hours were the worst in Harriet's life as Franny slipped in and out of consciousness, her contractions seemingly weaker each time. The doctor was full of the bluster and self-importance that Franny had hated, but she was too feeble to argue as he took charge of the birthing chamber, relegating the midwife to fetch and carry for him.

Regret filled Harriet's heart as she gazed at the beads of sweat covering her darling's face, her high colour and soaking chemise. This baby would never come; it would be trapped inside her forever, and both of them in a grave. Oh, but why had she wasted this summer on bitter thoughts and schemes for revenge? Why had she not done as Franny had, and surrendered herself to the simple joy of being together? Why had she wasted, *wasted*, what would very like be the last months of love they would know, and done more to make Franny happy?

It was all she could do not to drop to her knees at the bedside, but instead she sat still as stone, her hand enclosing Franny's weak one, waiting for the grip that came with each contraction, fainter every time. *Oh God, please let her live*, she prayed. *Please do not take her away from my vengeful heart. Let her live and I will never allow my soul to be distanced from you and from her by anger and bitterness again.*

Finally, with the aid of some instrument that Harriet dared not look upon, the baby was somehow pulled free, a bloodied scrap of a thing that was handed to the midwife while the doctor cut the cord that tied it to its mother. Harriet was relieved that Franny had fallen into a faint and would hopefully remember nothing, for the images would be seared into her brain forever.

A few moments later she heard the baby's cries and the midwife asked her to call for warm water so she could wash her. Her. It was a girl; a girl who would grow into a woman, and doubtless suffer as her mother had just done. Suffer all the injustices that went with their sex. And Harriet felt more helpless than she had ever done; beyond fury at the lot life had dealt her and every other female, at the unfairness of it all. And she could not help but weep, her pain turning in on herself for showing such weakness in the presence of a man.

The child's cries roused Franny a little and she looked around the room with fevered eyes. "The baby's alive?" she asked.

"Indeed so, and a fine little girl she is too, Mrs Coxe. Do you have a name for her?"

Franny frowned, as if not comprehending. "What is your name?" she asked the midwife.

"It's Eliza."

"Then Eliza she will be." Another contraction gripped her and she cried out weakly. "What is this?" she gasped. "Not another one, surely!"

"It is but the afterbirth, and it must leave the womb too, for you no longer have need of it. But once it is done, then you can rest."

"I do not want to rest, I want to die," Franny cried.

And Harriet cursed herself again, her silent weeping rendering her incapable of offering a single word of comfort.

CHAPTER TWENTY-TWO

The letter from Zephaniah Job was simple in the extreme; a request for William to attend as soon as was convenient, bringing with him samples of rope and being sure to send word in advance when the day might be. He would have showed it to Mary, but she struggled with her letters, so he read it out to her instead.

Her face looked pinched. "I thought you said Job was a smuggler."

"Not as such, although they call him the smugglers' banker. He has many business interests and great influence in the locality. You know his introduction to the sailmaker has already proved fruitful."

"Perhaps I should not worry…"

He kissed her forehead. "No, you should not. Especially when I am doing this to reduce our dependence on free trading."

She wrapped her arms around him, soft and inviting against his chest. "You are a good man, William."

"I try."

It pained him more than he would have believed that he was not telling her the whole truth. He could not share his fears that there was, indeed, more to this business than simply rope, although he was himself uncertain as to what it might be. Job may have decided to trust him, but whether he could trust Job… All the same, there was something about the man and his reputation that excited him when he knew it should not. To pit his wits alongside — or maybe even against — a personage so formidable would be a challenge indeed.

He hoisted Young Will onto his shoulders and led him across the farmyard, past the hayloft, from where the sweet smell of the newly cut fodder drifted, and on to the ropewalk where his foreman, Thomas Hichens, was feeding the strands of hemp through the metal plates, ready to be twisted. The building, little more than a wooden shed with open spaces for windows on the sheltered side, was some three hundred yards long and stretched across the top of the slope that led down to the Red River valley. Rather than disturb Hichens from his work he began to walk slowly along its length, explaining the process to his son. He was far too young to understand, of course, but one day this would be his inheritance.

After a while Young Will clamoured to be put down, and as none of the machinery was working William set him to run free. Hichens had completed his task and he joined him next to the cranking handle, where they discussed the differing thicknesses and qualities of rope he could take to show Job, and when they might be ready.

His business done, William took his son back out into the sunshine and looked around him. All this was his; as far as he could see towards the edge of Tehidy Woods and out towards where the land dropped away towards Portreath. The solid granite farmhouse and outbuildings, the ropewalk, the fertile acres of flat arable land had all been gifted to him by his biological father, although no doubt most thought he paid a rent, but the deeds were tucked safe in a metal box in the gorse cupboard next to the fireplace. It was his, and it would be Young Will's too.

The small hand in his, William strolled slowly along, stopping to point out a wren hiding in the hedgerow, her tiny black eyes peering out at them from the dark foliage. In the field beyond, the corn was beginning to ripen, its rich greenness fading into the gold that would see them through the coming winter. Yes, he was a lucky man indeed and he must not squander it.

For now he knew that was what he had lacked. A mother's love, a father's firm but fair hand. Yes, the Burgesses had taken him in, probably on sufferance, because his adoptive father had been more interested in furthering his political career, and his wife a weak woman who cared for little other than her own pleasure. So he had been left to the stables, then a brief but disastrous spell at Helston Grammar, from whence he had run away so often it was decided on pretty short order he would return to the stables again.

Had it not been for Franny, perhaps he would never have known affection at all, but the tiny tot who had taken to following him around had stolen inside his empty heart. Perhaps because something deep within him had recognised her as his sister, but more likely because they both preferred the company of animals to people, and later he had realised that she was as misunderstood as he.

He worried about her now; whether her confinement had begun and what would happen afterwards. Not only to her, but to the baby, who would be adopted, just as he had been. He only hoped Lady de Dunstanville had found a suitable place in a loving family, but his own experiences led him to fear otherwise. It was an uncertain world for unwanted children.

He looked at Young Will, the sunshine highlighting the hints of red in the curls inherited from his mother as he chased a butterfly down the edge of the field. His sons were wanted and he had to make sure they knew that; moreover, he had to make sure he was here to show them, and to teach them what they needed to know about life. He had to stop taking risks, that he knew. The question was, could he do it?

It was four days after the birth when Franny was recovered sufficiently to sit up in bed and utter more than a few words. Four anxious days for Harriet and also, she guessed, for Lord and Lady de Dunstanville, to whom she wrote daily. It was bad enough being here and watching Franny drift in and out of consciousness, too weak to even move, but for her mother all those miles away, it must have been almost unbearable. So much so that she half expected her carriage to appear, and that it did not seemed more than proof that her daughter's reputation was prized above her health.

Of course at no time had Harriet actually told her that Franny was in any danger, because the doctor had sworn it was not the case. The light fever had abated just a few hours after Eliza was born and had not returned, and her bleeding was not excessive. Franny was simply exhausted by the long labour and needed to rest.

Eliza had been taken immediately to the wet nurse who lived near the town square, which Harriet regarded as a very good thing. But once Franny was strong enough it would appear most strange if she did not ask to see her daughter, and Harriet was far from sure that she would. Perhaps she could put about that Franny was once again overwhelmed with grief for her late husband and did not want the further upset of seeing their child? That, at least, sounded plausible, and with luck the pretence could be kept up until they came to leave Torquay.

These thoughts and others more painful filled her mind as she wandered listlessly around the house, and took the air by walking as far as the headland. Here she had sketched with Franny, here they had laughed and talked, here they had kissed. And in those first uncertain days Harriet's anguish knew no bounds; she could still lose her darling, her one true love, and as the tears ran freely down her cheeks she prayed, nay begged, for her recovery. Oh, to think of those precious days she had wasted plotting revenge on Sir Christopher, when she could have been loving Franny better. From now on, she vowed that was what she would do.

It was as she was returning from one such expedition that she spied Ann running up the path towards her. Her knees threatened to buckle beneath her; what had happened to engender such haste? The blackest of thoughts filled her mind and she almost cried out with relief when Ann told her that Franny was awake and asking for her.

Franny was propped on a mound of pillows, her face white against them, while a warm breeze from the open window wafted the scent of gorse into the room. After taking her bonnet and shawl, Ann had left them so she was free to grasp both Franny's hands and kiss them tenderly.

"How are you feeling, my love?" she asked her.

"I cannot rightly say, but certainly better for seeing you. When I awoke and you were not here, I thought you had abandoned me."

"Never, my darling, never. But Mrs Whitney is insistent I take daily walks for the sake of my own health."

"Daily?"

"Franny, you have been away from us for four long days and five nights."

She shook her head from side to side. "I do not remember."

"Well that is a good thing."

"I think it is. Tell me, did the child survive?"

Harriet uttered a silent prayer of thanks. It really did seem that Franny could recall nothing of her ordeal and that, at least, was a blessing.

"She did, and she is with the wet nurse."

"She has a name?"

"You named her Eliza, after the midwife."

"I wanted to call her Harriet, or Jane for your mother."

"Oh, Franny, that is a kind and gracious notion, but I think Eliza is more suitable."

"Why?"

"Because … because … it may be easier to put this behind you if the child's name means nothing to you."

Franny's jaw set into a hard line. "I want to see her, all the same."

"And of course you shall. It would seem unnatural to others if you did not ask, although given your health we can perhaps delay it for a day or two."

"No. I want to see her now. Have Ann fetch the nurse to bring her here."

Weak as Franny still was, Harriet knew that tone of voice. It would brook no argument, but so grateful was she for her recovery, she was not minded to deny her anything she wanted. All Harriet desired was to be able to love Franny as she so richly deserved. Reluctantly she loosed their hands.

"I'll go and find her now."

Harriet stepped backwards in shock at the expression on Franny's face as the wet nurse placed the bawling red-faced bundle that was Eliza into her arms. She had expected her to recoil at the noise, but instead she rocked the baby gently, love writ large on every feature.

"There, Mama knows exactly what to do," the nurse commented as Eliza's wails subsided, "and baby knows who Mama is too."

Franny looked up with shining eyes. "She does. It is true." With the tip of her index finger she chased a tear from her daughter's cheek. "There, my dearest, no need to cry," she whispered, "Mama has you now."

There was nothing Harriet could do but stare. This was a completely unforeseen and a more than unfortunate outcome. She could not just stand by and watch her friend, her darling, her very dearest soul, develop an attachment for the child she must give away. Something inside her sensed it was already too late, but all the same she knew she had to try.

"Well, now you have soothed her, perhaps give her back to her nurse and rest a while."

Instead of answering, Franny looked up. "Harriet, isn't she beautiful? Eliza, this is your Aunt Harriet, Mama's dearest friend."

Harriet forced a smile. "She is indeed a most comely child." Which given her parentage was unexpected, but it was the truth. Now she had stopped crying, her eyes rested closed, with long dark lashes sweeping towards her elfin nose and mouth.

Franny picked up her hand. "And look, Harriet, such tiny fingernails, so perfect in every way."

"Yes, but you must not tire yourself…"

"I will never tire of looking at her. Not my whole life long." She glanced up at the nurse and smiled. "Perhaps we can offer you some refreshment? Harriet, ring for Mrs Whitney to take our guest downstairs."

Once they were alone Franny turned to Harriet. "I will not let her go. I cannot."

"Oh my love, I feared as much when I saw how you gazed upon her. But it will not be possible…"

"Then we must find a way. Please, write to Mama and tell her I wish to stay here with my daughter."

"But Franny…"

"Please."

There was so much pain in her voice that finally Harriet nodded. All it would do was prolong Franny's agony, but if she did not try she would never be forgiven, and that she could not bear.

"I will fetch my writing slope directly."

Franny nodded but her eyes were on the child.

Installed on the window seat to write the difficult letter, Harriet gazed out at the changing light on the water as the scraps of cloud scudded above. Franny was resting, the baby on the bed next to her, tucked into her arm. Harriet could hardly look at mother and child, lying together in perfect peace, such was the emotional turmoil filling her breast. That she had no way to stop the agonies that would follow was breaking her heart, her frustration at herself bringing her close to tears.

How strange that this, an affair with its roots in no more than curious experimentation and a quest for pleasure on her part, had led to a love that she had belatedly realised was worth as much to her as life itself. Indeed, what would her life be without Franny? And now she knew this was not about the excessive comforts she enjoyed living alongside her at Tehidy, this was about the woman herself.

She forced herself to think. Perhaps she should at first ask Lady de Dunstanville for a few weeks more at Torquay for Franny to recover. It would give Harriet an opportunity to consider the problem, maybe find a solution that eluded her now. But in that time Franny would grow even closer to her child, if indeed that was possible. Lady de Dunstanville was a mother too — would she perhaps understand her daughter's plight? But even if she did, what could she do? The fact remained that first and foremost Franny would be expected to do her duty as baroness when the time came.

But that could be a long way in the future. Maybe they could stay here, at least for Eliza's nursery years. Harriet began to see it in her mind's eye; that simple life Franny had come to love, the freedom to explore their passion for each other, for Franny to mother her child. And this time she would keep her promise to herself and to God; she would not allow the dark corners of her soul to blight their happiness one bit.

What then though? It would be infinitely crueller for Eliza to be turned away from a mother she would always remember rather than one she would never know. Surely it would be better for the child to be adopted as soon as possible … but that would pain Franny more than Harriet could bear. She might even be too weak to deal with the separation and pine away.

Franny opened her eyes. "Have you written to Mama yet?"

"In truth, I do not know what to say, how best to persuade her."

"There is no persuading to be done. You need only tell her I have decided to stay here with my baby and will not come home."

"Dearest, what if she makes you?"

"She can hardly send a groom to carry me screaming from the door."

"No, but she can dismiss the servants and stop paying the rent. The money I have in my reticule would keep us but a few weeks. Less if we had no roof over our heads and had to find lodgings. And it would soon get around the village that our accounts were no longer being paid."

Franny's brow creased into a frown. "But surely I have money if I'm to be a baroness?"

"Nothing that isn't under your father's control."

"I do not understand…"

"It is because we are women, Franny. We have no rights at all, everything is in the gift of men; our fathers, our husbands, if we had them… Only perhaps widows of our class enjoy financial freedoms."

"Then I will marry Sir Christopher, and then kill him."

"And end up with your head in a noose? What good would that do anyone? Franny, whatever we do we're trapped, do you not see?" Harriet could do nothing but burst into tears of frustration.

"Hush now," Franny said. "You'll wake the baby."

PART FIVE: 2020

CHAPTER TWENTY-THREE

I hang the sunset-coloured dream catcher on the pole balanced across the corner of the wooden box then pick up my camera. The late afternoon light is perfect and the purples and oranges reflect richly on the white-painted background, smooth and almost soft against its roughness. It's going to look perfect in my new online shop.

The online shop has been my half-term project and with school, such as it is, starting again tomorrow, I'm now on the last leg. Thank goodness Mani is dealing with the technical side of uploading my art to the website. It's not that I couldn't have done it, it's just so much quicker with his help.

It's a call from Mani that breaks my concentration.

"Hey, Carla — have you heard? As of this week we'll be able to meet in person. Outside at least. Isn't that fantastic?"

"That's amazing news. The government's road map out of this is on track then?"

"Looks like it. Apparently up to six people can meet outdoors. My manager's already arranged a working picnic in the country park for Wednesday afternoon. Provided it doesn't rain, of course."

He sounds so upbeat, it's brilliant. This will be great for Kitto too, not that I've heard from him over the last few weeks, but I didn't expect to. Since the tradespeople were allowed back to work apparently he's been helping Tia, a decorator friend of ours, to catch up with her backlog. He's probably trying to bed her as well, but I don't rate his chances; she's always been pretty picky with men, and good for her.

Mani is speaking again. "I'd love to ask you over for supper, but you'd need to come through the house to get to the yard, and I guess that isn't allowed."

"Then why don't you come here? I mean, I don't have much of a garden, but Mum and Dad do. Of course, I'd have to ask them, but I'm sure they wouldn't mind. I owe you such a huge thank you for all the work you're doing on my website."

"It's nothing compared to the thank you I owe you for keeping me sane through all this. Honestly, Carla, I really don't know what I'd have done without you."

"It's been my pleasure." And it has.

Mani arrives promptly at six thirty on Tuesday evening with flowers and a bottle of wine. Mum has covered the old table outside the kitchen door with a checked cloth and she places the brightly coloured gerberas in a vase in the middle, while Dad pours Mani a beer.

Some of Mum's nerves seem to have rubbed off on me, although I hope I'm hiding them as well as she is. It's really strange having someone other than Noel around after all this time, but Mani breaks the ice beautifully by talking about how great my online shop is going to be, and how talented I am.

"Of course, I've only seen photos of Carla's work," he adds. "I'm looking forward to being able to look at the real thing."

"We could always pull a box out into the yard," Dad suggests.

"Or I'll just fetch a few coasters from my workshop."

Mani grins. "That would be perfect."

I race across to the Granary and pick up four sunset coasters from the shelf next to the kiln. I look around. I want a piece to give to Mani too, something special, that will mean something to him. I drum my fingers on my work table. What about...

But then I know; an experimental dream catcher, gold and blue, with mica cut-outs of seals. It isn't perfect by any means, but it's right for him.

Once Mani has finished exclaiming over the quality of the coasters I hand it over.

"It's not the finished article yet, but if you like it, you can have it."

His face is almost glowing as he looks up at me, and I realise with a jolt that his aura is the faintest I've seen it, a shimmering pale green. "Hey, it's the seals," he says. "Like we saw the first day we spoke."

"It was why we spoke, if I remember rightly."

"Sure it was." If he grinned any more his face would split in two. "And I'm going to treasure this."

Mum emerges from the kitchen at that moment, carrying a huge dish of cottage pie, encrusted with bubbling cheese.

"Mrs Burgess, that smells fabulous," Mani tells her.

"Call me Elaine, please. You make me feel as though I'm about a hundred and fifty." She's almost blushing, but then Mani is a charming man. He's probably as nice to everyone as he is to me, and I don't know whether I feel sorry or not.

Over supper Dad asks Mani how he's been spending his time during lockdown.

"Well, my biggest project has been trying to trace my family tree. I know my ancestors emigrated from Cornwall, but I figured I needed to work back from what I knew to try to make the link, and it was something I could do online."

"How did you get on?"

"Pretty good, up to a point. I discovered my great-grandfather, Thomas Dolcoath, moved to Texas after the First World War to work in the oilfields, and I guess he wanted a change because his twin brother was killed in the fighting. So somewhere else on my wish list once we can travel again is to visit his grave in France. I also found his father Richard's birth records in Tennessee in 1873, and his parents' marriage the year before. But nothing older."

"Well maybe that was the point they arrived in the States. Mining here was struggling then and so many left for all over the world; Australia, North and South America. There are Cornish miners everywhere," says Dad proudly.

Mani frowns. "And yet I can't find a single person called Dolcoath here."

"Then how about this for a theory?" Dad is clearly warming to his task. "Perhaps when he arrived he took the name of the mine he'd worked in. He might have been say, Bill Trelawney, but if there was another miner with the same name where he found work he might have become known as Bill Dolcoath and it stuck."

"I never thought of that. I suppose there are no records of who worked in which mine?"

"That would depend on the owner, I guess."

"And the records would most likely be at Kresen Kernow if they exist."

Mani looks at me. "What's that?"

"It's the county's archive collection in Redruth, although goodness knows when it will reopen again. When it does I'll come with you to look if you like?"

"That would be great."

"You could try to track back our family too, Carla, see what you can find out about our smuggling ancestor."

"A smuggler? Wow." Mani looks impressed.

I laugh. "I told you we have a fine Cornish pedigree. It's always been rumoured we had a smuggler in the family, and while I was looking up Frances Basset in Mum's book I stumbled across a bit about him. I know it was the right guy because he lived here from the early nineteenth century. Got into all sorts of scrapes too, but he must have made a fair bit of money because he was able to buy inns at Camborne and Pool. I have to say, I would like to know more."

"I wonder if the tea caddy belonged to him?" Mum asks.

Dad shakes his head. "I doubt it. The trunk came from my mother's side of the family after all."

"That doesn't necessarily mean the contents did."

"True," Dad agrees.

Mani is looking slightly puzzled so I tell him about finding the Georgian tea caddy and that now more shops have reopened Dad has taken it to the locksmith in Redruth. "It's not an easy job to unlock it without doing any damage," I explain, "so it may be a while before we get it back. There's definitely something inside, and if it's the original glass mixing bowl and it's intact then it could be quite valuable."

Mani shakes his head a little sadly. "To have that kind of heritage in your family..."

"You have heritage too, Mani," Mum tells him, "and by the sound of it some of it is here."

As we wave Mani off across the yard in the dusk I wonder whether being with another family, in particular seeing us standing here as a unit, has made him sad. I think it would me, if I was in his position. Maybe he'll go back home and call his mother now, but whatever happens I'll drop him a message to check in before I go to bed.

Mum and I clear the table together, in the way we always do, except as we carry the glasses inside Mum says, "I think Mani likes you quite a lot."

"As a friend, maybe, but don't go buying a wedding hat because he has a fiancée back home."

She frowns. "How odd, taking a job over here when you're engaged."

"Maybe she was due to come over too but the pandemic stopped her. He was only here a matter of weeks before it started."

Mum nods. "That would explain it. But all the same, the way he looks at you…"

"Don't start…"

"No, don't," Dad interrupts. "He's a nice lad but I doubt he sees his future in Cornwall and I wouldn't want our Carla getting hurt."

I give him a hug. "You needn't worry about that, Dad. We're really just friends."

But seeing Mani tonight, his easy fit with my family, has once again made me question my feelings. If it wasn't for this Eloise in the background … but she is there, and that's that. No point in wanting what I can't have.

I clean my teeth and lie down on my bed, picking up my phone to message Mani, but there's already one from him: *Thank you for such a great evening. Your folks are just so welcoming.*

I reply: *You were the perfect guest. Mum was still fussing over her gerbera when I left. But I was thinking — I hope it didn't make you miss your family more.*

And then there's a silence, and I wonder if I should have said it, but finally he says, *I don't think I have ever met a more thoughtful girl than you. Yeah, you're right, it did make me a little sad while I was walking home but overall it was great to feel part of a family again, if only temporarily.*

You're always welcome here, Mani, and that's the truth.

Thank you x

I hug my phone to me for a moment, like a lovesick teenager, before throwing it across the duvet in disgust. No, no, no. This will not do at all.

CHAPTER TWENTY-FOUR

It rained earlier in the day and I'm going stir crazy indoors so I message Mani to tell him I'll walk over to meet him before we head back to the farm for supper. I choose the cliff path, even though the sea below is churning green-grey, silver spray covering the rocks and swirling into the cave in twists of dirty lace. Quite possibly it's William Burgess the smuggler's cave, and on a day like today if I half close my eyes, I can almost hear the shouts of the men as they wade ashore with their booty.

Having ground to a halt with his family tree, and with my online shop up and running, Mani has made a start at trying to discover the connection between Dad and William Burgess. Armed with nothing more than my grandparents' marriage certificate, he says he's finding it quite easy because we've always lived at Koll Hendra and it's a case of working back through the censuses. He's told me he wants to do Mum's side of the family too, and get it properly printed and framed to thank them for their kindness.

That kindness is about to extend, because it's just been announced that people living on their own can join what will be called a support bubble with another person or family. It's a great idea and will stop so much loneliness. Mum did briefly wonder if we should ask Kitto — I haven't been able to bring myself to tell her the extent of the rift between us — but when I shook my head all she did was grin and say that was perfect, because she'd rather have Mani instead.

I cut back across the field towards North Cliff car park, the grass damp beneath my feet. Sheep skitter away, the bleating lambs they were carrying three months ago already sturdy and strong. Time, which at first seemed to be endless, is running away with me, and I have important decisions to make.

The online shop is taking off quite nicely, but I wonder what will happen when people feel confident enough to shop in person once again. On the other hand, if the holiday trade does reopen at the beginning of July that's a massive opportunity and I've visited most of the craft shops in the area, with mixed success. Some already stock glass, and others want such an eye-watering share of the profit it's barely worth it. And although Dad has put in planning permission for change of use on the hayloft, it will be next summer before it's anywhere near ready.

Mani is waiting under the trees at the end of the car park, rucksack over his back. He never arrives at the farm empty handed, despite us all telling him he doesn't need to bring anything. He just laughs and says his mom would kill him if he didn't and he's mighty scared of her.

"You were looking very thoughtful," he says.

"Just thinking about the business, really. How I can get it off the ground in a meaningful way. But I guess I just need to be patient. It'll be hard to scale up too much until the hayloft is ready anyway." And until I've worked out how I'm going to afford a new kiln, but he doesn't need to know that. The farm was refused a government grant on a technicality to do with rates, but now Noel has applied for discretionary funding. I can't say I'm holding out too much hope.

"It must be frustrating though, when you have such a talent. But hey, I guess you're a talented teacher too."

We're following the narrow path through the stunted oaks and I look over my shoulder at him. "I've just fallen out of love with teaching, that's all."

"Because of the pandemic?"

"No, before that." I turn back and trudge on.

"Funny, isn't it?" he says. "How you think you really want something then realise it's not for you."

I'm about to question him when there's an almighty rustling in the undergrowth and a spaniel dashes out, almost tripping me up. It skids to a halt, panting, big brown eyes gazing up at me from a mess of auburn fur.

"Hey, I know this little fella," says Mani. "He lives just across the yard from me and he's always getting out."

As if on cue a woman's voice drifts through the trees. "Melba! Melba!"

I immediately think of peaches and start to giggle, but Mani has more presence of mind and grabs the animal's collar. "Over here," he calls. "We've got her."

A woman wearing loafers and jeans that look far too smart for walking the dog appears around the bend in the path.

"Damned animal slipped her lead again. Honestly, obedience classes can't restart soon enough."

She clips the lead to the collar and immediately the dog charges off, pulling her along the track ahead of us.

"Try a harness," I call after her. "It'll give you more control." But she ignores me.

"She could have at least said thank you," Mani says.

"I think she had other things on her mind, but you're right."

"She shouldn't even be here," he carries on. "They arrived a couple of weeks ago from somewhere upcountry. Apparently they're 'doing essential work' on the house."

"Now I wish we'd let the bloody dog go."

He shakes his head. "It isn't the dog's fault."

"Maybe we should have kidnapped it instead."

"That's your smuggling blood coming out," Mani laughs.

"I don't suppose I have very much of that."

"You do. I've established a direct line back to William Burgess's eldest son."

"Oh wow, Dad will be made up. Plus he's gone to collect the tea caddy; the locksmith has managed to open it so now we get to find out if it's worth anything or not."

"Will your parents sell it if it is?"

"They've given it to me actually, which is very sweet of them."

"So you get to keep it? That's so cool."

How can I tell him keeping it is something I won't be able to do? Even if it's worth just a few hundred pounds, that will be the down payment on the bigger kiln I'm beginning to need so very badly. Mani won't understand. Although he's never been so crass as to talk about money, he has the latest smartwatch and runs in top of the range trainers. Plus today he's wearing what I'm sure is an actual Ralph Lauren polo shirt.

I pull myself up short. Never before have I thought of anyone in terms of what they have — or more usually, have not. It isn't the way in Cornwall and it certainly isn't my way or my family's. So we stroll along the narrow track in companionable silence, listening to the birdsong and the shimmer of the breeze through the leaves, his solid tread comforting behind me.

When we arrive at Koll Hendra Dad is nowhere to be seen, but his car is in the yard so he must be back from town. Mum bustles out of the kitchen to greet us.

"Cold beers for the walkers?" she asks.

"Elaine, that would be fantastic. Thank you." Mani delves into his rucksack and pulls out a bottle of white wine. "This needs to go in the fridge as well. Carla mentioned Muscadet is your and Bill's favourite."

"You are so thoughtful, young man." She turns to me. "Have you told him yet?"

"Told him what?"

"About the support bubble. Mani, we'd love you to join ours if you'd like to."

His face clenches in on itself and for a moment I think he is going to cry. "You mean there's no-one else…"

"You're top of the list," Mum says firmly.

"I'm honoured."

I was right, there is the tiniest of chokes in his voice, and Mum reaches out and squeezes his hand.

"Welcome to Bubble Burgess, Mani. Right, I'll grab those beers so we can celebrate."

Once she's inside Mani turns to me. "You're sure about this too?"

"Why do you think I wouldn't be?"

"It was just the way … your mom kind of expected you to mention it to me and you didn't so…"

I grin at him. "I wanted to give her the pleasure. She's really taken to you."

He's looking at me, head on one side.

"We all have," I stutter, feeling myself blush.

"And I've taken to you." He's still looking at me as he says it, right into my eyes, but thankfully at that moment Dad strides from the yard.

"Brilliant! You're here. Now we can open the tea caddy."

"You mean you haven't looked?"

He grins. "I was tempted, but no."

The lid opens easily to reveal three compartments, but none of the glassware Mum was hoping for. The square one on the left is empty, as is the raised central area with its dropped down circle of unpolished wood for the mixing bowl, but on the right is what at first appears to be a piece of green and gold striped fabric, but when I pull it out I can see it's a small drawstring bag. And whatever's inside it is heavier than its size would suggest.

"This is where the weight comes from," I tell them, feeling the thick material. "It's the strangest shape."

The bag has a red elliptical base, the fabric stiffened, perhaps by some sort of card, but not before someone embroidered a beautiful horse's head on it. The work is so fine the beast almost seems alive, but I'll take a good look at it later. For now I set it down on the tea towel Mum has hurriedly fetched to cover the picnic table and begin to tease the gathered opening at the top apart. There's a stiffness born of age to the material and the cords running around the neck are made of strands of silk twisted together, so I want to be as careful as I can.

I am reluctant just to stick my hand in and pull whatever it is out, so I carry on gently pulling the drawstrings open until I can see inside. Even then I can't make out what it is, but it's definitely silver, so I reach in and pick it up gently by the strange dark pink handle at one end. I lift it free with a gentle tinkling sound, which comes from eight tiny bells attached to the widest part of its body.

"It's a baby's rattle," Mum breathes. "Well I never. I've seen some of these on TV and I bet the pink handle's coral."

"Any idea how old it is?" Dad asks.

"Not really. I don't think the basic design changed for generations." She holds out her hand and I rest it on her palm. "It's so intricate, it's covered in tiny carvings. Oh, and look, one end's a whistle. That is just so sweet."

Mani is standing a little away from the table and I turn to him. "What do you think?"

"Awesome. Completely awesome. I mean, just think, one of your ancestors could have been shaking that thing around hundreds of years ago."

"One of yours could have had something like it."

"I doubt it. We were most likely just poor mining folk."

"And we've always been poor farmers." Dad frowns. "It doesn't make sense."

"Except for the smuggler," I remind him.

"True. He had money. And of course it could have come from my mother's side of the family, and we know next to nothing about them."

"My next project, perhaps," says Mani.

"I don't know about that," Mum replies, "but *my* next project needs to be getting the potatoes on or we won't be eating tonight."

CHAPTER TWENTY-FIVE

The 4th of July brings the change we've all been waiting for; the pubs can open again, everyone can get a much-needed haircut, and very soon the tourists will start making their way back to Cornwall. Mani has been desperate for a British pint, but he has to hold off twenty-four hours so he can join his family online for American Independence and anyway, my guess is The Tinners was fairly messy on opening night.

As it is I hear Kitto's laugh before I even step inside the pub. Perhaps it was a bad idea bringing Mani here but I'd kind of had a bet with myself that Kitto'd be out in the boat. Obviously I underestimated the lure of a social life after the pubs have been closed for more than three months, even though most of his customers will now be up and running again themselves.

Inside The Tinners everything's different though, and I guess it will be for a while. The warm fug of beer has been replaced by a faint whiff of disinfectant, and no more than six can sit at a table. No-one is allowed to prop up the bar and there's a one-way system in past the toilets and out through the front door. The bar stools have been placed next to the pool table, which has been covered by a raised plywood box to make it the right height and around it sit the locals — my friends; Ray, Tia, Anna and Gun. And, of course, Kitto. We're going to have to walk right past them. I could have taken Mani anywhere and now I wish I had.

Ray calls out to me the moment I poke my head around the door. "Hey, Carla — you're our number six." He pats the stool nearest him, almost falling off his own, they've been placed so far apart.

"Sorry, Ray. There's two of us. And we're here for a meal. Guys, this is Mani. He's working over here for a while. Mani…"

"Carla, it's lovely to see you, hun, but can you sit down? We're not allowed to have people standing and chatting all over the place." Fi, the steely barmaid with a heart of gold has spoken and I slink away with Mani a pace behind me to a table for two in the far corner of the dining room.

"So, are those guys your friends?" Mani asks. "I feel a bit guilty you can't sit with them when you haven't seen them for so long."

"Honestly, I can come up here any day of the week and they'll be here. It's no big deal. Now, we need to find you a proper pint. Or you can work your way along the bar as I'm driving," I tease.

"I really don't think that would be a good idea. I have to work tomorrow. What's your most typical Cornish beer?"

Fi appears beside the table. "That'll be the Betty Stogs. What about you, Carla, the usual?"

"No, I've got the car so just an orange juice please, plenty of ice."

Fi waves at the chalkboard filling one wall. "Menu's up there. Seemed easiest under the circumstances. And I have to sign you both in for track and trace. What's your name, hun?"

"Mani. Mani Dolcoath."

"You're kidding me. Dolcoath with that accent?"

"My family emigrated to the States about a hundred and fifty years ago."

"Then welcome home."

186

"Isn't that nice of her?" Mani says as she bustles off. "You said this place is friendly and it sure seems that way."

"Friendliest pub in the world, I reckon, but I'm biased because it's my local, even though I have to drive twenty minutes to get here. Do you have a local at home?"

"I kind of used to when I was younger. There's a sports bar called Pennison's where my friends hang out. I mean, it's not the sort of place any of us would take a date, and that was kind of the point. If anyone was going steady they'd dip out."

"And was that why you stopped?"

"I guess. Even when I... Let's just say I haven't been there for a while. Maybe I just grew out of it."

"I find it hard to picture your life at home. You don't talk about it very much. Is that because you miss it?" I'm well aware I'm angling for him to come clean about his fiancée.

"It's not a conscious thing, not talking about it. And of course I miss my folks, but coming here was my decision. When I saw the job advertised it was as if everything was falling into place, almost like it was calling me." He laughs a bit self-consciously. "If that doesn't sound crazy."

I decide on the more direct approach. "No, I do get that, but what did your fia—"

"Pint of Stogs and an orange juice." Fi puts the glasses on the table in front of us. "Now, have you decided what you'd like to eat?"

Mani grins up at her. "I think it's going to have to be pie of the day for me."

"Good choice. It's chicken and mushroom. Carla?"

"I'll have the burger. Show my American friend here how they should be made."

"Oh, now come on. That's going a bit far." Mani laughs. "I doubt anything they serve up here could be bigger than a Texas burger. I've barely seen a cow since I've been here."

"Bigger isn't always better." My moment to bring up his fiancée naturally in the conversation has definitely passed, or have I chickened out?

Before the food arrives I excuse myself to take the now convoluted trip to the ladies, which involves going out of the pub's front door and back in through the car park entrance. Tia follows me outside.

"Nice date, Carla, he's gorgeous. Where did you find him during lockdown?"

"Not a date, just a friend. And I found him running on the cliffs. He arrived here from the States to work just before Covid hit."

Tia rolls her eyes. "Kitto's been telling everyone you've been breaking lockdown rules to shag him since Easter at least."

"He's been saying what? The lying little shit. Especially considering he was the one trying to persuade me to see him because he was lonely." I emphasise the last word by making speech marks with my fingers.

"God, not you as well." Tia laughs.

I sigh. "Seems there was quite a crowd of us. A woman we knew at school messaged me to see if I could get him to back off."

"That's Kitto for you though, sad case that he is. Still, it's good to see you and I don't want to keep you from Mr Hot. Come again on your own soon, won't you? Then we can have a proper catch-up."

Despite how much I'm fuming with Kitto I manage to be all smiles for Mani, and we fall into talking about the silver rattle we found in the tea caddy. Mum's been at it with her magnifying glass and as well as examining the engravings — there's even a gorgeous little unicorn at the whistle end — has tracked down the hallmark to Exeter in 1810.

"That does tie in with the smuggler, you know. Let me just check the family tree in my app." Mani taps on his phone for a few moments. "Yes, here we go, although it is too late a date for it to have been bought for your dad's ancestor, William Burgess, because he was born in 1807. He had two younger brothers and a sister, all born in a cluster at around that time, so perhaps it was for them."

"His poor wife. All those babies. Still, there was no such thing as family planning then."

"Women in particular didn't have as many choices as today."

"I often wonder if Frances Basset somehow deliberately avoided marriage because of that? On the other hand, much of her philanthropy in later life was directed towards children, so maybe she did come to feel she missed out."

Our conversation is interrupted by raised voices from the area of the pool table. To be fair, only Kitto's voice is raised — and slurred — and he's telling anyone who will listen he's going to have it out with 'that lying bitch'. I steel myself, this is going to be beyond awkward. Why the hell did I bring Mani here in the first place? There's a new pub in the middle of Porthnevek that does nice food…

Fi sounds almost angry. "Kitto — sit down or get out. One or the other. You can't just wander around in here like you used to. It's not allowed."

"Stupid Covid rules. You can't make me."

"I damn well can. And I can ban you. I can even call the police, so you'd better listen."

"Come on, man." It's Gun's quiet voice. "Come back home with Anna and me, have a bit of supper and chill. You don't need that hassle." I can almost see him winking at Fi as he says it.

"That's the most sense any of you have talked all night," she grumbles, but I'd put money on the fact she's winking back.

I hear the pub door open and close, three sets of footsteps on the gravel outside. I daren't look up at the window as they pass but I certainly owe Gun big time.

"Sounds like something was about to kick off," Mani says, thankfully oblivious to the fact we could have been in the middle of it.

I nod. "Gun's good at cooling things down."

"Gun? Doesn't sound like a suitable name for a peacemaker."

I shake my head. "It's because there are some people who think he's a bit shot away. He talks to ghosts, you see."

"No kidding!"

"No kidding. I've watched him sit in that corner over there and have a full on conversation with George, a miner who died about a hundred years ago."

"That does sound a bit shot away…"

What the hell would he think of my auras then? But I need to put this tactfully. Teasingly, even. "So you're not open to exploring the mystic side of your Celtic heritage?"

He frowns, looking down at his beer glass. "I don't know. I suppose, if I'm honest, it's not something I've ever thought about. Is that sort of thing common here?"

"No, I wouldn't say common, but you definitely come across people with a sixth sense like Gun's, or who have psychic or healing powers of some sort. Anyway, I don't see the harm."

"Me neither. Live and let live, after all."

But living with those things when they happen to you is a different kettle of fish entirely.

Despite his earlier protestations about having to work tomorrow, after we've eaten Mani takes his third pint into the beer garden. There's still plenty of daylight and if I wasn't so stuffed I'd suggest we went for a walk to the clifftop and back to watch the sunset, but we can do that another time. The white stars of jasmine scrambling along the fence perfume the air and the sky is that deepest of blues that can only happen just before it turns to night.

"This is the perfect English pub."

"Cornish pub," I tease.

"Sorry! I tend to think of a Cornish pub as being in one of those picture postcard fishing villages, right on the harbour so you can watch the boats come in. Although I'm yet to see anywhere like that."

"Then we ought to go sometime. But either soon or wait until September, when there are fewer tourists. Given people can't go abroad it's going to be rammed down here for most of the summer."

"You might sell more of your glass."

"I hope so. I've managed to get it into a few shops and I've taken the plunge and booked a stand at Truro market when they have one of their local makers' days. It's a bit of a risk but I'm hoping it will be worth it."

"You should sell truck loads, your stuff is so gorgeous. But then I'm probably biased." He snakes his hand across the table to hold mine. For an unthinking moment I hold his back, and then I stiffen. There's a reason he shouldn't be doing this, and she's called Eloise. But it's hard, so hard, because I want it too, however much I know it's wrong.

He pulls his hand gently away and I glance up to see his eyes full of longing and regret. But he should have at least told me he's engaged. It's so fundamentally dishonest of him not to, and I'm through with dishonest men, Kitto's behaviour tonight has only underlined the fact. Maybe Mani'll say something now, and I realise that all I want to hear is that he's calling it off with her.

In my dreams.

He clears his throat, and returns to our original conversation.

"If you'd like me to lend a hand with the market stall, just let me know." But he can't look me in the eye and the dark-fringed aura has reappeared. Guilty conscience perhaps?

I thank him and down my orange juice. "Right, drink up. Tomorrow's a work day, remember."

CHAPTER TWENTY-SIX

Kresen Kernow archives are open now too, although the appointment system they need with social distancing means I can't book us in for more than a week. It's a week during which Mani and I feel just a little stiff and strange with each other. Or at least, I do with him. There's a part of me that wants to come right out and mention I've seen his engagement photos on social media, but really, what would be the point? Even if he wasn't with someone, I don't want to take this any further. It's July already, and if he's only here for a year he'll be going home next March.

We spend a damp Sunday afternoon sprawled in Mum and Dad's living room, choosing the research material we want to study. The farmhouse feels like neutral ground where we're comfortable; I don't ask him across the yard to my place and I've never been invited to his. It's almost as though we're keeping a safe distance between us.

Sometimes I think it's because he has feelings for me in the way I'm trying not to for him, and then I berate myself because it's useless anyway. Sometimes I think he's a lying shit for not telling me about Eloise, and at other times I want to believe he's being completely honourable and not finishing with her in an email. I just wish, whatever's going on, he'd tell me — we're meant to be friends, after all. And I know there's something because, even though it's not as black as it was during lockdown, his aura is still pretty dark at times.

Mani looks up at me from the other sofa. "How long have we got at the research centre?"

"Just an afternoon session; two and a half hours, but we can always go back. Why? Is there a lot you want to see?"

"Someone's written a whole book on Dolcoath mine's history. It'll take more than that just to go through it."

"Most of it won't be relevant to our time period though. We only need to go up to … what is it? Eighteen-sixty-something?"

"True, but all the same…"

Inspiration strikes. "Have you checked online for it?"

"It's really old…"

"There are plenty of second-hand booksellers online. Especially now."

A few taps on his phone and he's found and ordered it. "Genius, Carla. I'd never have thought of it. Now I can concentrate on the other stuff."

"What's there?"

"Mainly plans and sett information, but there are letters and some legal documents too. It's hard to know where to start to be honest. I suppose I was hoping something would leap out at me, but of course it hasn't. How are you getting on with the smuggler?"

"There are too many William Burgesses for the search to be useful so I'm trying smuggling instead. I think I'll just order some books on the subject to scan through to see if I can find anything."

Mani laughs. "Where's your commitment? I know, you'd rather be making glass than trying to find out if there's a lost heir."

"A lost heir?"

"You know, to the Basset family fortunes."

"Their heirs weren't lost, they were just indirect descendants. And not very good financial managers either. There's nothing left for any heir to inherit, not even a title."

"No illegitimate children? No secret marriages?" he teases.

"Illegitimate children certainly don't count. They probably wouldn't even have been recognised, and what's more, that book of Mum's says there was no hint at all of Sir Francis straying, which was mighty unusual for the era."

"He probably found the right woman first time around, lucky guy."

"It could well have been a love match. His wife was the sister of a friend and although she was obviously well-to-do, she wasn't titled herself. Maybe because he'd been orphaned quite young he didn't have the weight of parental pressure on him so he was free to choose."

"I guess parental pressure was even worse then than it is today?"

"Is it still a thing?"

He rolls his eyes. "Try telling my mother it isn't." I could so easily ask him if she approves of his fiancée, but the words stick in my throat. I'm such a coward, this needs to be out in the open. This could be the way to bring it into the conversation naturally.

"So what does she do?"

"She drives Helen to distraction. She's only twenty-eight but anyone would think she's an old maid the way Mum keeps throwing her friends' sons at her. Especially the ones with Greek heritage. The thing is, it's pushing Helen away. Just as soon as she can afford it she says she's not only going to leave home, she's leaving town as well."

"So did your mother drive you away too?" I make it sound like a bit of a joke, but I want to know more about why he's here. I know he's told me about the job coming up, but something doesn't quite fit. A last taste of freedom before he ties the knot, perhaps. But will he admit it?

He speaks slowly. "Noooo … not exactly. I've had quite a lot of time to think about why I came since I've been here." He looks down at the carpet, pinching the bridge of his nose between his finger and thumb and frowning hard. "At the time it was an absolute gut reaction. I … I didn't think at all. I saw the job and it was all about making sure I got it." He looks up, smiles. "Forward motion, you know?"

"I'm not sure I do."

"Well…" Outside Sam barks and we both look towards the window. "Hey, it's stopped raining. Want to take a walk?"

He's changed the subject. This is avoidance for sure. But then he says, "I guess I find it easier to talk outside. Feels less intense, you know?"

"Sure. I'll get my coat."

We meet Dad in the yard, bundled into his waxed jacket, Sam capering around him.

"He's stir crazy, poor dog. If you're going to stretch your legs then we'll join you."

"We can take him if you like, Bill," Mani offers.

I laugh. "He'd never come. About a hundred yards and he'd been looking over his shoulder for Dad."

Mani glances at me, but I'm not sure if I'm misreading his look. "Well sure, Bill," he says. "It would be a pleasure to have your company."

In anyone's money, Kresen Kernow is an impressive place. Built into the crumbling ruins of a brewery in Redruth which was an eyesore for years, to me it's modern architecture at its best. And as it was only opened six months before the pandemic struck it still feels brand spanking new.

It's also eerily quiet. The car park is half empty and our footsteps echo across the courtyard. We stop and gaze at mellow old stones glowing in the sun and how well the large modern windows work with them. Then we don our masks and step inside.

The reception area is a study in more old stone and shining wood; floors, walls, staircase in rich bands of natural colour, colours that would never work in glass, yet are beautiful all the same. Light streams through the doors and from massive windows in the roof, and the centrepiece is a fabulous round reception desk. Mani stops in his tracks, gazes around, and says 'wow'.

It is wow, and I think that in Cornwall, especially the old mining areas, we need things to be proud of. There's deprivation and poverty here that the tourists never see and probably don't want to. I think of the students who will be leaving my school next month, many with little hope of an actual career of any sort, or even a steady job that lasts all year. What's the point of studying even something practical like design technology if they don't have a hope in hell of using it?

The thought rests like a pall of gloom over my shoulders as we are directed up the steps. To the left of the staircase is the library, with shelves filled with books about Cornwall, and I would love to be able to browse but that just isn't possible at the moment. Instead we head in the opposite direction and are seated in a clinical white space where a pile of books is waiting for me, and a veritable stack of papers and two leather-bound ledgers for Mani.

"I hope you don't mind," the archivist says as we settle ourselves on opposite sides of the table, "but when I saw what else you'd asked for I bought the Dolcoath board minutes for the 1850s and '60s too. The online catalogue isn't perfect yet, and they might help to tie some of the other information together."

"That is just so thoughtful. Thank you."

Once we are heads down over our material, I can't help but sneak a glance at Mani. Not having been able to get to a barber suits him, and his former crew cut has grown into a thick black mane that's grazing the collar of his polo shirt and flopping into his eyes. Every so often he sweeps it back with a long-fingered hand, which most of the time acts as a cradle for his angular jaw. I wonder how much easier it would be just to be friends if he wasn't quite so good-looking.

This is getting me nowhere, in more ways than one, so I return my attention to my first book. It's a slim volume with its focus around Polperro so I move swiftly on, rummaging through the pile to see if any of them at least has an index.

It could have been a needle in a haystack, should have been probably. But William Burgess is in the index of the third one I check and there are half a dozen pages devoted to him and his exploits. The first paragraph confirms he's my ancestor, with a mention of Koll Hendra as his HQ, together with a description so detailed that with any luck we might still be able to find one or two of his old hiding places. But it's how he came by the farm that stops me in my tracks.

It seems William Burgess was Francis Basset's illegitimate son.

But how? According to Mum's history book the man was a paragon of virtue. I need to get to the bottom of this, and the pile of books in front of me won't help at all. It's Francis Basset's story I need to understand right now.

"Mani!"

His head jerks up. "You found something?"

"Look at this." I push the book across the table, my forefinger indicating the paragraph.

"Do you think this is true?"

"I need to dig some more, but these books won't help. It's Sir Francis I need to find out about right now."

I know we're not meant to move around but the archivist has disappeared into a glass-fronted office so I thread my way between the tables until she notices me and comes out.

"I'm so sorry," I tell her, "but something I've found has pushed my research in a different direction. Do you have anything on Francis Basset, Lord de Dunstanville?"

"I'm sure we do. Sit back down and I'll see what I can find."

While I wait I offer to help Mani, but the stack of letters he gives me have no details at all of any of the miners. There must have been hundreds of them, most of them paid by the amount of ore they brought up, some no doubt moving from mine to mine when times were good, to get the best deal.

Paid. There's a thought. "Mani, I wonder if there are any ledgers showing payments to the miners? They might help."

He scribbles a note on his pad. "Good call. Although there is so much material here that might have to wait for another visit."

After a while the archivist returns with a couple of books on the Basset family, one little more than a pamphlet held together by brown paper and Sellotape. She sets them at the end of the table, away from where we are sitting.

"This little one may not look much, but it's an account of his early life written in Victorian times as part of a series about Cornish gentry. The other dates from the 1960s and is considered the best overall source."

I thank her and pick up the pamphlet. When it was written people may well have been alive who knew Sir Francis so it seems a good place to start.

It doesn't take long for me to discover the smuggling book was right. The first few pages are about his childhood and his education at Harrow, Eton alongside his cousin Christopher Hawkins, then Cambridge, and his love for the arts. For a boy who'd been orphaned at just twelve years old, it was probably a place to escape to.

Possibly a delicate boy too, because when he was eighteen he spent time at a farm near Helston, ostensibly due to poor health. Certainly he wasn't too ill to consummate a relationship with the farmer's daughter, one Emily Martin, who nine months later died in childbirth. In 1776 the shame her pregnancy would have brought upon herself and her family would have been huge, so she was spared that at least, but the upshot was that baby William was taken to Tehidy and adopted by the Basset's steward, Thomas Burgess.

I sit back in my seat. There's more than one source, and no doubt the other book will confirm it too. As much to myself as to Mani, I whisper, "It's true."

He looks up, eyes sparkling above his mask. "So that means you're ... the rightful Lady de Dunstanville." He bows his head. "My lady."

"Idiot. I am most certainly not, and anyway, the title through the female line was Baroness Basset of Stratton."

"I sit corrected. My lady."

I give him what I hope is a really withering look but he just winks. "You seem more upbeat. Have you found something?" I ask.

"Not for my side of the story, but a bit more about the Burgesses. There was a Thomas Burgess working at Dolcoath and I'm reasonably sure it's your family because his middle name was Parmenas. It's not the kind of name you forget easily, and I'm sure that was what one of the three children born at about the time of the rattle was called."

"It makes a change from all the Williams in our family. It's certainly unusual and I don't think I've ever heard it before."

"No, and it was seeing it that made me read the board minute more carefully. In 1865 our Thomas was appointed chief engineer at the mine. When I get home I'll get back on the family history website to see if I can trace him, although he may well have been Parmenas' son."

"Why not do it now?"

"I want to finish the rest of these minutes. With any luck I'll find a clue to my Dolcoath ancestor as well."

"Wasn't he called Thomas too?"

"Yeah, him and half the guys I've come across. Sometimes even as a surname. The mine captain at the time was called Charles Thomas."

"I wonder … and I could be barking up the wrong tree here … but could your Thomas Dolcoath actually have been somebody Thomas in Cornwall?"

Mani puts his head in his hands. "That only makes the whole thing even more impossible."

For the next hour I scribble down all the notes I can find on the Burgess-Basset connection. Dad will be absolutely fascinated and it means we can take the family tree back many more generations, because the births, marriages and deaths of the Bassets are bound to be well recorded. I can't wait to tell him, but I'm going to have to, because he and Mum are actually going out tonight. First time since lockdown and I'm glad they're getting their lives back too.

It's close to the end of our session when Mani speaks. "I've found our Thomas again. There was a discussion about who the next mine captain should be when Charles Thomas retired and he was definitely in the running, but in the end it went to Charles's son. Nepotism or what?"

"That must have felt like a kick in the teeth. If he knew."

"I think he must have. Two meetings later they were appointing a new chief engineer, so he obviously resigned. Still, he's an interesting footnote to your family tree."

We stack our books and papers at the end of the table as we were asked to do and head down the stairs and into the sunshine. Mani stretches, his polo shirt rising to expose a firm six-pack. I look away.

"Carla?"

"Hmm?"

"Now that we're allowed to mix indoors, I wondered if … you know … we could continue our research at my place? I can scrape together some pasta for supper and there are a few beers in the fridge. Unless, of course, you're busy?"

It's a straightforward enough invitation between friends, but although there's a shadow behind his eyes, there's a plea in them too and I notice he's clenching and unclenching his fist around his car keys.

"Sure," I say breezily. "I'd really like that."

CHAPTER TWENTY-SEVEN

Mani drops me home so I can collect my car and let Sam out for a nose around the garden. He seems lost without Dad, even more than usual because he's become so used to having him around all the time, and I wonder how the dogs people have bought during lockdown will manage when their owners eventually go back to work.

Work is something I've been thinking about too. I've decided to go back to school as normal in September — whatever they decide normal is — then, in December, I'll ask if I can go part-time from February. I'll have a few months to fit out the barn, design and make more stock, and find some extra retail outlets before the tourist season begins. It'll be scary living on half my salary, but my online sales are ticking along nicely so I'm determined to give it a go. And by then perhaps the farm will have been able to repay me.

There's a light drizzle falling by the time I get into my car. I'm not used to driving to Tehidy, and I've never visited the residential area, so I take a wrong turn and find myself in the almost deserted car park next to the café. As I'm turning around a light flashes on my rear windscreen; a dancing, clear white glow, and an intense feeling of fear causes bile to lurch into my throat, but then the light vanishes.

The car stalls. My instinct is to drive away as quickly as possible, but whatever I may or may not have seen has left me feeling pretty nauseous and I don't want to arrive at Mani's and promptly throw up. I need fresh air so I stumble out of the driver's seat and, gripping the open car door for support, gulp down some deep breaths to try to stop myself from retching.

After a while I am able to look in the direction the light came from, but there's nothing there now. Perhaps it was just my sidelights reflecting off the damp granite of the pillar that guards the entrance to the park. It has a coat of arms near the top, presumably the Basset's. And actually, mine now I suppose, so I take a closer look.

Although it's worn, I notice something I recognise straight away. On top of the central shield is a unicorn's head. Just like the one engraved on the mouthpiece of the whistle end of the rattle. The connection feels startling, but maybe it shouldn't. The rattle could even have been given to a secret grandchild by Francis Basset. I'll check some more images of the coat of arms when I get to Mani's place, then we can be sure.

I drive into the private residential area, past the modern houses that form Tehidy Copse, and I'm amazed how much green space is inside the enclosed area the public never sees. I park at the edge of the stable yard then crunch across the gravel, surrounded by cream-painted, slate-roofed buildings on three sides. In the centre of the courtyard are four square raised beds, each containing four balls of privet, their scent permeating the damp air as I walk past.

Mani's is one of just a few properties with an oriel window tucked under the eaves, and I spot it instantly from his description of the mounting block. The highly polished black granite looks very classy, despite Mani having dumped a plastic pot of trailing lobelia on the top step.

The front door opens straight into the lounge, and although he is all smiles as he ushers me in, the heaviness of the place presses down on me, an ugly echo of feeling that has nothing to do with the present and everything to do with the past.

At the other end is the conservatory he used for our video chats and I make a bolt for it.

"Let's sit out here, it's lovely."

"In this weather?"

"Oh yes, I love to hear the rain on a glass roof."

He takes what I say at face value and heads off to fetch some drinks while I gaze blankly at the small garden beyond, trying to steady my breathing. When he returns he assures me the beers are low alcohol so I'll be fine to drive, and I'm comforted by his consideration. But his aura is dark again, and I wonder if it's anything to do with living in this oppressive place. I'm already dreading having to walk back through the sitting room and I'm praying we won't be eating inside.

As soon as he sits down I tell him about the unicorn on the Basset crest on the pillar. His laptop is already open and he googles it. Sure enough, it's there in every image. Another link between the Burgesses and the Bassets; this time a tangible one.

"If we could prove the rattles' provenance it could be worth a lot more."

He looks shocked. "You wouldn't sell it though, would you?"

Of course I would, albeit reluctantly, if it could buy me a new kiln, but I mutter something about insurance and he nods.

"Have you made any progress since you've been home?" I ask.

"What, apart from running around making sure this place was clean for my lady's visit?"

"Mani…" My tone is perhaps a little more threatening than I intended.

"Sorry. But yes, I have, on Thomas Burgess at least. He was Henry's son, William the smuggler's middle boy, so Parmenas was his uncle. And Parmenas never married, so perhaps that was why he was named for him."

"Probably."

"Anyway, Thomas was born in 1841 so he would have been really young to be a mine captain in 1867. On the other hand, he was also young to be the mine's chief engineer so he must have been something of a whizz kid."

"What happened to him once he left Dolcoath. Can you tell?"

"Well here's the thing; he's not on the 1871 census. His brother, yet another William, is running an inn at Pool, but no sign of our Thomas."

A penny begins to drop, a linking of two stories, or leastways, one giving a clue to another. "Unless ... he emigrated somewhere, like your ancestor. But how would we find out?"

"My ancestor was Thomas ... but then, as I said before, from the mine records half of Cornwall was called either William or Thomas. But at least we have a surname too — Burgess, and there are ship passenger lists we can search online."

I take a sip of my beer. "Go on then."

It doesn't take him long, and he swivels the screen towards me. "Got him. Thomas P. Burgess, mine engineer. From Cornwall, England, intending to make his home in the USA."

"One step closer."

"To what?"

I can't help myself from grinning. "To you being your own bloody lost heir, not me."

"They do say ... six degrees of separation and all that... OK, let me think. Immigration records. Where was the ship headed? Right... Wilmington, North Carolina... But it's going to take a while to check through these and I'm getting hungry."

"Then why don't I do it while you sort out some supper?"

"Good call, I can hardly send you to my kitchen, can I?"

"Certainly not. I'm more than happy here." Hopefully he'll take the hint when it comes to eating our food.

He does, and just as I've worked out the best way to search the immigration database, Mani returns with a bowl of Greek salad, two small plates and some cutlery.

"Move that computer out of the way and I'll fetch the carbonara."

"Mmm … one of my favourites. If we're going to be related, then I'm glad you can cook."

He screws up his face. "We'd be really, really distant cousins, right?"

"Distant as distant can be. Especially once you go home to the States."

I listen to his footsteps cross the wooden boards of the living room. Why the hell did I say that? This house has put me on edge, as has Mani's darkening aura. It was barely visible most of the day, but here, now…

A bowl of carbonara lands in front of me and it smells delicious, so I help myself to salad and we tuck in. I ask him if he planted up the pots in the garden himself, and if he likes the way his neighbour's clematis has colonised his side of the fence. He asks me what my next glass designs will be, but I can tell he barely listens to my response, which isn't like him.

I finish my meal and put down my fork. "OK, Mani, are you going to tell me what's wrong?"

"How do you mean?"

"You know what I mean."

He pinches the bridge of his nose. "Yeah … yeah … I guess I do." He stands. "Let me clear these and make some coffee, then we can talk."

I smile up at him. "That sounds good to me."

I gaze at the darkening sky as I listen to the clatter of dishes from the kitchen, and then the whoosh of a coffee machine. I suppose I shouldn't have expected instant from a guy like Mani.

After a while he reappears at the conservatory door. "I've put coffee in the living room. It's getting too cold out here."

"No, I'm fine…" But already he is back inside, holding the door and waiting for me to pass through it.

OK, I can do this. All he's asking of me is to go into a room with an oppressive atmosphere and listen to him. I should be focusing on what he's saying, anyway, not the room. Do that, and I will be fine.

The coffee cups are on a side table between where the two right-angled sofas meet. The fact it's dusk and Mani has set the lamps quite low isn't helping, as the corners of the room away from the conservatory doors ooze blackness. I don't know why this is happening. I've never felt anything like it before.

All the same, I turn to him and smile encouragingly. He can't quite smile back.

"It's time I levelled with you, Carla. In some ways I feel I've been less than honest, and you and your family have become real important to me so it doesn't sit well."

"I get that. You seem like an honest guy."

"Thank you. I am, really. Straight up as they come."

"So what haven't you told me?"

He rubs his index finger across the furrows on his brow. "That I'd like us to be more than friends. Almost from the moment I first saw you, and as I've got to know you… I would like more, but there's…"

I think of the night in the beer garden when he tried to hold my hand. Out of the corner of my eye I see a flash of bright light and I feel myself stiffen.

"See," he says sadly, "you've done it again, like you did outside The Tinners. I can see it isn't what you want, Carla, and perhaps I should have kept my mouth shut, but when you asked it seemed like an opportunity to get it out in the open. I suppose I hoped…"

The quivering mass of light seems to be growing, hovering near the bottom of the stairs. I can't take my eyes off it. I'm hot. I'm cold. My heart begins to pound. I can't be here… I just can't… I'm going to throw up all over the carpet any minute.

I stand. "I'm sorry, Mani. I'm so sorry … it's … it's not what you think but there's just no way I can stay here." I grab my bag and make a lunge for the front door, flinging it open and running across the courtyard. The only thing on my mind is to get away. Throwing myself into my car, I breathe a silent prayer of thanks my dinner stayed in place. The engine starts first time, I slam it into gear and race away.

PART SIX: 1810

CHAPTER TWENTY-EIGHT

Although it was late in the day, Zephaniah Job received William warmly in his study. It had been a long journey and William was looking forward to his bed at The Three Pilchards, but Job surprised him by his offer of refreshment before they set out.

"Our business is not to be undertaken here?" William asked.

"I would prefer you to see to what use the rope would be put, after all, you seemed curious last time. In addition I think it wise to discuss your samples with the men who will be benefiting from their undoubted quality."

William bowed his head a little, but not too much. The man had not even asked if his mount was sufficiently fresh, unless, of course, he already knew that he had changed horses at the inn at St Keyne, leaving Liberty in the care of the groom who he felt he could trust. With his horse, if nothing else.

There was something about Job's manner that made William uneasy, and this strange plan of his to ride out put him on his guard. He was polite, punctiliously so, and affable in his own quiet way, yet William sensed much was hidden behind this polished front. He had heard rumours the man had been forced from St Pirans, rather than chosen to leave. And if they were true there was indeed a ruthless iron fist beneath that fine calfskin glove.

The sun was already low in the sky behind them as they left Polperro, climbing between the granite cottages on either side of Talland Hill, then along a sunken lane, the horses' hooves silenced by the soft rutted earth beneath the rippling green canopy of beech and oak. Skirting the grounds of Killigarth

Manor they trotted across open fields, the corn all but ripe and swaying in the breeze, the sea the deepening blue of dusk beyond them.

As they descended the track the pair of coves that made up Talland Bay appeared below them, the nearer a long funnel low to the beach, the further almost perfectly round but with a perilous rocky shore. Job reined in his horse and raised his eyeglass, scanning the coastline towards the next headland where a compact brig, its sails hanging slack, was anchored a few hundred yards offshore. As they watched, a rowing boat detached itself from the ship's long shadow and progressed towards them.

"Let us go. We shall be drinking the finest French brandy within the hour."

To William the beach looked too exposed for such an operation in what were still, after all, daylight hours. A band of woodland ran down the valley, with a sunken lane towards the village on the other side, but both could hide foe as well as friend. His unease increased and, while he was scanning the terrain to imprint it into his mind, something caught his eye.

"Wait!"

"Are you afeared, man?" asked Job, turning in his saddle.

"No, but there was a flash of light, up towards the church. A flash like an eyeglass might have made, reflecting against the setting sun."

"Then it is not of any great concern. The vicar is our man. As are the villagers, the whole valley. There will be no betrayal here."

"Betrayal, no. But force to silence men, perchance, on the part of the preventatives?"

"They know better than to try in one of my strongholds. Come, there is no time for further delay. We must be on the beach when the boat moors for the captain will be on board to meet you."

Job had never struck William as an incautious man, but now he was hastening into a potentially dangerous situation. Was it only his arrogance making him so bold? Or could it be the local excise men were in his pay as well? He was not the smugglers' banker for nothing, and perhaps favours could be done, one way and perhaps another, as well as money and contraband changing hands. Could his capture be one such favour? Could this all be an elaborate trap?

But no, he was exaggerating his own importance in this part of Cornwall. Even so, much as he wished to conclude the sale of his ropes he did not wish to ride into any sort of trouble, so he hung back a little, continuing his assessment of the ground for the best means of escape should the need arise.

Job turned in his saddle. "What are you waiting for now? I tell you, the cove is secure."

"All the same," William replied, "something is making my gut uneasy, and over the years I have learnt to trust my gut. I have come here to ply an honest trade, not to become embroiled in something I do not understand."

Job was clearly becoming riled. "Do not come the moralist with me, man. Your reputation precedes you. I know who you are — and what you are too."

"That I very much doubt." William murmured it quietly to himself, but Job's ears were sharp.

"Perhaps my trust was misplaced, after all."

"And mine alongside it. I will go no further."

"Well, I do not advise you to go back."

William glanced over his shoulder the way they had come, only to see two mounted men appear on the ridge of the hill behind them. Much as they blocked the track behind, Job's horse blocked his way in front, so William urged his mare over the low hedge and raced down the field towards the bay, hoping the mare was up to the challenge.

She did not disappoint him and they galloped down the slope, expecting at any moment to hear the sound of gunfire behind him, but it did not come. He almost had time to wonder if he had been mistaken, but then three mounted preventative men burst from the cover of the trees below the church, just half a field away from him as he passed the second cove. There was a boat already drawn up on the shingle; a boat he hadn't seen, and the men unloading it returned fire. William hesitated for a moment, just long enough to see an exciseman catapult backwards from his horse, clutching at his chest, then he spurred his mount away into the sunken lane, praying there were not more preventatives hiding there.

His luck was in, and he gave his horse its head through the village, galloping past low cottages into the deepening dusk. He was riding east, that much he knew, towards Looe, where he could follow the valley back to St Keyne. But what if the preventative was dead? William, a known smuggler, had been in the vicinity, indeed had perhaps been placed there deliberately. What if they came after him for it? It was a crime the perpetrator would swing for, nothing was more certain.

He had to keep riding, to get away. Trees and hedges flashed past but after a while he knew his horse could gallop no longer and he slowed to a trot. Liberty would be waiting for him at St Keyne, but who else might be there? It was not a risk he cared to take, neither did he know where best to lie low, so his only option was to leave the area.

Exhaustion and the sick feeling that filled him when the thrill of a chase left his body befuddled his brain. But this chase had not been thrilling and the predicament he was in made it hard to think. To be taken for something he had done was one thing, but to be accused of something he had not… But he had not ridden close enough for the preventatives to be sure of his identity, and the shots had come from the beach. No wonder Job had been in such a hurry to place him there. All the same, he needed a sound alibi, so that if they eventually caught up with him he had every chance of walking free.

Only one place came to mind. If he rode as hard as he dared push his horse then he would be in Torquay before dawn, and if he was seen about the village early in the day, if Franny could be persuaded to tell her maids he had been there all night… Perhaps, perhaps it would be enough. The reality was he had no better choice.

CHAPTER TWENTY-NINE

The early dawn had already claimed the pink-gold sky and the chatter of birds was filling the trees as William circumnavigated Torquay and approached Fern Cottage across the heath. He was beyond tired as he tethered his similarly exhausted horse to a tree in the orchard and headed towards the house in the hope of finding some water and no early rising servants.

Instead he found Franny, standing at the open front door with a baby in her arms.

"Good morning, William," she said, as though she had been expecting him. "Have you come to meet Eliza?"

He could not help but smile at her, pale and drawn as she was. "And to assure myself of your good health."

She shrugged. "They're going to make me give her away, William, and I cannot do it."

William shook his head. "They should never have shown her to you, then you would not have known. It is beyond cruel."

"I insisted. I was curious. Curious to see what I had produced. And of course, the instant I saw her I loved her."

"Oh, Franny, I am so sorry it has come to this."

"Sometimes I think it would be better to end both our lives than to be parted, but Harriet tells me it would hardly be fair on Eliza, and of course it would not sit easily with my faith."

Not an overly religious man, nevertheless William said, "And your faith will surely sustain you."

"Pah! How can that be? Food and drink are what sustains one, William."

This was the Franny of old and he was glad to see it. "Talking of which, I have a thirsty horse in the orchard."

"There is water in a trough in the yard behind the house. You can lead Liberty there."

"Not Liberty, but a hired mount, although a good one, for I have ridden all night. Franny, please tell no-one I arrived this morning. It would be better if the servants understood I was here before midnight."

"But the guest room was not prepared…"

"Tell them I slept in the parlour."

Her eyes narrowed. "Of course, William, but in return you must do something for me. You must find a way to help me to keep Eliza."

After seeing his mount had slaked its thirst and rubbing her down with handfuls of grass William returned to the yard and sluiced his face in the trough, trying to rid himself of the overwhelming desire to sleep that had come upon him. He was no good to either himself or Franny in this state and had there been a stable he would have gladly stretched out in the hay and allowed oblivion to claim him.

He could hear the housekeeper and maid talking in the kitchen, so he walked around to the front of the house and let himself in through the door, and thence to the parlour where he took a chair in front of the empty fireplace. Floorboards creaked over his head; whoever was in the room above was up and about so he would do well to snatch what sleep he could before they came downstairs.

He woke to find Harriet standing in front of him, glaring angrily while repeating his name.

He struggled to his feet. "Good morning Miss Le … Buller. I hope I find you well."

She folded her arms. "Mrs Coxe informed me that her cousin had arrived during the night. Please join us in the dining room for breakfast."

"Thank you." He put on his jacket, which he had abandoned on the sofa, and followed her across the hall.

Franny was already seated at the table, with Eliza in a wicker basket on the floor close by. They made small talk until the young maid left them, while Harriet poured the coffee. William would have preferred a jug of ale, but given the tension in the room decided not to impose further on their hospitality.

"So have you thought of anything?" Franny demanded.

"Not unless he thinks while he's asleep," her friend countered. "I found him snoring in the parlour."

William applied himself to buttering his bread, then reaching for a slice of cold beef to accompany it. "Am I right in assuming that your father is unwilling to let you stay here?"

Harriet snorted. "Quite unwilling, as you put it. So unwilling, in fact, he has demanded we return before the month is out or he will cut Franny off without a penny."

"And that is our problem," said Franny. "William, do you have any money you could give us? You are a man of business, after all."

Harriet's hand fluttered to her mouth. "You cannot ask him that, Franny."

"Why not?"

William turned to her. "There are those who think it indelicate to even talk about money amongst friends, much less ask for it. But I take no offence for I can see how desperate you are. But that is by the by; with a family of my own to care for I have little enough to spare. Certainly not enough to provide for another household."

"We could do away with the servants."

"Franny, we would starve. Have either of us ever cooked a meal, laid a fire? Laundered a dress?"

"Well, just one maid then, like William has."

The older woman turned to William. "You see how impossible it is to find a solution. Do not think for a moment that I am not as desirous of Franny keeping Eliza as she is herself, but I see no plan which could work."

William nodded. "I share your sentiments exactly. I know how my Mary would pine if she had to give a child she had birthed away to strangers; I swear it would break her, and likely me as well. Indeed, we still mourn the girl who was stillborn to us almost two years since."

A thought began to take root in William's mind, but it was an outlandish one, and one he would not speak of. To give a child away to strangers was one thing, but to give it to friends, to neighbours, to be raised close by… But no, without Mary's consent he would not dare to offer that hope.

But Franny had seen it too. "Then you and Mary can take Eliza. You would have your girl and I could see my daughter every day. It is the perfect solution." She looked down at the basket. "I told you, my dearest, that William would not fail us."

Harriet looked from one of them to the other, William silently willing her to find some objection. Instead she said slowly, "The plan has some merit."

"It is not one I could agree to without Mary's consent."

"But she is your wife!" Franny burst out.

"Not my chattel," he replied angrily.

"Quite so," murmured Harriet.

William nodded. He could not tell them his story, the story of not being wanted by his adoptive parents, of being forced upon them. Yet all the same, perhaps his real father had done it to keep him close; so he could watch him grow, and see the

219

kind of man he would become. Perhaps now history was repeating itself.

"Very well," he said. "I will talk to Mary, and if she agrees, I will speak to Lord de Dunstanville."

"But why?" Franny asked. "He will only refuse."

William folded his arms. "Those are my terms, take them or leave them."

"And your alibi?" Franny asked.

Damn, he had thought she had forgotten it was part of a bargain, especially given Harriet's words about him arriving in the night.

"If I am arrested, albeit falsely, you will have no hope of keeping Eliza at all," he told her.

CHAPTER THIRTY

William planned to leave Torquay well before dawn the next morning, but he absented himself from Fern Cottage for much of the day, generally making sure he was seen around the town and partaking of a hearty dinner and several tankards of ale at the inn. The desperately sad atmosphere at the cottage had made it uncomfortable for him to be there, but he returned for a light supper before the ladies bade him good night and good travels, then retreated upstairs.

Franny turned back as she left the room, taking his hand. "For friendship's sake, William, please speak favourably of our scheme to your Mary."

He looked into her red-rimmed eyes and promised, "For friendship, and for Eliza, I surely will."

He removed his jacket and loosed his stock, but still he could not settle and he prowled around the room. It was simple and homely, a far cry from what Franny was used to at Tehidy, but the furnishings were well maintained and the rug in front of the fire of good quality. The curtains were yet to be drawn, and he settled himself on the window seat to watch the dusk claim the bay.

In order to do so he had to move Franny's sketchbook, and he started to flick through it. Clearly it had been a new one to come here, for the first pages contained soft seashore scenes, a botanical sketch of a fern, and a view of the orchard. Thinking what an accomplished artist she'd become he continued to turn the leaves until his fingers faltered on a portrait. A half-height portrait of Harriet wearing nothing but a cotton chemise.

The intimacy of it shocked him to the core. The curve of her breasts was apparent through the thin fabric, her nipples standing so proud he had to look away. He was no prude when it came to women, but no lady should be drawing or be drawn like this. No lady should even have seen these things in another.

But Franny clearly had. As the sketchbook attested, she did not draw from her imagination. In fact, nothing he knew about her suggested she imagined anything at all; even as a child she would not read or listen to stories that were 'made up'; such things were beyond her comprehension.

He turned the next page more cautiously, this time confronted by Harriet wearing nothing but a pair of earrings, her shoulders and breasts completely naked for all to see. Then, after a watercolour of a rose he recognised from the front garden, and a sketch of a fishing smack, were a pair of curled female legs and feet, one stockinged and one not, and it was not hard to guess whose they were.

Franny's portrayals of her friend were disturbingly erotic. Oh, not in the way they aroused anything in him, but they were clearly how his friend saw her companion, nothing was clearer. As was the fact that, given her subject's state of undress, her affections were reciprocated. Unless such sketches were simply how bored, wealthy ladies filled their time, but he had never heard of such a thing.

He had, however, read about the rather scandalous Ladies of Llangollen, who apparently lived openly in the same way as a married couple, although denying any impropriety. Franny had spoken of her desire to live here with Harriet and bring up her daughter — had that been what she had meant? If he were to creep upstairs now, would he find them sharing a bedchamber?

William had no desire to do so. The fact that this was useful information to squirrel away for a time it was needed came to him more from habit than anything else. He would not, could not, expose Franny; if he failed to persuade Mary about Eliza then she would need her friend's comfort more than ever. Whatever the truth of their relationship, a mere sniff of scandal would force the Bassets to send Harriet away.

Everyone needed someone, and throughout his childhood Franny had been his only friend. The strange and at times unfathomable life he had been given by his father had been a lonely one, but now he hoped it had sprung from a need to keep his child close. The thought warmed him more than anything, the fact he might have actually cared enough to do so. To him it was a debt of honour he should repay through Franny and her child if he possibly could.

It was still in the forenoon when William arrived at St Keyne. He had no desire at all to be in what he viewed as Job's territory, but he could not leave Liberty here indefinitely. Common sense told him his visit was a bad idea, but if he exercised sufficient caution, he hoped that all should be well.

The graveyard was tucked into a secluded crook of land behind the church and bordered by trees, so it was to one of these he tethered his mount before proceeding into the hamlet. If anyone was watching and waiting for his return they would be expecting a man on horseback, but there was no-one about and the only sounds he could hear were the ringing blows of hammer against anvil from the smithy down a narrow lane next to the inn.

He glanced into the low windows as he went by, but the parlour was empty, save for the serving wench, slumped half asleep on a stool next to the barrels. He doubted any preventatives were hiding there, waiting to pounce, or she would not be dozing about her work, and he quickened his pace around the corner and into the stable yard.

The groom was pulling water from the well and nodded in acknowledgement while he completed his task.

"Come for your horse, have you?" he asked. "You were meant to be bringing one back."

"I have, and she is tethered in the churchyard. Let us say I thought it wise to exercise a degree of caution in coming here." He leant against the wall, where he had a clear view of the whole yard and an escape route back into the lane.

"Ah, yes. It was said you ran into a little trouble with the preventatives down at Talland."

"I did not run into trouble; trouble ran into me while I was about my honest business. I simply had the misfortune to be in the locality when shots were fired with unfortunate consequences."

"Misfortune? Poppycock. Job had you there for a reason, I'll be bound. That excise man had caused him trouble before but he would have no wish for another of his own men to swing." He spat on the ground. "But no matter, because I told the old gossip who told me he must be mistaken, because you were here in the stables that evening, yarning with me over a flagon of ale, before riding your own horse away as dawn broke."

William was still cautious. Why would the man go to those lengths for a virtual stranger? Was the trap becoming ever more elaborate? "Then I thank you, but I do wonder … the tip I gave you last time was not so very generous." He smiled, his eyes still darting around him, every nerve straining for signs of danger.

"Ah, you can prick down your ears, Mr Burgess. I have no love for Job and his gang. They pulled the most devious trick on my sister's husband when a preventative was shot in a battle over one of Job's ships. Whole of Polperro were in hiding, I reckon, with excise men and soldiers everywhere, so Job told Roger to turn king's witness against the man who fired the shot, and after the trial he would set him up with a new life in the Americas. But where is he now? In Newgate gaol for his own protection, and the man he turned in hung for his crime and his widow left to beg. It was a bad business all round."

Almost to himself William murmured, "Then he is capable of such things."

"And worse. But his hands are always clean, mark you. Always clean. Now take your horse and ride from here. It would not be wise to return."

The groom disappeared into the stables to saddle Liberty, but William remained alert in the courtyard. Swallows swooped from a nest in the eaves, their young now fledged. Summer was drawing on. His corn would need harvesting soon and the simple thought warmed him. Was he beginning to tire of danger? Certainly this sort of danger, where he could not weigh the risks.

From now on he would be a rope maker and farmer, and his sons would be rope makers and farmers, and he would bring them up to conduct their affairs with caution. Their lives were far too precious to him to do otherwise.

CHAPTER THIRTY-ONE

William rode into Koll Hendra's yard just after sundown, bats swooping from the eaves in the warm air. But he had hardly noticed the gathering dusk, as throughout the long ride home he had attempted and failed many times to find the right words to persuade Mary to take Eliza. Yes, his wife had a generous heart, but it was a great deal to ask when she had lost a daughter of her own and still hoped for one to cherish.

Hearing Liberty's hooves the stable boy emerged from the tack room, bleary-eyed with sleep, and took her reins. William thanked him for his trouble and walked slowly towards the farmhouse. A lamp still burned in the kitchen so he opened the door and went in.

Mary was sitting in her chair close to the fire, which was banked down to an orange glow that caught the lights in her hair, brushed out ready for bed. He was ready to bed her too, to lose himself in her softness and warmth, but he could not do so with the question he had to ask so heavy on his mind. For a moment he wondered whether it would be better to wait until morning, but to do so seemed somehow dishonest.

She smiled up at him. "I am so glad you returned tonight. I had almost given up hope."

"I said I would not be long away." The words came out a little harsher than he had meant and he sighed. "It has been a tiring day."

She stood and moved towards the pantry. "I would wager you are hungry. There is bread and cheese, some ham freshly roast this morning."

"Thank you."

She set a jug of ale in front of him and took the carving knife from the drawer, slicing the meat in great folds. When she had finished she looked up. "William, what is it? You have not kissed me, barely spoken."

"I have something to ask you. A great thing, a thing that you must feel free to refuse but it would please me if you did not." How stiff and formal he sounded, as though he was a puppet and someone else was pulling his strings.

"Then as it is clearly making you out of sorts you had better ask it and be done."

He leant against the dresser, nursing his ale. "On my travels I came across a baby girl in need of a home. She is but a few weeks old. She would never know she was not ours…"

Mary frowned. "To replace the girl we lost not two years since? William, how could you think of it when we can still hope for a daughter of our own?"

"That thought occurred to me too, but one does not preclude the other."

"No … and yet … William, if I am honest, this is most strange. You have never shown any interest at all in a child other than your own."

She was right, of course, and she was going to turn him down. Yet for Franny's sake he had to try harder. He had never seen her tears before, not even when her first pony had died when she was but eight years old, and he knew if she were never to see Eliza again it would break her heart. And of course, he had her leave to tell Mary the truth if need be. But to make sense of it all there were two secrets he would need to share.

He cleared his throat. "And if I told you … that I share a blood link with this child…"

"You… you…" Mary stuttered, her knuckles white around the handle of the knife.

What on God's earth? And then he realised how she had taken his words. "No!"

"You bastard! How could you? When I was carrying your child at that." Gripping the knife harder she raised it and lunged for him, but he was quicker and slid through the door and into the night, her furious cries following him.

He stood for a while with his back against the warm stones of the farmhouse wall, sweat dripping down his spine making him shiver. For all the words to have chosen … but he had never thought she would believe that of him. And yet she so easily had. She was never going to forgive him, not unless she would let him explain, and at the moment that seemed most unlikely. After he'd run from the kitchen he'd heard her draw the bolts across, and anyway, it would be most unwise to try again when she was so angry.

Resigning himself to a night in the hayloft he sluiced his face in water from the horse trough to clear his head then climbed the ladder to bed down in the sweet-smelling straw, the gentle shuffling and snorting of the horses below soothing him. He was back to his childhood, to a place he had felt secure, understood by beasts if not by man. Yet understood by Franny and he could not let her down.

Despite his tangled thoughts exhaustion claimed him, but it was still full night when he awoke. He had to talk to Mary, had to make her listen to the truth. However strong his bond with Franny, he was a grown man now and his wife and family came first. They needed him. And he needed them.

His sleep having cleared his head, he crossed the starlit farmyard. Guessing the scullery window might be open to let in the cool night air he levered himself up and clambered through it, dropping onto the stone floor beside the sink. Here he removed his boots and crept up the stairs, avoiding the third and sixth ones which always creaked, praying the boys would not wake.

On the narrow landing between the rooms he heard Mary's weeping. He closed his eyes. He had caused this anguish and now he must put it right.

Their bedroom door rattled but she did not hear him, prone as she was with her face buried in the pillows on his side of the bed. It was not until he sat down that she twisted towards him.

"Get away from me," she hissed.

Obediently he dropped to the floor, kneeling as if a child at prayer at the side of the bed. "Please, Mary, hear me out."

"Why should I?"

"Because the baby is not mine."

"Then why did you say it was? You've had hours now to concoct some lie, while I've been weeping over your faithlessness."

"I did not say she was mine; I said she shared my blood. Please, listen to me. Let me tell you the truth, although perhaps it is a truth I should have shared with you long ago."

She sniffed. He sorely wished he could see her face through the darkness, but now she seemed minded to listen he did not want to break the spell by pausing to light a candle.

"I was not born a Burgess. I was adopted as an infant after my mother died in childbirth and some time later I discovered I had a half-sister and the baby is hers."

"But why did you not tell me this? Why see her in secret, pretending you are selling rope when all the time I feared you were smuggling." Despite her copious tears she still had the strength for anger of a sort and it showed in her voice. He dearly wanted to hold her hand, but it was far too soon for that sort of comfort.

"Because I promised my father, my birth father, I would tell no-one. Least of all his legitimate daughter who has known me as a friend all her life."

"A friend?"

"Franny."

There was silence as she took the information in. After a while William said, "This farm, Koll Hendra, we are not Lord de Dunstanville's tenants, it is ours, by way of a gift. Or more likely a bribe to keep my mouth shut."

"How … how did you find out who you were?"

"I guessed. I came to look a little like him and my upbringing having been so unusual I began to wonder. Then one day I went into the house and saw a portrait of Lord de Dunstanville as a young man and I became more certain. So I asked him, and rather than deny it he told me it was the truth, that my mother had been a dalliance when he was but a youth. She was not of his class; he had ruined her but he never would have married her, even had she lived."

"But why did you keep this from me?" There was a hiccup in her voice as she tried to suppress a sob.

"Because I swore faithfully I would tell not a soul. But now it has come to it, you are more precious to me than any promise I made to him."

Her hand crawled from the bedclothes and reached for his. It was damp and hot, and he held it tightly, resisting the urge to cover it with kisses.

"So what of Franny? She has followed her father's licentious ways?"

"Not at all. She was taken against her will, and I think perhaps she does not truly understand what happened, which is a blessing indeed. Of course, Lady de Dunstanville had to send her away and she has been in Torquay these last months with Miss Lemon for company. But now the time has come, she does not want to give Eliza up."

"Of course not. She is a mother," Mary murmured.

"But neither can she take her home. Nor will her parents permit her to stay in Torquay as she wishes. She will be baroness in her own right one day and has her duty to fulfil."

"So she wants us to take her child."

"Yes. Because she knows we will love her as our own. And that she can see her regularly, know she is safe and watch her grow. And of course, although Franny does not know it, Eliza will be with kin."

Mary rolled away from him, onto her back, but her hand was still in his. "There is a great deal to think on before I give you an answer."

"I know. And if I am asking too much of you, then I understand."

He dropped into a sitting position on the floor and rested his head on the counterpane near her chest. He was beyond tired now, but somehow he dared not climb up next to her.

After a while she said, "William?"

"Yes?"

"Have you any more secrets you are keeping from me?"

"No."

"Do you promise?"

"On my life."

"Then come to bed."

CHAPTER THIRTY-TWO

William watched as Lord de Dunstanville rode across the downland towards the cliff where he was waiting, sheep scattering in his path. While not the horsewoman his daughter was, he was still accomplished in the saddle as a gentleman should be, and despite his small stature and fifty-odd years there was a vigour about him, even from this distance.

"Good morning, William," he said as he drew his mount to a stop. "I have to say I am rather baffled by your choice of meeting place."

"And yet you came. For which I thank you."

Father and son looked at each other, but there was little affection in their faces. Perhaps, William thought, the respect he felt for Lord de Dunstanville was mutual, but for more than that he could not hope.

"It is a matter of some delicacy, so I thought it better to talk where we could be sure of not being overheard."

"Delicacy that will affect my pocket?" William could tell he spoke only partly in jest.

"Delicacy relating to your daughter."

Lord de Dunstanville shifted in his saddle. "Oh?"

"Mary and I would like to adopt her baby."

"The devil, man, how do you even know?"

"You should not be concerned, my lord. You understand perfectly well that I can keep a family secret."

"Hmph. But all the same…"

"I know because Franny would not have left without saying goodbye, so I made discreet enquiries as to where she might be. I had business in the direction of Torquay so decided to pay her a visit and of course the reason for her sudden departure became more than clear."

"And you have told no-one?"

"Only my wife, for the decision to adopt the baby had to be hers as well."

"And if my answer is no?"

"Then I would beg you to reconsider."

"On what grounds?" There was a combative ring to Lord de Dunstanville's voice which put William on his guard. He needed to somehow appeal to both sentiment and logic to win him around, and if he could not do so the future would be bleak indeed for Franny. Perhaps that would be the place to start.

"First, for the sake of your daughter's health, my lord. She tells me she will not be able to bear being parted from her baby completely and I believe her. We both know there are certain ways that she is not, perhaps, as strong as other people, and I am worried this would affect her badly."

"So you claim to know my daughter better than I do?"

"Only insofar as I have seen how she acts as a mother and I have to say, her tenderness surprised me."

"I suppose it is natural in a woman." Pursing his lips in thought, Lord de Dunstanville looked past William and out to sea. "In any case, the ties of blood are strong."

Much as he wanted to know if that was the reason his father had kept him close, William did not speak. Such a question would be seen as impertinent at the very least and he could not jeopardise his negotiation — if, indeed, negotiation was what it was — at such a delicate stage.

Eventually Lord de Dunstanville said, "And if I were to agree, what would be the arrangement? I cannot have Lady

Frances traipsing over to Koll Hendra at every opportunity; tongues would be bound to wag."

"Perhaps she should continue to visit no more and no less than has been her norm when out riding. I am fairly sure she will accept any reasonable stricture rather than give her child up to strangers."

Lord de Dunstanville half smiled. "I think we both know that what my daughter sees as reasonable is rarely the same as others see it."

William nodded. "And we also both know that once she gives her word on a matter she keeps it."

There was another long silence, both men gazing over the sparkling ripples of the ocean below, the heat haze blurring the horizon.

"And what would you gain from this?" Lord de Dunstanville asked. "I take it money would need to change hands."

"I had not thought of it. I act as I do to spare Lady Frances undue pain, and you are already sufficiently generous to me, my lord."

"Hmph. Let me think on this. Much as you needed to ask your wife about the baby, it would be unwise of me not to seek Lady de Dunstanville's counsel on this matter. I will send word once I have made my decision."

"Mary and I, we would raise Eliza as our own…"

"So you have said. Good day to you, William." He turned his horse and began to trot away, then stopped. "Thank you. Thank you for your consideration towards my daughter."

Harriet gazed at the Sherborner's thin back as he retreated along the path to the village. Again there was no letter from William and it was cruel of him to string Franny out so. Had he done anything to secure their plans at all? Had he forgotten about it completely? Or was he still trying to work out how to play this matter for his own best advantage?

She had never understood Franny and William's continued friendship; he was but a steward's son who had thrown away his chances in life to waste his time in the stables. But nevertheless he had prospered, no doubt due to the loyalty of his father, now an MP, to Lord de Dunstanville's political views. Not to mention his own nefarious activities as a free trader. No wonder she was finding it hard to trust him with the one plan that could salvage any scrap of comfort at all for Franny. But she had no choice in the matter. Despite her misgivings, he had to succeed.

She gathered her shawl around her shoulders and was about to return inside when she heard hoofbeats in the lane and her heart quickened. Instead of writing had he come himself to tell them? To take Eliza to his wife? She prayed silently for good news, but when she raised her head it was not William before her, but Lord de Dunstanville himself, accompanied by a groom, albeit not one dressed in the Basset livery.

She dropped a swift curtsey to cover her confusion. "My lord."

"Good morning, Harriet. I will come straight inside, if you please. My man will see to the horses."

Harriet stepped aside. "Indeed. We have but a modest establishment, but there is an orchard to tether them and a trough in the yard behind the house for water."

The hall was dark after the bright sunlight, but Franny, her face as white as any ghost, was already at the bottom of the stairs, clutching the newel post.

"Papa? Oh, Papa, have you agreed?"

"You forget yourself, Frances," he said stiffly. "Where might we talk?"

Harriet ushered him into the parlour, with Franny trailing behind, then she rang for Mrs Whitney, instructing her to prepare some refreshments for their guest.

"You have ridden far this morning?" she asked.

"Not a great distance. I am on my way to London, but currently enjoying the Champernownes' hospitality at Dartington."

"You will be away from Cornwall for long?" Harriet asked politely, settling her hands quietly in her lap, while Franny hunched on the window seat, knotting her fingers together one at a time, then unclasping them in the same careful manner.

"It is hard to be sure, but I would wager two or three months at least. Lady de Dunstanville sails from Truro next Wednesday to join me, and requests that you board her boat at Plymouth the following day."

Before either Franny or Harriet could speak, Mrs Whitney returned with Phoebe, carrying trays with jugs of barley water and ale, and some plates of fruit, cheese and bread.

As soon as they had left, Franny burst out, "But what of Eliza?"

Lord de Dunstanville gave his daughter a piercing stare. "Whether she remains in Plymouth or travels to Koll Hendra rather depends on whether you agree to my stipulations."

"I will agree to anything to keep her close," Franny said.

"You must, however, listen carefully and note what I am going to say. Firstly, you will remain in London for at least two months so there is no suspicion of you and the child arriving in Portreath at the same time. Secondly, once we return to Tehidy you will carry on your life as before. You will not pay frequent calls on the Burgesses and you will pay no special attention to the child when you do."

"But am I not to hold her, kiss her darling face?"

Her father sighed. "Franny, you must understand that from the moment you hand that baby into William and Mary's care she is no longer your child; she is theirs. They will be the ones to protect her and guide her as she grows, indeed it is my wish that she will never know they are not her true parents, although of course a suitable story has been prepared to quell any gossip that may arise." He looked into Franny's anguished face and his expression softened. "My dear, this will not be easy, but it is the price you have to pay. If you cannot do it, then it is better to give up your child completely."

"That I will not do," Franny whispered.

Harriet wanted more than anything to take her hand, to comfort her, but dared not in front of Lord de Dunstanville. So much had changed since they had been here, in their habits and in her own affections, she was afraid she might give herself away.

"Then you agree?"

"I have no option."

"Very good. I will send word to William to accompany you as far as Plymouth when you leave here. Now I must be on my way as my hosts prefer to dine early."

All three stood and Franny rested a hand on his sleeve. "You do not wish to see your granddaughter?"

"I have no granddaughter," he replied with great dignity, but Harriet detected a slight catch in his voice. "No granddaughter, no son, only you, my dearest. And I rue the day I invited that man into my home only for his despicable actions to cause you such pain."

He turned on his heel and they listened in silence as his riding boots retreated down the hall and the front door open and close softly behind him.

CHAPTER THIRTY-THREE

The wheels of the coach stopped creaking as it drew to a halt, the only sound a whinny from one of the horses. Harriet looked from the window; Plymouth was spread out below them, an untidy straggle of houses around the Hoe and numerous craft of all shapes and size at anchor in the harbour, but today it was not in her soul to be curious about them. Today her darling Franny's heart would surely break, and her own along with it.

The carriage door opened and William climbed in, seating himself opposite Franny. "It is time we went our separate ways."

Franny was pale as death, clutching Eliza tightly. "No."

From her corner of the carriage Ann let out a sob, covering her mouth as Harriet glared at her. Her emotional outburst was not helping.

Harriet leant across and patted Franny's arm. "I'm afraid you must, my dear. It is the only way."

Her face was twisted with anguish. "I know, I know. But I am not sure I can. Father was so cruel, saying I could never hold her again."

"Cruel for you, but not for Eliza," William said. "Mary must be her mother now, for it would confuse her to have two. She must grow up never even suspecting we are not her true parents. A child needs to know where they belong."

He said those last words with a passion that surprised Harriet. William was normally such a measured man. Perhaps the emotion in the carriage was affecting him as well?

"A child needs her mother's love," whispered Franny.

"Mary is her mother now." His words were spoken gently but there was a look of steel in his eyes.

"It cannot be…"

"It must be. Franny, I know the heartbreak this will cause you, but your father is right. There is no other way for you to be able to watch her grow in safety and in love."

Silence filled the coach, heavy and dark, at odds with the pale morning sunlight outside.

Finally Franny said, "Please do not think I am ungrateful. I will be indebted to you and Mary to the end of my days. But my heart will never mend. It will be an empty and barren place."

It was Harriet's turn to stifle a sob, mainly for Franny's pain but in part for herself. Did this mean there was no place for her, either? But no, that was a selfish thought. Franny needed her more than ever now, and whatever it took, however long it took, she would remain at her side giving her the love she so badly needed. She had already wasted far too much time.

William reached to take Eliza from Franny's arms. "Come along now, Franny."

Harriet held her breath, but Franny simply nodded and passed the sleeping bundle to him without so much as a glance, let alone a kiss.

As William took her he said, "I promise you I will love her as if my own blood flowed through her veins."

But there was no answer from Franny. She stared directly ahead, not even looking as he descended the carriage and disappeared from view. Harriet heard him instruct the driver to make haste to the port, and the creak of the carriage wheels filled the silence as they started to move.

PART SEVEN: 2020

CHAPTER THIRTY-FOUR

The farmhouse is in darkness when I get back from Mani's place, still shaken by the flashing white lights I saw. I cross the garden to open the kitchen door to let Sam out, then sit at the picnic table, head in my hands. The man I am coming to love has just tried to tell me he has feelings for me, and I ran away because I was spooked by something that probably wasn't even real. How can I ever put this right?

I try to recall his words, but everything blurs in my memory. There was something else he was trying to tell me, most likely about Eloise, but now I'll never know, will I? He'll never want to clap eyes on me again after tonight, that's for sure.

I rest my forehead on my arms and sob. After a few moments I feel Sam's wet nose nudging my hand and I sit up to stroke his silky-soft head. He rests his chin on my thigh and looks up at me. He probably only wants a biscuit, but right at this moment I'd rather think he's giving me what comfort he can.

Leastways it's enough to stir me into action, so I take him inside, give him a treat from the box on the dresser and watch as he settles down in his basket. Then I trudge across the yard into the Granary and lock the door behind me, before heading for the kitchen and opening a bottle of wine. It's absolutely the wrong thing to do and I know I'm running a huge risk of drunk-messaging Mani, but I need something to calm me or I will never sleep.

The need to make contact with him is overwhelming. I imagine him in that horrible house, all on his own, thinking he's screwed everything up between us. With a shaking hand I pick up my phone and type: *I am so, so sorry. It's not how I wanted it to be.*

I'm about to send it when I read it again. That's not right. He might think I'm referring to what he said, rather than how the evening panned out. I could say I was feeling ill, but that would be a lie. Or I could tell him the truth. That a strange light bouncing around on the bottom of the stairs, that he couldn't see, freaked me out so badly I had to run away. I don't think so.

But whatever I say, it's going to sound bad. Either he'll think that I don't reciprocate his feelings, or that I'm a heartless bitch, or that I'm a complete fruitcake. But what do I want from this message, except to make both of us feel a little better? What do I want to happen next?

And suddenly I know, beyond the wine and beyond any doubt. Beyond any fear of his going away. *I'm so sorry, Mani. Can we start again?*

I can't say I slept and I'm not even sure I dozed, but when I hear Dad and Noel chatting in the yard I know it's time to get up. I scrabble on the floor for my phone. Nothing from Mani. When I swing my legs over the side of the bed every part of me seems to ache, so instead of a shower I decide to wallow in my misery in the bath.

I throw on some sweatpants and a T-shirt before I allow myself to check my mobile again. It's going to be that sort of day if I let it. Maybe that sort of week. I feel like sobbing into my tea, and my toast gets stuck in my throat. There's no way I can work on my glass this morning. I don't have an ounce of creativity left.

I can empty the kiln though, a job that always lifts me. I've had to make more of my mackerel design, the green and blue shot through with silver-grey that I worked on during those first days of lockdown. The coasters shimmer in the light as I hold them up to check them, glorious as the sea itself. I can understand why people buy them, it's as though I've managed to lock a tiny slice of Cornwall into the glass.

I scribble the thought in my notebook. Maybe I need something like that, a sort of slogan or tagline? Maybe that's what I should do today to distract myself; work on marketing, and perhaps set up the social media accounts for the business that I've been promising myself. Recently Mani's been helping me with the technical stuff and I feel myself slump again. What I don't need right now is to be alone.

I pack the tiles into boxes and carry them through to the living room, averting my eyes from Gran's photo. It's her fault I see things I shouldn't. I didn't ask for this. But perhaps the problem is, I didn't ask her enough about it when I could.

Right. Today. First and foremost I need to tell Dad about the Burgess-Basset connection. He'll be tickled pink and making him happy should make me feel better too. I spotted him just a few minutes ago walking the cauliflower field beyond my kitchen window, so I pull on my wellies and head off to join him.

A gentle sunshine warms my back and the plants around me exude the bitter tang of brassica stems. They look almost ready to me, their heads creamy and full, so Dad's probably trying to work out when he'll need to coax the old harvesting machine into life. One of these days it will point-blank refuse, then it will be more money to fix it, or perhaps admit defeat and hire a contractor.

As soon as he sees me, Dad calls across the field. "Hi Carla, how did you get on yesterday?"

"Found some very interesting stuff indeed. Mind-blowing, actually, and it goes a long way towards explaining the rattle."

He waits until I catch him up. "Well?"

"How about William Burgess the smuggler was Francis Basset, Lord de Dunstanville's, illegitimate son?"

"I suppose it might have been rumoured…"

"I cross-checked the sources. There's a whole story behind it, and it seems to stack up." So I tell him about young Francis' affair with the farmer's daughter and its sad outcome, and how the child was adopted by the Basset's steward, Thomas Burgess.

"Well I'll be… That's incredible."

"It explains the rattle too. I'm pretty sure it's the same unicorn from the Basset crest on the whistle, so it could well have been a present from Lord de Dunstanville to his illegitimate son or grandchildren. It must have been quite galling to have four male heirs who could never inherit the title."

"It explains the farm too. It never made sense how this smuggler guy came from nowhere and suddenly he owned it. Even if he had the money to buy, the Bassets would have had no need to sell. Just wait until I tell your mum she married into the gentry." His grin is as wide as I've ever seen it. "I'll have some fun with this."

"How did Mani get on?" Dad asks. "Or should I wait until he comes over later to ask him?"

I shake my head, the cauliflower nearest my left foot becoming the most interesting thing in the world. "He won't be coming." I can barely choke out the words. "We had a … we had a…" But what did we have? I look up at Dad and my tears spill over.

"Carla, love, what happened?" He wraps me into one of his amazing hugs and I cry all the more into the soft brushed cotton of his work shirt as he pats my back. Sam appears from the hedgerow where he's been sniffing around and leans against our legs.

I have to talk to someone, especially about the strange lights I saw, and Dad fits the bill. He's the link between Gran and me, so maybe he's even seen something like it himself.

I sniff and look up at him. "Remember Gran saw people's auras?"

He sighs. "I think I can guess where this is heading. She told me you saw one once when you were a child, when that friend of yours was being bullied. Am I right in thinking it wasn't a one-off?"

"Nowhere near. And Gran knew that. I mean, it doesn't happen often and when it does I shut myself off from it, walk away. I don't want to know about that stuff, Dad, I don't want it. But now I wish … I wish I'd asked her more."

"So what happened with Mani?"

"I've always been able to see his aura, right from when I first bumped into him on the cliffs. He was so sunny and smiley, but his aura was dark. Which kind of made sense when I found out he was here all on his own in lockdown. And it has been better recently … well … lighter and paler … sometimes I don't even notice it…" I'm stumbling over my words and he hugs me tighter to him again.

"Last night Mani asked me over to his place for supper, and the moment I walked in, the house felt oppressive, heavy. Evil almost. I'd never felt anything like that before and it freaked me out. We sat in the conservatory, though, and that was fine, but Mani's aura was really dark, so after we'd eaten I asked him what was wrong.

"He said he'd explain over coffee, but when we went back into the living room the feeling was worse than before ... and then these strange white lights appeared... I'm so scared. What the hell are they? And why am I seeing them?" I'm close to sobbing again, but he tilts my face up to look at him.

"Listen to me, Carla. Your gran did talk about seeing lights, especially after my father died, and she found them a comfort. She said they were souls seeking her out and she was blessed to be able to see them."

I pull away. "I don't feel blessed. I feel cursed. And last night, because of them I ran out on Mani when he was trying to tell me something really important. He must hate me right now."

"Have you explained to him what happened?"

"Of course not. He'd think I'm a right fruitcake. But I don't know what's worse, that or him thinking I'm a heartless cow. I did message him to apologise, but I haven't heard anything back."

Dad looks thoughtful. "You're fond of him, aren't you?" I nod. "Well, you probably don't want to hear this right at the moment, but maybe this is a blessing in disguise. He's a lovely young man, Carla, but sooner or later he'll go back to the States and I don't want you heartbroken when he does."

"I know. You're right, of course." I try to smile. "Voice of reason as ever, Dad."

"Voice of reason, shoulder to cry on, and lord of the manor to boot." He laughs and I join in, but my heart isn't in it and he knows, so he tucks me under his arm and we talk about the cauliflowers, and the goats, and what we're going to do next with the hayloft, as he continues his inspection of the crop.

CHAPTER THIRTY-FIVE

"Hey, Carla, I've made the connection."

Mani's number on my screen is the last thing I expect to see as I settle down with Mum to watch a rerun of *The Durrells*, followed by a double helping of vintage *Downton*, so I leave her to it and go to sit on the bottom of the stairs.

"Sorry. I'm at the farmhouse and Mum's watching TV. What have you found?"

"That Thomas Burgess is Thomas Dolcoath."

"That's incredible! How did you link it all up?"

"It's taken me most of the day, on and off. But in a nutshell, I traced him from the ship at Wilmington as Thomas P. Burgess and his immigration record said he was heading for Claiborne County in Tennessee. So I dug a bit into its history and at the time there were three big mines around Powell River and that rang a bell. It was where my first American ancestor was born."

"Oh wow ... you must have been excited."

"I tried not to be. Loads of Cornish miners must have emigrated there, so I went back to Richard's birth certificate and although I hadn't realised it before, his father's name was written as Thomas P. Dolcoath. What's more, his date of birth was the same as Thomas Burgess's, so I reckon it's pretty conclusive."

"That's some sleuthing, cousin." I'm trying to sound upbeat, and I really am pleased for him, but all the same I'm wondering what he'll say next. Or what I should say.

"So what have you been doing with yourself today?" he asks.

Moping around, missing you? "Chores, mainly. Unpacked the kiln, did a bit of marking, walked the fields with Dad. He's absolutely made up about the Basset-Burgess connection, he hasn't stopped ribbing Mum about marrying into the gentry." A thought occurs to me. "And now I can tease you too."

"Like cousins do," Mani murmurs. "Well, cousins it is then. I'll let you get back to your programme, Carla. Have a good week."

"And you."

But I sit on the stairs for quite a while, phone in hand. He's made the first overture, we're going to be friends of sorts, but once again it's lumpy and awkward between us. I push the thought that I still want more to the back of my mind. Dad's right, after all. Mani will go back to the States. Maybe even to Eloise. While I need to get on with my life here.

As the country begins to ease out of lockdown and the trickle of visitors to Cornwall becomes a flood, I try as hard as I can to put Mani out of my mind. I go up to The Tinners when I know that Kitto will be at sea. Tia persuades me to join her for an early morning swim at Porthnevek, and even though it's getting on towards the end of July, bracing isn't the word. I venture into school to look at my GCSE group's projects, now covered in a light sheen of dust, so I can give them a final mark. And when I shed a tear or two in the workroom, I have to accept it will take a while to get back on an even keel. Longer for my students who've had their lives disrupted by Covid, though.

It's when I spot a seal basking under the cliffs in Basset's Cove that I have an idea. I check the tides and ask Mani if he'd like to meet for a picnic on Friday night. He hasn't been in touch since his call, but I figure it's down to me to make the next move. Maybe I should stay away, but somehow I can't. If he says no then I'll know where I stand.

We arrange to meet at seven. I'll bring the food, and he'll bring the drinks. I pull myself out of my torpor to make an asparagus and salmon quiche. Buoyed by the fact it doesn't fall apart and looks quite edible, I set to work on some potato salad, then cook some green beans and toss them in lemon and olive oil. It feels good to be cooking for someone else, but as I pack the picnic box the thought of being alone for the rest of my life overwhelms me and I find myself dashing away tears.

This self-pity will not do and I wonder if I'm brave enough to rekindle the conversation Mani tried to have with me before the strange lights intervened. I hear Dad's voice in my ear, telling me he'll be going home to the States, but then it strikes me; is that the way in? The reason I ran? Then I can admit I feel the same but I can't face the hurt? And to be honest, that's very close to the truth. I know if I went just half a step further I'd love him too much and I don't think I'm that brave. I need to channel some Frances Basset and be happy on my own.

As I set out down the drive, past Tehidy's East Lodge and along the side of the golf course, I try to find the right words. It's only when I see Mani waiting for me at the corner of the woods that I realise the only thing I can do is play it by ear. His aura is as dark as it's ever been, but still he's smiling. We're in the same place, for sure. But can we reach each other?

We walk through the dappled sunlight beneath the slender trunks of the stunted trees that occupy the seaward side of the woods, and Mani tells me he's started to look up Georgian silver rattles on the internet. Apparently some are quite valuable, and the Exeter hallmark will make ours more so.

We decide on a spot above the cove where we're most likely to see a seal. Sitting on the rabbit-cropped grass a few feet apart, Mani pulls a bottle of wine from his rucksack and makes over-generous comments about the quiche as we try not to look at each other. He spills my drink as he pours it, and swears. My hand trembles as I hand him the salad and I know I have to say something. Even if the upshot is that one or both of us gets up and walks away, it has to be better than this.

"Mani, can we talk about what happened at your place?"

His head jerks up from his plate. There are dark circles beneath his eyes, as well as the green-black dullness around his head. "You think?"

"We may not want to, but we need to. However much we try to pretend it isn't, it's making things awkward between us and I don't want that."

"It's my fault. I should never have said…"

"No," I interrupt. "I'm glad you did. It made me realise … well, kind of face up to … how I feel about you."

"Which is?" He's so tense he makes it sound like an accusation and I almost lose my nerve.

"The same as you, I guess. More than cousins, more than friends, but … but I can't take it any further, Mani. Not when I know you'll be going home next March."

"And that's why you ran out on me?" He looks away for a moment, then turns back. "I don't know whether to be angry or relieved. You've put me through hell this last week, do you know that? Why couldn't you have said then what you're saying now?"

Because of the weird lights dancing a jig at the bottom of your stairs? Because your house was pressing in on me like thunder? I swallow hard.

"I'm really sorry. It was a stupid thing to do."

"You knew you'd hurt me and you didn't even attempt to explain until now. All I did was try to tell you how I feel. I didn't deserve that."

"Mani — whatever I may have done, you had no right to say anything at all. At least I'm single and can make my own choices; you're engaged to someone else."

He recoils as if I've shot him. "How do you know about that?"

"So you did try to hide it from me."

"No … no … but I don't understand…"

"Social media. It was on a profile of yours."

"But I haven't logged into my accounts for years."

"There's an engagement photo of you and your fiancée."

"She isn't my fiancée anymore."

"Oh." What else can I say? I'm not going to apologise again, especially as I might get my head bitten off. I pick a corner of pastry from the quiche and crumble it between my fingers.

After a while Mani says, "Do you want to hear about it?"

"OK." I wish I could sound more gracious.

"Part of the reason … no, let me be honest here … most of the reason I came to Cornwall was to get away from the whole sorry mess. Eloise and I were an item in high school, our moms are friends, we grew up in the same community. We drifted apart when we went off to college but then, about three years ago, we got back together and fell properly in love. Or so I thought. Our families were delighted, we got an apartment, started to plan the wedding. Future mapped out." He takes a gulp of wine.

"Then, just after Thanksgiving, I found she was cheating on me, so I shipped out. I was just about holding my shit together when she started to call, saying she'd made a mistake. But how could I trust her? Then Mom piled in, telling me to take her back. That I just couldn't handle. I needed an escape route, so here I am."

"Oh, Mani, I'm so sorry you went through all that. It must have been awful, especially having your mum take her side."

He shrugs. "Question is, Carla, what are *we* going to do?"

"In what way?"

"Well, it's out in the open we have feelings for each other, but you have a very valid reason not to commit and I respect that. Really I do. The last thing I would ever want is to hurt you."

"And I you," I whisper.

I don't know what else to say. I gaze down into the cove, and to my amazement not one, but two seals have appeared on the rocks below, fresh washed by the receding tide.

"Mani! Look!" I point, then glance up at him. He's grinning.

"Perhaps the fact they're a pair is a good omen and I'm not saying that to pressure you. I think … I think that now we've been honest with each other we'll be able to continue as friends, for the moment at least. Are you up for that?"

"Yes. It's been pretty rubbish without you."

"Likewise."

When Mani arrives for Sunday lunch he's full of smiling politeness, although his aura tells me a different story. I guess the fact he's a master of deception when it comes to his feelings bothers me too, but aren't I doing the same? We're both pretending to my parents that nothing has changed, except we tease each other over-loudly about being cousins.

He's completed William Burgess's family tree, linking it to his own, and down our side as far as me. He's printed it off on sheets of A4 paper taped together, and unfolds it on the kitchen table for us all to study.

It's a marvellously detailed piece of work, with dates of birth, marriages and deaths. He takes us through Dad's line first, six generations of Burgesses farming Koll Hendra before him, and we have a little giggle about how soon after his grandparents' wedding his father was born.

"No wonder there was always an icy atmosphere between them," Dad chuckles. "They probably weren't suited at all!"

Up until Dad's generation it was always the eldest son who took on the farm, and he explains to Mani that his brother Howard never wanted to be a farmer.

"He's seriously clever, my brother, like Carla is. Would have been wasted here. He was the first of the family to go to university, but it's going to right itself when Noel takes over. Thinking about it, we'd better add him and his brood too as he'll be running this place when I hang up my wellies for good."

As Dad and Mani complete the bottom corner of the chart, my eyes stray to the top. There's something not right, but it takes me a while to fathom it. But once I have seen it, it becomes screamingly obvious. Eliza Burgess was born on the 9th of July 1810, and her brother Henry just four and a half months earlier. If that's right, there is no way they can be brother and sister.

"Mani, these dates of birth ... how certain of them are you?"

"As certain as I can be. They come from the baptismal records from Illogan church."

"Well, either there's a mistake, or Henry and Eliza can't have the same mother — he's not five months older than her."

"Hold on, I've saved it in my app." He taps on his phone, hair flopping into his eyes in that adorable way it does, and a surge of emotion rushes through me. Under the table I dig my nails into my palms. I promised myself a forever man who can commit, and Mani isn't him.

He angles his phone towards me, leaning so close I can feel his breath on my cheek. "The text is pretty small, but it's legible. Look, there's Henry Burgess — 26th of February. Now, scroll down. Not far. Eliza Burgess, 9th of July. Now you've pointed it out I don't know how I didn't notice it before."

"So who was the other mother?"

"One of them is most likely William's illegitimate child," Dad says and grins at Mani. "If it's Henry, you could be on the wrong side of two blankets."

"His poor wife," Mum says. "I'm glad I wasn't around then, because I'm not sure I'd have stood for it."

I trace my finger over the chart to find her name. "Mary probably didn't have any choice. Where could she have gone? She'd have had no money, no rights... God, I can see now why Frances Basset decided to stay single."

"It's different nowadays though, isn't it?" Mani says. "Marriage is an equal partnership. Or should be." He's looking straight at me, and there's almost a question in his eyes. I hold his gaze for a moment, then have to look away.

"Like Mum and Dad," I say.

Dad laughs. "Perfectly equal, just as long as I remember Elaine's the boss."

CHAPTER THIRTY-SIX

It takes just two weeks of school in September for me to consider handing in my notice there and then. Masks, bubbles, the constant Covid testing. I gag every time I stick that damn swab thing up my nostrils. I hate not being able to see my students' expressions behind their masks. I hate the fact that I can only have half a class in the workshop at any one time. And, to make matters worse, the rule of six has just been reimposed, which means any social gatherings of more than six people will be against the law. It looks like we're in for a bumpy winter.

In The Tinners on Thursday night it's my turn to be grumpy, while Kitto is all charm and smiles as he arrives with a beautiful tourist on his arm. I try to put on a happy face, especially when she seems so nice, but as I'm nearing the end of my second glass of wine I text Dad to ask him to collect me early. I just want to go to bed and get this horrible week over with.

The situation with Mani isn't helping either. He still comes to the farm every Sunday, and sometimes we see each other in the evenings to head out for a walk, or sit outside a pub somewhere and chat. We're friendly, but holding ourselves apart from each other and I know that's down to me. The looks he gives me sometimes when he thinks I won't see — and sometimes when he knows I will — would melt an ice maiden's heart at twenty paces. And I'm not an ice maiden, am I? I'm just trying to prevent myself from getting hurt. Except it isn't working.

To my surprise, when Dad picks me up outside The Tinners, instead of heading home he turns down the valley into Porthnevek.

"Thought we could have a walk on the beach," he tells me.

I mumble my agreement. Not that I was being asked in the first place.

Music pumps softly from Stars, the bar just above the beach, and a gentle breeze licks our faces as we head out between the cliffs. A spaniel runs circles around its owner, punctuating the air with excited barks, and right on the shoreline a couple walk barefoot through the surf hand in hand.

As we head past the rocks that guard the bay and out onto the sand Dad says, "So are you going to tell me what's wrong?"

"Rubbish week, that's all. I've already said how difficult it is at school with all the Covid restrictions."

"Sounds as though it's time for you to hand in your notice, love."

"I can't do it just like that. It's too much of a risk. You know my plan is to go part-time if I can in the spring. I can't be without any money coming in at all, so I'll just have to stick it out."

"What about if I told you we've finally received our grant, so we can repay you?"

"You have? Really?" It would make all the difference, but I can barely believe it.

"I wouldn't say it if it wasn't true. It just popped into our bank account today; no paperwork, no nothing. But it's there."

"Oh, Dad."

Beyond the waves the clouds are streaked with orange as the sun sinks behind them. There's nothing to stop me doing this now, nothing at all. Except perhaps the terror of standing on the precipice; my reasons and excuses stripped bare. The fear in my heart that I cannot do it.

"Dad, I'm scared."

He folds me into his arms and I rest my cheek on his shoulder.

"Do you want to tell me why?" he asks.

"Because it's down to me, isn't it? I'm going to have to step outside everything I've ever known. What if ... what if it doesn't work? What if I run out of ideas? What if I make loads of stuff and no-one buys it?"

"Then you'll have tried, and you will know. If you don't try, Carla, your life will be full of if-onlys and what-ifs, and I don't want you to live like that."

I look up at him. "I'm not sure I'm that strong."

"Carla, you are. I know you can do it. You are your gran through and through and you make me so proud, but at times you're a little like me — a bit too cautious, a bit too sensible — a bit too much of a Burgess farmer, generations just plodding along. It's time for that to change, for you to take that leap of faith. And if it doesn't work out, well, Mum and I are here to help you pick up the pieces."

I squeeze my arms around him as tightly as I can. "Thank you for believing in me. I'll think about it, really I will."

"Not too hard or too long, Carla. Just do it. Channel a bit of our smuggling ancestor and take a risk for once, see where it gets you."

I wake at five in the morning, clear headed and completely sober. Which is surprising, given I had a few more glasses of wine with Mum and Dad before bed.

I am going to take that risk. I'm going to give in my notice. In fact, I'm going to write the letter now and hand it to the head the moment I arrive at work. Get it done. I know in my heart it's right. And there's something else my heart knows too; that one big risk might as well lead to another. And if, in a year's time, I am sitting here penniless and with my heart in tatters, at least I will have tried. I might have regrets, but as Dad said last night, at least I'll know.

Mani unwittingly plays right into my hands because at lunchtime there's a message from him on my phone, full of excitement as he's found a virtual antiques' fair at the weekend, with experts giving valuations for charity. Perhaps we could log on and show them the tea caddy and rattle? When I text back he tells me he'll cook me lunch on Saturday, then we can take our place in the online queue.

Can I go back to his house? At some point I'll have to if I want things to progress between us. 'In for a penny, in for a pound,' Gran would have said, so instead of an excuse I type *Yes please.*

Actually clapping eyes on the place, it doesn't feel so easy. I sit in the car for quite a few minutes, gazing across the sunny courtyard at the benches and colourful pots outside some of the houses, trying to convince myself that Mani's place, with its overflowing lobelia on the mounting block, is not in shadow. And of course it isn't, not any more than the others facing north anyway, so I pick up the tea caddy from the passenger seat and stroll across the gravel as though I haven't a care in the world.

The sun streams through the conservatory doors and there's only the slightest residue of the oppressive atmosphere I felt before. Maybe it was just … but I don't know what it was. Right now it is barely apparent, which leaves me to concentrate on what I will need to say to Mani at some point today. Which is just as terrifying.

I put the tea caddy down on the shelving unit in the conservatory and follow him into the kitchen. It's a small, bright room at the back of the house with white units and tiles. A casserole is bubbling on the stove.

"Wow," I tell him, "that smells amazing."

"It's gumbo. I thought I'd cook you something traditional from the American South."

"So what's in it?"

"Bell peppers, celery, onion, chicken, shrimp … a few spices too. I just hope this is as good as my mom's, because I couldn't quite get all the right ingredients."

"You must miss your mom's cooking."

He shrugs. "Of course I do. By the way, I need to tell you. I've booked my flight home." He pauses. "I mean, just for a visit. I'll be coming back."

"You had me worried for a minute there."

"Did I really?"

"Yes, you did, if you must know. And I think … I think you said it that way deliberately."

"You see right through me."

I take a deep breath. Now is the time to take the plunge. "I had a long chat with Dad this week, about taking risks. Big ones. I handed in my notice at work yesterday."

"Carla — that's amazing. When do you finish?"

I reach out and put my finger on his lips, ever so gently. That questioning look is back in his eyes, questioning and just a little bit wary.

"It's the other risk I want to talk to you about, Mani, the one I'm prepared to take with you. But that depends on whether you're in."

His breath is warm against my finger. "You know I am." He reaches behind him to turn off the gas under the pan then slides his arms around my waist. "Are you really sure about this? I can't have you breaking my heart, Carla Burgess."

"And I can't have you breaking mine."

My chest feels tight, and as he pulls me closer I can feel the heat of his body through his shirt. Then lips are on lips and I taste him for the first time; gumbo spice, and salt, and something I know is uniquely his.

The kiss draws me into him, the muscles of his back taut beneath my touch. It's heady stuff, but it doesn't matter; we've both been waiting far too long. I'm barely aware that he's teased my top from the band of my jeans but his fingers exploring my spine are electric, although somehow I manage to pull away a little to loosen his belt.

"Carla … are you sure?"

"Why do you keep asking me that?"

"Because if this isn't as important to you as it is to me…"

"It is. I promise you."

"Then let's do this properly."

He grabs my hand and starts to lead me into the living room. I stop. Past his shoulder the light has reappeared, far more intense than it's ever been, spinning and swooping, its focus the tea caddy that has somehow ended up on the floor.

"Carla, what's wrong?"

My teeth start to chatter and I can barely speak. Mani's grip on my hand tightens, and his voice seems to come from a long way off when he repeats his question.

"You'll think I'm crazy. There's a weird light … a presence … something in this house…"

"A what?"

"I don't know. I don't know." I bury my face in his sweatshirt to find his heart is thudding almost as hard as mine. This needs to stop. But how? How?

I take the deepest of breaths and turn back to the room. Below the light a yellowing sheet of paper flutters on the floor. Is that it? Is that the reason? With trembling fingers I pick it up, and the light vanishes. Completely vanishes, as if it had never been.

My knees crumple and I'm on the floor, next to the tea caddy. It's on its back and I turn it over. The wooden floor of the central portion where the bowl should have been has popped out, revealing a cavity beneath. "The light led me to it. It must have knocked it off the shelf," I whisper.

Still Mani is silent. Have I lost him? Does he think I'm absolutely crazy?

Slowly he sits down next to me, cross-legged on the floor and takes my hand. "Has whatever it was gone?" he asks.

"Yes. As soon as I picked up the paper."

He nods. "So what does it say?"

I unfold the note and hold it where we can both see it. The writing is small and faded, but angling it to the light I can just make out the words.

Dear William and Mary,

I write in humble and grateful thanks to you both for giving my daughter a home, and the enclosed is a Christening gift. As you know my father is keeping me in Kensington until after the service but Eliza will be in my heart and mind then, as she is every day.

Franny

"So Eliza was the adopted child," Mani says.

"And not William's bastard either, given she is thanking them both. That must have made Mary's life easier. But I wonder whose..."

We stare at the letter for a long while, then Mani removes it from my hand and puts it back in the tea caddy, along with the rattle and reticule.

"That is for another day. As is the valuation. The virtual antiques' fair lasts all weekend — we can log in tomorrow. But, for now, I need to know what happened back there. You're still white as a sheet."

I look at him. "I've been hiding it from you, Mani. That's why I ran out on you before. The real reason. I've been feeling something in and around this house, and seeing strange lights. Today was the strongest but now..." I struggle to find the right words. "It's gone, and somehow I know that it won't come back."

"So no more freaky stuff?"

"I can't guarantee that. Dad said Gran used to see these lights too. And auras. I see auras as well... I saw yours ... the day we met." I can't look at him, but then I feel his arms around me as he sighs.

"I'd be lying if I didn't say it's weirded me out, but it must be so much worse for you, to live with this sort of stuff all the time."

"Luckily I don't. I can count on the fingers of one hand the times I've seen auras and, well ... I've learnt to largely ignore them."

"But what do they mean?"

"I don't know and I don't want to. Gran understood them, but I've never courted that knowledge. I ... I mean, I'm glad I've told you, before ... we go any further ... so you can decide... The lights were different. It felt more like a presence. But now we've found the note, I think whatever it was has been put to rest. The question is, Mani, has what I've told you put an end to us as well?"

Mani is quiet for a moment, but then he wraps his arms around me and I melt into his comfort and warmth. "Like I said, you're the one who has to live with it. I just want to support you. To be with you. But I am wondering if you have any more secrets you're keeping from me?"

"No."

"Do you promise?"

I look up to see that he's smiling, so I kiss him gently on the lips. He responds in kind and relief floods through me. "Is that your answer?" he murmurs, as his hand slips towards my waistband.

"Smugglers' honour."

"Which given our heritage, will have to do."

And together we roll onto the soft carpet, laughing. Laughing and so, so much more.

We don't get around to eating the gumbo until about seven o'clock, Mani dressed in a sweatshirt and shorts, pretending to grumble about how stodgy it's become, and me wrapped in his dressing gown and a warm fug of loved-up drowsiness.

The mysterious note lies on the arm of the sofa, and once we've finished eating I pick it up and reread it.

"Kensington isn't much of a clue to track Franny down," Mani says.

"No, but it's safe to suppose her father was a man of some substance if he had two houses. If she'd just been a village girl she'd have been hidden away during her confinement, or even cast out entirely, but that clearly wasn't the case here. And anyway, she probably wouldn't have been literate."

"And if the Christening gift she mentions is the rattle we found, she would have been very wealthy indeed."

"You don't think…" The thought is a heady one, but entirely possible. "You don't think she was Frances Basset, the future Baroness Stratton herself? I mean, that rattle carries the Basset unicorn, and Franny could be a diminutive term for Frances. You never know, despite the social differences, she might have been on good terms with William Burgess because they were both brought up at Tehidy. I wonder … the Bassets most likely had a London house. Is it possible to find out where it was?"

Mani jumps up and heads for the conservatory to fetch his laptop. I don't mind being alone in this room now; the oppressive air has vanished completely and there's a sense of something new awakening, although that could just be how I feel projecting out to fill the space. It wouldn't be a bad thing if it is.

As I gaze around, something catches my eye, something that looks like a small roll of paper, half hidden under the unit where Mani's television sits. It looks yellow with age, and that's what makes me jump off the sofa and pull it out.

"Is this yours?" I ask him.

"Never seen it before in my life."

"Then it must have come out of the caddy too."

It's sealed with an old-fashioned blob of wax. I run my fingernail under it carefully, telling Mani I don't want to break it.

"Look at it carefully, Carla. Isn't that the Basset crest with the unicorn?"

"Franny. Lady Frances." I breathe.

"It's more evidence, certainly."

I continue to work at the seal, while Mani types away at his computer. I have just reached a particularly delicate stage when he yells, "Got it!" making me spill the paper roll onto the floor.

He apologises, with a touch of his fingers to my cheek that fizzes through me. "Here we go… I had to search 'de Dunstanville London' in the end. A property listed as Stratheden House in Knightsbridge. Is that even close to Kensington? I don't know London at all."

"They're next to each other, but…" I bend to pick up the paper. The seal is almost off and with a final gentle lever it comes free, dropping into my lap.

"No … no, it's here, further down," Mani continues, pointing at his screen. "Kensington *Road*. I guess that would be an easy mistake to make, particularly if Franny was feeling emotional."

"Poor Lady Frances. I wonder what happened?"

"Well I would have thought that was obvious."

I give him a nudge. "No shit, Sherlock. It just seems at odds with the fact she never married."

"Perhaps news of what had happened did get out?"

"Maybe, but she would have been about thirty when Eliza was born. In those times, a proper old maid. It still seems surprising she didn't marry earlier."

"Well, I guess we'll never know."

"When she was baroness she founded several schools locally. She must have liked children. Poor woman."

"Yes, it must have been tough watching your child grow up so close to hand."

"But better than giving her away to strangers."

"Maybe."

I turn my attention back to the paper and begin to unroll it. It's stiff with age, but the quality is good; a fine parchment almost, and inside is a pencil sketch of a little girl, perhaps three years old, sitting on a rock on the beach, the cliff line behind very familiar.

"That's Portreath. From the Carvannel Cove end." But it isn't all. The child looks familiar too, the style of sketching…

I'm trying to work it out as I unroll the final curve of the paper. At the bottom right is the word 'Eliza', at the bottom left, the initials 'FB'.

"That's all the proof I need," Mani says.

"So she did see her daughter."

"At least close enough to be able to draw her."

"She was pretty good at it too."

I'm still frowning. "I've seen sketches like this before. Mani, what have you done to my brain? I should know."

He holds up his hands, laughing. "Don't blame me." I drop a kiss onto his nose. Not his lips; that really would spell more trouble and I need to think. Then I have it. I know exactly where I've seen the other sketches; there are three of them in a single old oak frame, above mum and dad's bed.

"Got it!" I tell Mani. "They're at Koll Hendra. She's a bit older in all of them, but it's definitely the same child."

"Oh my…"

I turn to face him properly. "I'm so pleased Franny was able to have some sort of relationship with Eliza, even if it was just as a nice lady who came to sketch her sometimes."

"It must have been so tough though, not being able to tell her who she really was."

I nod, thinking back to the bright light. It was only because of its antics we made the connection. In some strange way I struggle to understand, I wonder if it was Franny? Did she want posterity to know she was Eliza's mother, even if her child never did? Did she need to tell someone in her family, so we could add it to the tree? After all, both of us are Burgesses and through that connection, Bassets.

"What happened to Eliza?" I ask. "Did you get that far with our family tree?"

"Let me take a look." A few clicks later it's on the screen and I lean back into him. "Yes, she married a Sidney Tolcarne in 1838. Let me see if I can find the source material." I nestle in further, nuzzling his neck just below the line of his stubble. "Now you're the one doing the distracting," he complains with an exaggerated sigh.

"Don't mind me." I'm tempted to snake my arm under his sweat top, but I want to know about Eliza too.

"OK, I have the marriage certificate. To one Sidney Tolcarne, a mine captain from Pool. She did well."

"So did he, only he never knew it," I reply.

"As long as they were happy."

"I hope so, and I hope Lady Frances found a way to be happy too."

He leans forward to put his laptop on the floor then turns to me, running his finger around the edge of my face and across my lips.

"Carla?"

"Mmm?"

"Are you happy?"

"Why would I not be?"

"Seriously, are you really happy to be with me."

I put my hands on his shoulders. "Yes. It's been too long coming, Mani Dolcoath, but I guess I was just too cautious."

"And I guess I was too. But now we're here, it doesn't feel like so much of a risk after all."

"It feels right, properly right, and we're very lucky."

He nods, runs his fingers down my neck, and we begin to kiss again.

"Two lost heirs," he murmurs. "Except now we've found each other."

HISTORICAL NOTES

I initially chose Tehidy as the location for my second Cornish Echoes romantic mystery because I love walking in the wooded country park that surrounds the private estate where the house once stood. It is such a beautiful place, just a couple of fields' distance from the cliffs between the fishing port of Portreath and the notorious Hell's Mouth. Rugged and wild, it is everything I love about the north Cornish coast.

When I started to research the hugely influential and wealthy Basset family who lived there in Regency times, I was rather intrigued to find that their only child, a daughter, had never married. I could not understand it; she must have been one of the most eligible matches of her time, especially as her father had a second baronetcy created to pass through the female line. Why hadn't anyone snapped her up? Why hadn't her parents made sure she produced an heir?

The answer is, of course, that I do not know, but there are clues in the historical record. Contemporary accounts describe Lady Frances in her twenties and thirties as not the most pleasing to the eye, shall we say, but also most definitely lacking in social graces. On the other hand, she was known for her good works, taught at the local Sunday School, and when she became Baroness Stratton founded several other schools in the locality.

The family history also suggested there was mental illness on both sides, so I decided to give my version of Franny some form of neurodiversity to explain her lack of social understanding. I have absolutely no evidence at all she was in a lesbian relationship with her friend and companion, Harriet

Lemon. Indeed, after Lady Frances' mother died, Harriet married her father with unseemly haste and there must have been a great deal of bad feeling, because the older Bassets removed to London, leaving Baroness Stratton alone in Cornwall. Neither, of course, are there any grounds to consider Sir Christopher Hawkins a rapist, although he and Lord de Dunstanville were bitter political rivals and did, indeed, fight a duel in March 1810.

This being a Cornish Echoes tale, I wanted to find a smuggler. Imagine my delight when researching Georgian and Regency Portreath I discovered they had quite a notorious one, William Burgess, who lived on a farm on the fringes of the Tehidy estate. He would have to be my man, and in the depths of Truro library I found a slim self-published volume of his family history. He was none other than Baron de Dunstanville's illegitimate son. Yes, really; that part of the story is true and corroborated by several different sources — a cast-iron incidence of truth being stranger than fiction. I used the Burgess family tree in this book as the basis for Carla's.

Zephaniah Job is another real character, although he was perhaps less directly involved in smuggling than the man in my story. He was known as 'the smugglers' banker', the money man financing their activities, and certainly had fingers in many local pies around Polperro, while wearing a cloak of impeccable respectability.

Tehidy House must have been a wonderful place in Regency times, filled with sculptures and paintings, and every latest comfort including oil lamps, wallpaper, a state-of-the-art water closet, and even a cottage by the beach at Carvannel Cove. As well as being a keen bather, Lady Frances was apparently a talented artist, having painted a panel for the family chapel. Sadly, it no longer survives, nor does any painting of her as an adult that I can find, although there are Gainsborough portraits of both her parents. I also discovered that her maid was called Ann.

I have tried to make as much of the incidental historical detail as accurate as possible — it's part of the fun for me, to wrap my story around the people and happenings of the day. I have, of course, taken a few liberties for the sake of the plot, for which I make no apology. I do write stories, after all.

A NOTE TO THE READER

Firstly, thank you for taking the trouble to buy and to read this book. I really do appreciate it, because without readers, where would authors be? We write our stories to share them, after all.

The Lost Heir is the second Cornish Echoes novel, but they are not a series and do not have to be read in order. Rather, they are a loose collection of tales set in great Regency houses of Cornwall, then and in the present day, and I hope you enjoy them. If you would like to find out more about the history, some historical notes follow. Given this book is set in Portreath, quite close to the fictional Porthnevek of *The Forgotten Maid*, a few minor characters do have very brief walk-on parts and I could not resist taking readers back to The Tinners again. It was nice to see Anna and Gun from the first book still together five years later (as I absolutely knew they would be).

The contemporary strand of the story is set during and just after the first Covid lockdown in 2020; I didn't choose to do so for any reason other than it suited the plot so well. I know that period may bring back painful memories for some readers, but I wanted to bring out the positive aspects of lockdown (as I remember it in Cornwall) as well; communities pulling together, the incredibly good weather, and space and time just to walk and think and be.

A book is never written in isolation, and I live in dread of forgetting to include someone important when writing the thank-yous. Obviously, my editor at Sapere Books, Amy Durant, for commissioning the novel, for her patience, and for fostering a real family feel amongst her authors.

For author friends who have helped along the way: Cass Grafton, with her expertise in matters Regency, Alexandra Walsh for introducing me to Zephaniah Job and for beta reading, Morton S Gray for aura advice and for taking me to a ropewalk, Carol Thomas for finding a teacher willing to talk to me about school life during lockdown, and to Kitty Wilson and Polly Heron for their endless support.

For the invaluable assistance I have received with my research: Tim Janaway on behalf of the residents of the private estate at Tehidy Park, the invisible people at Cornwall Libraries for providing me with the books I needed at the drop of a hat, the staff at Kresen Kernow for their friendly welcome, and Rosalind Waite-Jones for sharing her inspiring memories of teaching during lockdown.

Friends have rallied around too: Marsha Smith for checking Mani's dialogue and Sally Thomas for beta reading. My husband Jim is unfailingly patient and always deserves a mention; it isn't always easy living with an author. Sadly, while I was completing this book, we lost one of our friends from 'The Tinners', so this one's for you too, Rixy!

If you would like to find out more about my books, written as both Jane Cable and as Eva Glyn, please contact me via **Twitter: @JaneCable**, **Facebook: Jane Cable, Author**, or **my website**. I am also happy to visit book clubs and libraries, virtually or in person.

Jane Cable
Cornwall, 2023

janecable.com

Sapere Books is an exciting new publisher of brilliant fiction and popular history.

To find out more about our latest releases and our monthly bargain books visit our website:
saperebooks.com

Printed in Great Britain
by Amazon

49233789R00155